Work
Nights

Work
Nights

Erica Peplin

GALLERY BOOKS

New York   Antwerp/Amsterdam   London
Toronto   Sydney/Melbourne   New Delhi

G

Gallery Books
An Imprint of Simon & Schuster, LLC
1230 Avenue of the Americas
New York, NY 10020

This book is a work of fiction. Any references to historical events, real people, or real places are used fictitiously. Other names, characters, places, and events are products of the author's imagination, and any resemblance to actual events or places or persons, living or dead, is entirely coincidental.

First Gallery Books hardcover edition June 2025

GALLERY BOOKS and colophon are registered trademarks of Simon & Schuster, LLC

Simon & Schuster strongly believes in freedom of expression and stands against censorship in all its forms. For more information, visit BooksBelong.com.

For information about special discounts for bulk purchases, please contact Simon & Schuster Special Sales at 1-866-506-1949 or business@simonandschuster.com.

The Simon & Schuster Speakers Bureau can bring authors to your live event. For more information or to book an event, contact the Simon & Schuster Speakers Bureau at 1-866-248-3049 or visit our website at www.simonspeakers.com.

Interior design by Kathryn Kenney-Peterson

Manufactured in the United States of America

10 9 8 7 6 5 4 3 2 1

Library of Congress Cataloging-in-Publication Data is available.

ISBN 978-1-6680-5087-3
ISBN 978-1-6680-5088-0 (ebook)

Work
Nights

october

I WAS A LONELY PIECE OF GARBAGE AND ALL I WANTED WAS TO BE touched. Not in a gross way. I just wanted someone to touch my arms, my hands, and other places like that. I started wearing short-sleeved shirts on the train, hoping someone would bump into me. It happened eventually with an old woman. She didn't move her arm, so I didn't move mine, and for the next three or four stops, we sat like that with our arms touching. It was nice. Her skin was soft and warm, and when she got up with her plastic bags and cane, I wanted to follow her. I thought I could help her up the steps, walk her home, make soup.

I worked in an office where people coughed and the printer broke. I'm not sure why the printer was always broken. A man with a mustache came to fix it but the next day it would break again. I could hear it from my desk, gasping and wheezing in the copy room. My destiny was to become that printer, a faulty engine filled with faded colors that pretty soon nobody would need anymore. It's not like I was special. The city was filled with people like me. People who woke up in the morning and put on a mostly clean shirt and walked to the train with some kind of bag. Tote bag. Messenger bag. Exercise bag. The train was filled with so many people carrying bags you'd think we were going somewhere but we weren't going anywhere. We were just going to work.

The only thing that made going to the office remotely worthwhile was my fixation on a twenty-three-year-old intern named Madeline Navarro who had seemingly no interest in me. We'd met briefly in the dining hall and I fell in love with her for no reason. I just liked her sad mouth and faraway eyes and tiny black miniskirt that no woman on my boring floor would have had the guts to wear. We talked for twenty minutes next to the salad bar and she told me about her room in Bushwick, her love of foreign film, and her family dog in Guatemala that her mother had named Cat. She gave me her number and we'd gone out a few times and even though we hadn't touched or kissed and whatever we were doing couldn't have been called dating, I still wanted her more than anyone I've ever wanted in my life.

My crumb-filled keyboard was on the nineteenth floor of the famous Newspaper building where nothing interesting happened. No stories were written, no hard questions were asked, no Pulitzer Prizes were won. I'd actually stopped telling people I worked at the Paper because it only led to their disappointment. I didn't write or do research or take pictures or do anything that required an iota of talent. All I did was sell ad space, filling the Paper and its website with exactly what readers least wanted to see.

The only good thing about the nineteenth floor was the light that blew in through the floor-to-ceiling windows and moved every minute of the day like an animal presence in the room. It stretched across Operations in the morning, cast shadows over Legal in the afternoon, and occasionally burned into people's eyeballs so badly they had no choice but to move or go blind.

I was waiting for something, or maybe nothing, when Samantha, a nice, pretty girl who made multimillion-dollar ad campaigns for Windex and told stories about getting too drunk to open her front door, rolled over to my desk and said, "I think Joy's asleep."

Joy Platt was my boss, a kind old woman with many beautiful wigs, and if she was asleep, I was all for it.

"Must be tired," I said.

Samantha stared at me and blinked a lot, which meant she was annoyed. She wanted drama. It was her reason for being.

"Don't you want to check on her?" she said.

Reluctantly I put away my phone, which I'd been using to draft halting one-word messages to Madeline, and went over to Joy's cube, hoping the sound of my heavy boots would wake her up so I wouldn't have to nudge her out of her dreams.

Joy was lying facedown on her desk.

"Joy?" I said in a little baby voice that did not belong to me. "Did you fall asleep?" I poked one of her shoulder pads and when she still didn't move, I knew something was wrong. I looked down at her hands, veiny and pale and dangling over the floor, and that's when I knew she was dead. A better person would have checked for a pulse or screamed for help but that wasn't me. I stood and stared and went back to my desk.

Samantha watched me coming as she reapplied her lip gloss, eager to hear news and make herself shiny.

"She's gone," I said.

"She left the building?"

"No, she's—" I made that hand gesture like you're cutting your own throat, and Samantha rushed to pick up the phone.

A few minutes later Joy Platt's shriveled body was carted off in an elevator, and by the time she'd reached the lobby everyone knew I was wrong. She wasn't dead. She was just old and overworked. Strained and sore. Dehydrated and faint. Whatever it was, her desk was empty and I had nothing to do for the rest of the day, the near-death of a salesman being, if nothing else, an excellent excuse not to work.

My commute home to Brooklyn took a little over an hour and I spent most of it reading the train's advertisements for solutions to problems I didn't have. Sleep apnea, drug addiction, erectile dysfunction. It made me jealous. If only I could have had all my problems concentrated into a single nonfatal disease, I could call someone and complain, or better yet, I could move back home to Michigan, eat chicken broth, and recover with dignity. Instead I was strapped with an entirely amorphous feeling of unwell and no idea how to change.

I got off the train in Bushwick and followed the rest of the commuters up to the street. Warm smoke from the taco truck blew in my face and gave me a small burst of comfort. I lived on a treeless block of drab apartment buildings in a neighborhood so different from Times Square, so crooked and peeling and falling apart, that I clung to it like an antidote against the billboards and chain stores. In that part of Brooklyn, clothes still hung on clotheslines, feral cats slept under parked cars, and families gathered in Maria Hernandez Park to share the most amazing-looking cakes.

As soon as I got home, though, I never felt entirely at home. This was my own doing: I rejected any homemaking impulse that might have made me feel too tied down, and my room, as a result, had nothing but an IKEA bed with broken slats, a pile of overdue library books, and two narrow windows I covered with beach towels because I was too lazy to buy curtains. I might have taken them down once in a while but I had grown to dislike sunlight and how it lit up all my dust and hair on the floor, like a spotlight trained on my indifference.

Laurel Yang was my friend and roommate but she was also busy all the time. A short and stocky visual artist who made her own clothes and mutilated our apartment floor, she'd turned her room into a toxic home studio full of wooden boards and power tools and huge pink-and-purple canvases that doubled as tables for her pencils and paintbrushes and six open bottles of rubber cement. She also thrived in huge social circles, cozying up to the drunks at the gas

6

station and her rich friends from art school without differentiating between the two. She'd gone to a famous college on the East Coast, but she refused to say its name, preferring instead to write on her CV: *Laurel Yang went to school.* Her canvases were sprawling asymmetrical things made of blankets, plastic bags, and dirty napkins she took out of our trash. I loved her art for its chaos and filth, but she rarely sold anything because she never tried.

"I think you're a genius," I told her all the time.

"Ugh" was all she ever said. "That word is so problematic."

Laurel happened to be home that night, wearing a crop top she'd made out of bright-yellow string and sanding a ceramic bowl.

"It looks useful but it's not," she explained. "It has secret holes."

"So when you pour a bowl of cereal . . ."

"All the milk comes out. And the milk is the art. *Not* the bowl."

Since our apartment was gross and had nothing to eat, we went out for drinks at a bar we liked with comfy stools and free popcorn. After taking turns complaining about our jobs—Laurel worked for an artist who hired random art school grads to meticulously glue together shards of broken glass—we went through every girl in the room and decided which ones we wanted to date. Laurel had big, roving animal eyes that were good at prowling around and analyzing people. It was fun to be around her because she embraced a lot of things that freaked me out, like karaoke and flirting. I picked a bookish girl with glasses. Laurel picked a hot dyke in a varsity jacket. Then we didn't do anything. We just sat and speculated about the reasons they would be terrible to date.

"Too high-maintenance."

"Too clingy."

"Too kombucha."

"Too boy band."

What I couldn't tell Laurel because it was too sincere was that I already had a crush but we weren't together. We weren't dating. We were barely texting. But she was still a presence in my life, or really in my mind, and I thought about her so often that there was no room for anyone else.

"Should I get a therapist or buy a wood cutter?" Laurel said, picking at a popcorn kernel stuck in her mouth. "They cost the same and I can't afford either so I'm only getting one."

"Get the wood cutter."

"Because talking is a waste?"

"Yeah, and the wood cutter will be so loud you won't hear yourself think."

Another round of drinks appeared, our hypothetical dates left, and pretty soon it was time to get deli sandwiches and go home.

"I think Madeline lives around here," I wondered aloud, despite knowing exactly where Madeline lived, having long ago overheard and instantly memorized her address.

"Who?" Laurel was unwrapping her bacon and egg hero and biting, it appeared, into the foil.

"No one," I said. "It doesn't matter."

I had to be careful around Laurel. The pink and blue streaks in her hair and stick-and-poke tattoos that went up and down her arms gave her an aura of queerness that I seemed to lack. And Madeline, a girl who dated men and wore tiny skirts and carried lattes around like a prop, was decidedly not queer.

"Look at the moon," I said, pointing up at the half-moon revealing itself behind hazy clouds and telephone wires. "It's so pretty. I want to write a poem about it."

Laurel looked surprised. "You write poetry?"

"Used to," I said. "My notebook ran out of space and I never got around to buying a new one. Plus poetry is embarrassing."

"I know what you mean," she said. "Whenever I sit around with my clay and sing to myself it's embarrassing too."

"But it makes you feel better?"

"Hard to say. I feel pretty shitty most of the time."

I was hungover and vaguely miserable the next day when Bekah Rake walked over to my desk and said, "I think I'm your new boss? I think you work in Fashion now? I think you work with me and Tom?"

I'd never actually spoken to Bekah but I'd always admired her glamorous boredom from afar. She was like Cher from *Clueless*, an obscenely pretty girl whose complete ignorance of the real world in no way dampened her social or professional success. "Can I be honest?" She leaned over so her face was close to mine and I had a split-second fantasy where we kissed. "Vanessa told me you were in the *other* corner so I spent like *an hour* looking for you." She made a face. I made a face back. United in dislike for our frumpy supervisor, I felt a jolt of hope. It didn't seem out of the question that we might fall in love, run away, and never set foot in our stupid office again. "I'm telling them to move you. You need to sit near me in Luxury. Have you met Tom yet? Let's go look for him. I think he's back from Milan."

I hadn't spoken a word but it didn't seem to matter. As I followed Bekah past the copy room, the mail room, and the break room that always smelled like tuna, I had the unassailable certainty that I was being carted off to a new beginning. The future was a matter of destiny I had no say in creating. I would follow powerful women with color-treated hair down long hallways, the silent and obedient peasant with a ponytail.

"You're going to love Tom. He never gets mad. He's just crazy all over the place and super ADD so you have to babysit him." Bekah crossed into the Luxury section of the floor, a cluttered continent of felt-walled cubes, dated computer screens, and ergonomic rolling chairs that looked exactly the same as Packaged Goods, Healthcare, and all the other ad categories that divided the nineteenth floor. "Stuff gets lost all the time so you have to take care of him and treat him like a kid or else things fall through the cracks."

Bekah slid open the door of the messiest office I had ever seen. The walls had been rendered invisible beneath maps of Ireland, printed song lyrics, expired work calendars, concert tickets, and a blown-up school photo of a pimply smiling teenager. The desk was equally covered in things: business cards, remote controls, coffee cups, multiple pairs of glasses taped over the nose, and a stack of hardcover biographies, all of them new and most likely stolen from the review pile in Editorial. A balding middle-aged man sat in the middle of it all, frowning at his keyboard as he typed an email in all lowercase letters with his stubby index fingers. He looked like someone's dorky dad, rumpled and rosy-cheeked with an endearing beer belly.

"You're back." Bekah moved a pile of newspapers off a chair and sat, serpentine and bored. "Did you bring me something from Milan?"

Tom rubbed his eyes until his face turned red. "Emily called me six times about Gucci, Prada doesn't want the sponsorship, and you have to talk to Erin about Chanel." His shirt was covered in crumbs. His inbox had forty-four thousand unread messages. His fingernails were bitten to nubs. Whoever Tom was, his professional life appeared to be imploding.

Bekah looked at the ceiling in adolescent annoyance. "*Erin's* at Gucci, *Emily's* at Prada, and this is Jane Grabowski, our new media planner."

Tom burst into song. "*Sweeeeet Jaaaaane…*" He was still imitating Lou Reed and patting a pile of *Women's Wear Daily* when the fan in his laptop turned on and he looked at Bekah with fear in his eyes. "What's that? What's that noise?"

Bekah sighed, annoyed again. "Your laptop overheated because you put papers all over it." She scattered the papers and revealed an old issue of *Chic*, the Newspaper's monthly fashion magazine, which I had spent the last four years ignoring.

"Do you love it?" She held it up like it was her most beautiful friend.

"It's definitely lovable," I said.

She stood and her height was staggering to remember. It felt profound to have to look up so high just to see a face. "Take it," she said. "Study it. Memorize it. This is about to be your life."

Orange plastic crates were waiting for me when I got back to my desk. Samantha was typing in slow motion, the universal sign for *I just got a manicure*.

"I can't believe you're moving," she said. Her voice was sweet, as if all that time we'd spent typing and ignoring each other was really the sound of us becoming friends. "If you get a view of the Hudson, I'm gonna be pissed."

I moved into my new desk with a view of the Hudson while Ellie Banning stood over me sipping tea from a speckled mug that said *Cape Cod*. Her desk was next to mine and it was so clean it looked fake, with its color-coordinated folders, neatly tabbed to-do lists, and photographic shrine to her underweight boyfriend. She was the most dedicated planner at the Paper and I could tell by the humorless way she said "Hi" that she was someone I should never displease.

"I hope you're ready for a change," she said. "Fashion's not for everyone."

Ellie shouldn't have intimidated me—we had the same job and we'd started around the same time—but she carried herself with the unconditional niceness of someone who was raised religious and the secret meanness of every nerd with pent-up rage. "I sent our rates to Chanel, by the way," she said. "Tom came over here freaking out so I just did it. You should talk to him. I think he thinks I'm you." She tied her frizzy hair back into a bun so tight it looked masochistic and I cringed at the thought of anyone mixing us up. Ellie wore earth-colored sweaters and ballet flats and looked like a middle school guidance counselor, whereas I dressed more like a sophisticated janitor in black lace-up boots, black pants, and white collared shirts.

"We sell to super important clients around here so the planners end up putting out a lot of fires. What was your category before this again?"

"Nonprofits," I said. "United Way, Red Cross, Goodwill, all that trash."

I smiled at my joke. Ellie did not.

"Those accounts are small," she said. "What were your plans worth? Like twenty thousand? I just submitted a campaign to Tiffany worth two million."

Karen Vitelio came in at ten thirty, the latest possible time a planner could show up without seeming to have completely given up.

"I want to friggin' shoot myself," she said in her stale cigarette voice. "I talked to Vanessa for an hour last night about the goddamned merry-go-round. It doesn't work. Clients hate it. We have to get rid of it." She collapsed in her chair with her legs splayed and her arms hanging over the armrests, a middle-aged mom crucified by exhaustion.

"I like the merry-go-round," Ellie said. "We can put videos inside it."

"Videos?" Karen sat up, seething with disbelief. She wore the same black hoodie, black stretchy pants, and black eyeliner every day and nobody questioned it because she'd worked at the Paper for eighteen years and had the general air of being able to beat someone up. "That unit is a piece of crap. They can't even fit a friggin' logo inside it."

I vaguely knew what they were talking about. The merry-go-round was a digital ad unit that our managers were supposed to sell so that readers scrolling through the Paper could decide, in the middle of reading an article about melting ice caps, that they should buy a new mattress.

"We can discuss it with Vanessa at the planner meeting," Ellie said.

"Fuck Vanessa," Karen said. "She doesn't know shit." She flicked her stringy black hair over her shoulders and clipped on a headset that made her look like a cashier at a mid-nineties clothing store. "I told Vanessa she's got to hire another planner supervisor or else I'm gonna quit. That job's been open for months. How are we supposed to get anything done if we don't have a friggin' supervisor?"

I pinned up the postcards I'd saved from the move: Hopper's *Sun in an Empty Room*, Goya's *Madhouse*, Bosch's *Garden of Earthly Delights*. They were all gifts from Laurel, likely stolen from the Met gift store, and I wasn't particularly attached to them but they still gave me small comfort, like a quiet refutation of all things corporate—all these old paintings of loneliness and hell.

"Overtime's a whole other thing," Karen said. "It's illegal is what it is—making us work late and not paying us a cent. It didn't used to be like this. We used to work until five and the computers would shut off. They didn't pay us overtime but they didn't make us do it either. That was before your time, in the old building. God, I miss that place. There was toxic mold in the walls but they let us keep ashtrays in the bathroom stalls."

Ellie squeezed a drop of lavender lotion into her palm, the diligent mouse to Karen's cussing megaphone.

"What I wanna know is this," Karen went on. "What the heck are we gonna do about it?" She crinkled open a paper bag and pulled out a donut. The smell of it was overpowering, sweet and tragic. "I'm sick of being a servant to all these spoiled twenty-two-year-olds. That's all they do now. They just keep hiring kids."

A maintenance guy appeared to take away my empty crates. He

looked at the ones on the other side of the station, piled high next to Karen. "Should I grab those too?" he asked.

"*Shit.*" Karen swung around and looked at her crates as if only just remembering they were there. "I still got to go through those."

"I'll come back," the guy said, and Karen seemed pleased, knowing he'd forget. Ellie looked at me with buggy eyes.

Hoarder, she mouthed.

Bekah clomped past the filing cabinets in a leather jacket with a hundred useless zippers, buckles, and belts. Her mouth was big with lipstick. "I've been trying to call you," she said, crinkling her button nose. "Does your phone not work or what?"

I held the receiver to my ear. It sounded like nothing and I was tempted to lie, to make her think my phone worked and never get a phone call ever again.

"You're right," I said. "It's dead."

Bekah frowned and the pointy silver buttons on her leather jacket looked suddenly like nails growing out of her skin. "Well," she said, "that needs to be fixed."

I sent an email to IT asking for help getting my phone to work and someone named Dee responded: Call me.

Too proud to ask Bekah or Ellie if I could use their phones, I found Alvin in the mail room. He was the five-foot-tall religious fanatic who sorted everyone's mail.

"Hello, Miss Jane," he said. "What can I do for you?" He addressed everyone by "mister" or "miss" and it made him seem gentle and slightly dumb.

"Can I use your phone? I'm supposed to call someone named Dee."

"Dee Pedersen," he said. "Fifteenth floor. God bless her. She gives me pens, tape, markers. You can use my phone. Whatever you need, Miss Jane, I'm happy to help." He pulled up his sagging cargo pants and surveyed his fluorescent-lit counter, piled high with newspapers and sticky notes asking him to send out a hundred different things ASAP. "We are walking miracles fished from the stream of God's loving river. Do you know about Saint Francis and the light he always saw?"

"Hi, Dee?" I spoke into the ringing phone, pretending not to hear.

I got up for lunch around one, when I knew Madeline might be in the cafeteria, and Ellie looked up at me with a puzzled face. She was clearly monitoring my every move, waiting for me to screw up so she could tell HR.

"I'm just going down to lunch," I said.

"You're lucky," she said. "I never have time for lunch."

"You want me to bring you something?"

"I wish. It's too hard to negotiate my allergies with all of those contaminated serving spoons."

"I'm sorry."

"It's fine. Just be careful. The vegetarian soup is definitely *not* vegetarian."

The dining hall was a light-filled arena of round tables, red carpeting, and intelligent, journalistic conversation in which I took no part. I got the same sandwich I got every day—turkey and Gouda and whatever crappy lettuce came with it on a salty, dried-out brioche—and joined Samantha and a few other planners from the nineteenth floor. They formed a trio of glossy young women with straight hair, perfect teeth, and amazingly toned upper arms, and I'd secretly nicknamed them the Stepford Planners because their personalities were more or less interchangeable.

"I can't believe Bekah got promoted."

"She used to cry at her desk."

"I used to sit next to her. She used to look for other jobs."

The Stepford Planners spoke in declarative statements and ignored their soup to eat exclusively the saltine crackers that came with it, spilling crumbs across the table and somehow getting none on their vibrantly colorful skirts.

"Are you ready to work for Arthur?" Samantha said. "They just wrote about his birthday party in the *Post*. He rented a male strip club and every power gay in the city was invited."

"The scar under his eye is from a botched nose job."

"He dated Anderson Cooper."

The old men who spent every lunch hour playing chess turned to see where the shrill, feminine voices were coming from. The dining hall was in some ways a battleground between the young and the old, and the young always won. They were louder and faster and they never seemed to notice the judgmental looks coming from the graying, middle-aged tables behind them.

I got up to find Madeline and recognized the editor of the Books section sitting across from her in comfy-looking corduroys and a big green basketball jersey.

"I just wanted to say," I spoke to the older woman, "your section is my favorite section of the paper."

The editor looked surprised, like maybe she wasn't used to being accosted so close to a vat of ketchup.

"Really? That's nice to hear." She got up with her empty tray and walked toward the elevators that would deliver her back to the editorial side of the building—the thoughtful, idea-driven side, which was kept, by ethical standards, as far away from advertising as possible.

"Something crazy just happened," I said to Madeline, who was moodily poking some sushi with a wooden chopstick. "I got transferred to Fashion. The guy in charge is some famous gay dude who dated Anderson Cooper."

"Huh."

"I bet I could talk to someone and get you transferred up there. I mean, if you're interested. We make pretty big campaigns for companies like Tiffany and Chanel."

"Maybe."

Her eyes refused to look at me, and whatever sheen I thought my life might have taken on from working in Luxury vanished so quickly that I probably should have quit on the spot. There was something inherently wrong with me. Something no job or haircut or date with a girl could fix.

"Some missionaries were giving out pamphlets on the street today," she said. "When they saw me coming, they looked away. They didn't even try to give me anything. It was like they knew I was ruined. They didn't want to bother."

"I bet they were intimidated," I said. "You're so cute. They were probably confused. Like, how did this angel get here? We should avoid her in case she's an emissary of God who will tell on us for having snacks in our purse."

She glanced at her phone, checking the time.

"Why don't we have a prayer session tonight," I said. "We could meet at a bar. Drink some communion wine."

"I don't know if I can."

"Should I text you?"

"If you want."

She collected her empty soy sauce packets and I felt like an idiot, just standing there and watching the way her hands moved. She did everything gracefully. Even throwing stuff away.

Bekah online-shopped for throw pillows for the rest of the afternoon while I wrote ten different messages to Madeline and erased them all immediately. *I want to see you* was too direct. *You're on my mind*—too cute. I settled on *Hey, let's get that drink* and buried my phone in the back of a drawer so I wouldn't keep checking it every five minutes. Ellie looked away, so I knew she'd been watching, but maybe she was right to be suspicious. I took shortcuts. I took naps.

"I have a dumb question," I said.

She swiveled in her chair to face me, excited for my dumbness.

"Is Arthur a real person?" I asked.

"Arthur Truman," she announced, "is the SVP of Luxury, and that"—she pointed at a glass-walled showroom of midcentury modern furniture—"is his office. He's actually not here right now. Why? Do you need to talk to him?"

My ears burned at the thought. I wasn't afraid of powerful people. I just didn't like them.

"He's related to the president," Karen said. "The one who dropped the bomb and killed all those people."

I looked to Ellie for confirmation and she'd already pulled up a picture of the thirty-third president on her screen. "It's true," she said. "They have the same nose."

I checked my phone to see if Madeline had written back and found nothing. It was hopeless. But that was our relationship. It followed an unspoken rule that said we were allowed to ignore each other for long periods of time because we weren't actually dating. We were consenting adults in an entanglement that involved getting drunk, flirting mercilessly, and revealing nothing real about ourselves.

Bekah chirped at me from her cube. "Janey, do you have a minute?"

I got up and went over to her cube only to find her, inexplicably, on the phone.

"My boyfriend wants to go to Bar Harbor but I'm sick of seafood. . . . I know, right? Why do they call it *aioli* when it's literally just mayonnaise."

She laughed while I stood next to her and waited. I didn't mind being ignored. It was sort of nice to be invisible for a while and just watch the sunlight slowly move across the carpet. Four or five minutes must have passed before Bekah hung up.

"I hate Arial," she said.

"The girl from Armani?"

"No, the font. I wish we could all use Times New Roman and be done with it."

She pulled out a metal filing cabinet so I could sit and I felt my insides constrict, knowing she was about to assign some cryptic task and make me stay late enough to hear the vacuum cleaners roaring.

"How long have you lived in New York?" she said.

It was the first personal question she'd asked and it felt like a trick.

"Four years," I said.

"That's too bad. Your first year in New York is the best. I wish I could do it again. I went out, like, every night. Are you single?"

I nodded.

"I'm lucky I met Devin. So many weird guys used to come up to me at bars and I was always like, *Ew, why are you talking to me?* I have a theory about why it's hard to date in New York. It's because you have to fight to make it here so everyone's super ambitious and it makes people selfish. Do you meet guys on apps or what?"

"I date girls."

Bekah blinked. I had strayed from the script and become a social deviant, but some part of her must have known it was coming. My clothes were plain and loose, the heels of my shoes were trodden flat, and my hair was perpetually tied up because it had given up on being down.

"Congrats," she said, sounding bored. "Guys in New York are the worst."

I glanced at the time, fully prepared to leave, considering it was after five, and she started filling a Post-it note with specifications for a million-dollar plan. She needed five budgets, geo-targeting, video capability, multiple sponsorships, and LVMH rates. Her handwriting kept getting smaller. She flipped over the Post-it and wrote on the glue.

"Does that make sense?" She handed me the note. I couldn't read a word.

"Totally."

The office emptied out as I worked on Bekah's bloated plan and stayed late enough to learn that whenever the overhead lights stopped sensing movement, they turned off and cast the station into a series of shadows. The darkness felt deliberate, like the building was trying to erase me, and I knew if I sat in the dark for long enough, a succubus was going to rise up and drag me down to the basement where they kept the broken desks. So I waved my arms to turn the lights back on every five minutes, and by the time I left for the night, the only planner left was Ellie, tirelessly scanning a fifty-page PowerPoint for her boss, Diana, in the copy room.

"Don't stay too late," I said.

"I don't mind," she said, with enough sincerity that I wondered if a demanding office job was a sort of salvation, saving us from having to ask ourselves what our efforts might really mean.

Once a month, when Laurel wasn't home, I called my parents to let them know I was still alive. The only annoying thing was that I had to call them one by one because they'd been divorced since I was nine, so I'd gotten used to describing most events in my life twice, modifying details to appease or provoke each listener. First I called my dad, a retired stock photographer who took walks at the mall and grew tomatoes in the yard. I loved talking to him because he was easy to get along with and our conversation never lasted more than five minutes.

"You forgot to tell Nancy happy birthday."

Nancy was my stepmother. She'd been married to my dad for fifteen years but I'd only started accepting her in the last two.

"I'm sorry. I forgot. I've been swamped at work. I just got transferred to a new department."

"A promotion?"

"Kind of. I'm going to be working in fashion."

"That doesn't sound like you."

"It's not. I actually have no idea what I'm doing with my life."

"You could always move back home."

"That's never going to happen."

He scratched his beard and I could tell he was in his faded armchair, probably watching MSNBC with a book about World War II in his lap.

"Would you say a robot could do your job?" he said.

"Probably."

"I read an article that said if your work is mostly on a computer, it won't be long before you'll get replaced."

"Why are you telling me this?"

"Things change. Just be ready."

"Thanks, Dad."

He sighed again, sounding relaxed. "Well, make sure you get enough to eat out there. And don't forget to call Nancy."

"I won't. I'll call as soon as we hang up."

"Good. She's been a part of this family for a long time and it means a lot to her when you make an effort to include her."

"Definitely."

We hung up and I called my mother. Neurotic and single for the last twenty years, she picked up after the first ring.

"I met someone," she said, her voice a little breathless, as if I'd caught her in the middle of a jog when really, I knew, she was probably just in the middle of heating up a TV dinner. "I'm a little nervous to talk about it because it's all happening so fast, but he just came over one day to look at the crack in the front step and I answered the door in my workout clothes and you know how I look in my workout clothes, I don't look cute, but we stood and talked for an hour."

"Can I say something?" I interrupted. My mother had a habit of falling in love with men, sharing their biographies with me, and then dumping them the minute she remembered how much she loved living alone. "I'm happy you met someone but I actually called because I have news."

"I know, I feel like everyone has news right now. Like with Doug, that's his name, we already went out for dinner twice. He has a daughter about your age. He lives in Parkdale, so pretty close."

"Mom! I'm trying to talk."

"I am too! I feel like you never listen."

"I listen. I'm listening. I just wanted to let you know that I work in fashion now. So my job is completely different."

"Honey, that's wonderful. Did you get a raise? If you didn't you should still ask because you don't want them to think you're one of those girls who never speaks up."

"It's not wonderful. I hate fashion. It's completely vapid."

"Well, if it's so terrible, why don't you get some new clothes and introduce yourself to the writers? You're so pretty and outgoing, some editor is bound to notice you."

"That's not how it works."

"But you're so creative."

"I'm actually not."

When Bekah's blond crown of hair rose up from her cube, I assumed she was coming over to congratulate me. I'd sent her the million-dollar plan for Chanel the night before and felt proud of the work I'd done.

"The plan is all wrong," she said. "I told you to use that new unit."

"The corkscrew?"

"No."

"The cyclone?"

"No."

"The escalator?"

"The escalator sucks."

I was trying to remember more of the units I'd heard Ellie say into the phone. There were hundreds and she had somehow memorized all of them.

"The merry-go-round," Bekah said. "Put that on the plan."

Karen was outside smoking, but I could still hear her raspy voice. "Karen said it doesn't work."

Bekah frowned. "Don't listen to Karen. This is Fashion and we can do whatever we want." She padded back to her cube, and for the rest of the day I was convinced everyone in the office was evil. A belief that was strengthened when Ellie announced that Samantha watched movies at her desk.

"It's not right," she said. "She watched *Love Actually* yesterday— the whole thing—and today she's watching *Pretty Woman*."

"I fucking hate that movie," Karen said.

Ellie strangled the dregs of her chamomile into her mug. "Jane, you used to sit next to her. Did you used to see her watching movies?"

I was well acquainted with Samantha's movie-watching. I watched them with her.

"Not that I can recall," I said. "I was pretty focused on my work."

I excused myself to go to the bathroom and zoom in on pictures of Madeline. I loved her moody lips, her pointy eyebrows, and the smirky, knowing look she wore in every photo, as if deriding the very act of picture-taking itself. There was so much I still wanted to know about her. What kind of shampoo she used, what her handwriting looked like, whether or not she'd ever been to Coney Island. To know her better was always the goal, but I knew at the same time that familiarity would be the death of us. Preserving the mystery was the only way to keep love from getting ruined.

Tonight at 9, I wrote to her in an emphatic tone that in no way belonged to me. I was just pretending to be someone else. Courageous and decisive. Meet me at Birdy's. You're not allowed to say no.

I waited in the echoey bathroom stall, crouched and pathetic.

Fine, she wrote back, and in that moment, my phone was no longer just a phone. It was a chalice. A love letter. A crystal ball. I'll wear something cute for you, but you have to be nice.

Back at the station, a mission-style lamp in Arthur's office gave his room a menacing glow. The air also smelled rich, musky, and masculine, like the stump of an old tree mixed with whiskey and hair gel. Arthur had been in there at some point, that was clear, but where he'd gone after was a mystery. That's how it was with powerful people: their authority so often seemed to lie in their ability to disappear.

When he finally flew past the station in a tight-fitting cream-colored suit, he was on the phone.

"She needs to rectify the terms of our partnership and stop self-medicating." He threw back his head and laughed and a part of me was mesmerized.

"I've always wanted to know how old he is," Ellie said, glancing at his long legs, resting serenely over the top of his desk. "I'm guessing forty but he acts younger."

I studied him through the glass walls of his office and he really did look like a prince. His pores were so open, I imagined they had mouths that could talk to him, laughing at his jokes and offering sage business advice.

"He could be one of those rich guys who's fifty but passes as thirty," I said.

"What if we're all wrong," Karen said, "and he's actually dead?"

Ellie's boss, Diana Sands, was the only one brave enough to go in there and say hello. She stood in his doorway and adjusted her pink satin headband as they discussed key takeaways from Italy.

"Lago di Garda is overcrowded."

"I got sick of pasta."

"It's so hard to get out of Venice."

As they continued to complain about the diminishing benefits of first class, their entire lives flashed before my eyes. He knew the difference between brandy and scotch. She owned a kimono. Their lineage went back to Charlemagne and the Vanderbilts, to men who rode horses and women who carried parasols.

Karen got up and tapped on Arthur's door. "I'm lookin' for the big calendars," she said. "You got any of the big calendars? I got the small ones but the big ones are the best."

"Sorry," Arthur said, and anyone listening could tell that he wasn't. "I haven't seen any calendars."

I often thought half the reason people moved to New York City was to feel better than other people. They wanted to live in a place where they could make tons of money and then feel famous for having made it. Arthur was one of those people. There was a glimmer in his eyes that signaled to anyone who looked at him that his life was bigger, brighter, and richer than theirs could ever be. It must have been exhausting, actually, to eat, bathe, and sit in first class knowing all the while he was above every pinprick of reality on the ground below.

Madeline was late to the bar. I told myself she wasn't doing it on purpose. She was just trying to look cool. But the longer I waited, the more the street came to seem demonic. Strangers stood around, cackling and blowing smoke. A truck driver yelled at a biker and the biker yelled back. I stood under the bar's ripped awning and looked at the bouncer. A big woman whose boredom was also big. She looked like a dyke so we exchanged head nods, and when I asked her where she lived, she started talking to me like she'd been waiting to talk all night.

"I'm Dominican," she said. "I don't drink but I smoke a lot of weed. One day off a week is all I get and nobody is allowed to bother me because all I want to do is watch TV. *Game of Thrones. Walking Dead.* I live in the Bronx. It takes me two hours to get home on the train and do you know what I do?"

"What?"

"Watch TV on my phone."

Madeline walked up in tight black jeans with a rip in the knee. It was a beautiful rip that only a designer could create.

"I'm having a crisis," she said. "Someone at the Paper said I was bisexual and I was like, no, that's not right, but then I didn't know what to say. What do you tell people you are?"

"I tell people I date girls," I said. "That way there's no label."

"But if you *had* to have a label, what would it be?"

"I don't know," I said. "A blob."

The bouncer was watching us. I guess we were her TV.

"Sometimes I think I have to know what I am so I can tell people," Madeline said. "But nobody ever really knows who they are. It's all just words. Relationships are abstract, you know? I think I'm post-relationship."

"I agree," I said. "Coming out is a lie. We're all nobody."

I held open the door, a performance of chivalry as sincere as it was ironic. As she passed me, I leaned in and smelled her hair. It was smooth and black and chopped clean above her shoulders so it bounced when she walked.

The bar was crowded with awkward dates and dudes with neck tattoos, so I told Madeline to find a table in the back. I tried to get the bartender's attention but he seemed to be going out of his way not to notice me. I hoped Madeline wasn't watching. She probably never had trouble getting drinks when she was on dates with guys. When the bartender finally came over, I caught him glancing at Madeline and it gave me a terrible sensation of power. She was feminine and pretty and I had the urge to lean over the lemon wedges and tell him to back off.

She was looking at her phone, texting and smiling, so I assumed she was flirting with someone else. I couldn't even be mad about it because monogamy was something we made fun of all the time. Marriage, kids, anniversaries, Super Bowl parties, trips to Montauk—it was all a bunch of crap—all those Crate & Barrel benchmarks to forming a life. But a stubborn part of me still wanted her to like me and only me.

I sat next to her on the bench along the wall and put our drinks on the table.

"What do I owe you," she said.

"Just your undying love and devotion."

She took a sip of her drink and winced.

"I gave that to you last week," she said, "when I told you I didn't like whiskey."

"Forgot about that."

"Yeah, right. You're probably just mixing me up with your other dates."

"You? Never. I only see you, Madison."

She swallowed down the rest of her drink and leaned against my arm.

"Can you please sedate me," she said. "I slept for two hours, my roommate hates me, and my internship sucks. It's boring and basically unpaid but I still take a car there almost every day. Is that bad?"

She shrugged off her tiny denim jacket and I looked at her shoulders, the bones beneath her tank top moving this way and that.

"Yes," I said. "You are deranged."

She started touching her hair, playing with the loose strands that fell around her ears.

"I'm sick of working in media," she said. "All I do is add keywords to cooking videos. It's like, I didn't read Deleuze in college just to be able to optimize some video about mushroom risotto."

I stared at her face. She had the perfect face.

"I'm gonna quit," she said. "It feels unconscionable to spend one more day in a place so bad for my mental health."

"How much longer is the internship?"

"A week."

I laughed so hard I knocked the table and got the feeling that maybe Madeline was the one. She was just so strange and spoiled and funny. It didn't seem out of the question that we'd one day be shriveled old ladies in a bed together, telling our grandkids who were half AI about that one date we went on when Grandma Jane made Grandma Madeline drink whiskey and Grandma Jane almost spilled a table full of drinks.

"You can't quit," I said. "Everybody hates their jobs but we all keep going to them anyway. That's what being an adult is."

She petted one of her eyebrows, thin and finely plucked. "I still want to quit."

"What would your parents think?"

"They don't care what I do. They just don't want me to go back to Guatemala."

"Because . . . of the violence?"

She laughed and shoved my knee under the table.

"No, you idiot. It's nice where we live. It's just super gated and all the girls I knew growing up got married and had babies and my parents don't want that for me."

"That happened to the girls I knew in Michigan. The whole baby-husband pipeline."

"It's not the same. There's the whole machismo culture."

"So no gay bars?"

Her eyes turned to slits. "You wouldn't last a day."

We got another round and the room turned warm and velvety.

"I have a theory." She jabbed at her ice. "I think you're a vampire."

"Oh no." I pretended to be offended. "You think I'm a cliché?"

"I've never seen you eat. I have no idea where you sleep. And I've never seen you in daylight. I've only seen you at bars or in horrible office lighting."

"Maybe that's because I don't like sunlight," I said. "It's overrated."

She smiled, and there was something profound about the way she did it. How small and sly it was, and slightly condescending.

"You sound insane," she said.

"I'm serious," I said. "Sunlight is for happy people. So is hugging, brunch, and the beach. I hate all of those things."

She laughed and crossed her legs, and when her clean white tennis shoe touched my boot in the forbidden dark beneath the table, I started to feel hopeful, like this might be the night we finally kissed.

"Do you get along with your parents?" I said. "Do you believe in God? How do you feel about death? Do you like showers or baths?"

"Stop asking me so many questions. You sound like my therapist."

"I'm interested in you," I said. "You're an interesting person."

She brushed her hair back and I stared at her neck. I had the urge to do something but I wasn't sure what. She scooted closer to me and I reached for her hand. It was small and soft and I was about to tell her how much I liked her when she yawned.

"It's late. I'm calling a car."

"That's absurd. You live three blocks away."

"But it's after midnight."

"I'm walking you home."

I closed the tab and left the bartender a big tip, hoping Madeline would see. She was standing by the door.

"I can't believe you're making me walk," she said. "I hate walking."

She sighed as I led the way down Myrtle, a loud avenue made louder by the aboveground train that sounded like the end of the world every twenty minutes.

"Walking at night is the best," I said, gesturing toward the liquor store and food trucks and garbage bags piled high along the curb. "There's so much to smell and hear and see."

"You sound like Willy Wonka."

"A beloved alcoholic," I said. "I'm touched."

We slowed down in front of her place, a massive brick building surrounded by a tall black metal fence so suburban moms would feel better about letting their kids live near a needle exchange. Madeline had already told me that her building used to be an opera house, and ever since, I'd felt sorry for the ghosts. Former sopranos, divas in their time, now forced to witness millennials playing Xbox and having drunk sex.

"How are you getting home?" she asked.

"I might stay out," I said. It wasn't true, but with girls like Madeline, it was best to lie.

She typed a code into the gate and looked back at me like a chore.

"Thanks for helping me realize I have no identity," she said.

"Anytime."

The gate closed in my face with an absurdly loud clang.

Karen clipped on her headset, took a bite of donut, and said, "How was your weekend?" For a second I considered telling her the truth: that I got rejected by a girl, ate a hot dog from 7-Eleven, and watched a four-hour Criterion movie about abortion with a blanket wrapped around my head.

"Good," I said. "How was yours?"

"I," announced Ellie, who had not been asked anything, "had the worst weekend of my life." She tugged on her tea bag. "I had to spend the night at the hospital because I got too close to a plate of walnut brownies. If I so much as smell a peanut, my breathing passageways close. I can't have nuts or certain oils or meat."

"You're allergic to meat?" Karen asked.

"No, I just don't like it."

Bekah called me over to her desk. She was wearing a tight black dress with white ruffles around the hip that made her look like an expensive baked good.

"Quick question," she said. "Have you been reading your emails?"

"Always," I lied.

She unpeeled the lid of a yogurt, licked it, and stuck it to a piece of paper that looked important.

"I need you to redo the plan for Chanel. Paris wants something different but they won't say what, so just make a new one and send all the *Chic* magazines with Chanel ads to their office on Fifty-Seventh. Rudy has them in the archive. He can help." She crossed her legs and coughed in my face. "I'd get them myself but I think I'm getting sick. I'm trying not to overexert."

My chest tightened with rage as I rode the elevator down to the archive and stopped thinking Bekah was attractive. Her freckled arms were future cancer, her straight white teeth were the result of orthodontic privilege, and her promotion was nothing but further proof of the whole working world's preference for pretty people.

Rudy Marini was biting into a bagel as I approached his enormous back. He was the surly human snowman in charge of the company's archive. Affectionately described by HR as the most important archive in the history of American journalism, it had nevertheless been moved to increasingly obscure parts of the building until one day it was at the very bottom, in a large and windowless basement that smelled like a burp.

"How's your lumbar?" I asked Rudy, having overheard from Karen it was the ailment of the week.

He wiped the cream cheese off his hairy fingers and seemed glad. Not so much to see me as to be able to talk about his chronic pain.

"It's getting worse," he said. "I can't empty the dishwasher without going numb."

"I'm sorry to hear that."

He rubbed his elbow.

"As long as I'm down here," I said, "do you think you could help me get some magazines for Bekah Rake?"

Rudy groaned. "I thought she was a planner."

"She got promoted."

I followed him down a long aisle of teetering filing cabinets and watched as he pulled out a drawer filled with exactly the magazines Bekah needed. It was actually amazing. The way his whole life seemed to have melded with his collection so that every newspaper represented another day he'd spent in his rolling chair, eating a breakfast bagel and complaining about his back.

"I hope you feel better," I said, wheeling the magazines away on a cart.

"I won't," he said, and as I boarded the elevator going up, I felt strangely soothed by the reminder that I wasn't the unhappiest person in the building.

I went through *Chic* magazines for the next few hours and fell into a daze. Every page sold the same dream of gauzy sundresses, sheer evening gowns, and silky jumpsuits, and the goal of it all seemed to be a kind of death state that involved lying by a pool with your eyes closed, sweating in a sauna until you forgot you had a body, or drinking so much champagne that you stopped hearing your own words. Was that the goal of luxury? A kind of comfortable nonexistence?

Bekah came over with a lint brush to check on my progress. She rolled the brush over her torso, armpits, and breasts. It felt vaguely inappropriate to watch.

"Just so you know," she said, "you have to send those magazines yourself. Alvin can't do it because he's too slow." She peeled her furry tape off the roll and held it in the air. It was the most disgusting thing I'd ever seen, this flag of dead skin and old hair. "Here," she said, handing it to me. "Can you throw this away."

Alvin was in the mail room, scuttling between tasks with the devotion of an ant.

"Miss Jane." He took the magazines out of my hands. "I can send those for you."

"I got it!" I yanked them back and felt suddenly unable to look at him. His wire-framed glasses were making me sad. He tried so hard but he made so many mistakes.

"Are you sure, Miss Jane? I'm happy to help."

I looked for a marker, checking the drawers and the cupboards, but I couldn't find any. The mail room had every office supply ever invented except for a single permanent marker.

"You look lost," he said. "What do you want?"

The question was simple. What did I want? I couldn't imagine telling someone so full of conviction that I had lost faith in wanting, that I no longer knew what kind of person to be.

"When I kept silent my bones wasted away," he said. "Doubts, regrets, fears, all those things I had to admit."

He took a Sharpie out of his pocket and gave it to me.

"If you don't transform your pain, you will transmit it."

"Totally," I said, copying down Bekah's addresses. The smell of the marker was sweet and sour and I wondered how many more zip codes I'd have to write before I got high.

Madeline's short, dark braids and all-black clothes appeared at the edge of Tech and I rushed over to her, not wanting Ellie or Karen or anyone else in Luxury to see me blushing in front of an intern who was arguably not supposed to be on our floor.

"Sorry if I was a bitch the other night," she said. "I think I'm anemic."

"I always forget what that means," I said.

"It means I'm tired all the time."

"Isn't that everyone?"

"Cassandra said I have to eat more protein."

"I thought it was spinach."

"I think it's both."

We looked down at her shoes. They were black loafers that she'd paired with small and frilly white socks.

"At least you look cute," I said.

"Thanks, I think so too."

She reached for my wrist and held on to it for a second. My sleeves were rolled up so she was making contact with my skin, and even that pathetically short sensation of touch made my entire body want to shake.

"How about we get some protein after work," I said. "Like a rotisserie chicken we can take to the park."

"You're such a weirdo," Madeline said, smiling as she walked away.

The sun shriveled over Jersey and I knew Madeline was a fake, a flirt, and a tease. Nothing about my life in the office would change. The furniture was nailed to the floor. The elevators could only go up or down. The conversations in the hallway would always be the same ("Is your internet working?" "My internet's not working." "Is it raining?" "Got any fun plans this weekend?").

Disparaging my job, my future, my posture, and my ponytail, I passed Schnipper's on my way out of the building, and as I hurried past the hamburger fumes, I hopped over a massive puddle and looked down just in time to see a cockroach lying on its back. It was waving its string-bean legs in the air and I should have kept walking—that bug's life meant nothing, no more than mine or anyone else's—but instead I stopped and stared at him and wanted to yell at all the people passing, *What is wrong with you? Isn't anybody going to help this cockroach?* Then I stepped over him and went down the subway stairs.

Madeline was "still sick" on Friday night and I didn't believe her. I wanted to get a can of soup just to walk it over to her apartment and prove she wasn't there, and I might have done it if it weren't for Laurel. She was halfway to Fort Greene on her beat-up bike and texting me at red lights to remind me that it was Gay Shabbat. A dinner party thrown once or twice a year by our chef friend Maxine and the sort of event where you needed support, another body in the room to protect you from all the beer breath and gossip.

I took the bus down to Vanderbilt and was standing on the corner and feeling very adult because I was holding a bottle of wine when Laurel pulled up on her rusty bike.

"Is it red or white?" she said in a blunt, mocking voice.

"I don't know what color it is," I said. "The bottle's green."

"Do you know how to open it?"

"No."

"What if I made you open it in front of everyone?"

"I would cry."

Maxine lived on the third floor of a creepy old brownstone where the rent somehow wasn't insane. She split the place with her Craigslist roommate, a big, sad Canadian girl who was painfully in love with me. I'm not saying that to brag. She just very badly wanted to talk to me about her family in Ottawa and show me things in her room.

"I invited that girl I went out with last night but it's weird," Laurel said, locking her bike to a squat metal fence that said NO BIKES.

"Why's it weird?"

"I don't want to kiss her."

We stood in front of Maxine's door and looked at the eight different buzzers.

"I think it's two-something," Laurel said.

"I thought it was three."

I took out my phone to write to Maxine.

Hey hi Happy Shabbat! What's your apt #?

As soon as I hit send, my phone died.

"I guess we'll just have to wait until someone comes down," I said.

"Or we could go home."

"Let's do that."

We turned to leave and Maxine opened the door in a greasy white tank top that showed off her long armpit hair. She worked in the kitchen of a Michelin-starred restaurant, which made her glamorous, but she also didn't shave or shower regularly and she pretty much always had food stuck in her teeth. "I'm so glad you guys came," she said, hugging us with her cut-up chef's arms. "I got three hundred dollars' worth of meat."

She led the way up the stairs and we followed the smell of her BO. It was actually comforting, how carefree and pretty she was and how she always smelled like a twelve-year-old boy. "My roommate's going to be especially glad now that Jane is here." She smiled at us over her shoulder.

"Sucks for her," Laurel said. "Jane's obsessed with a straight girl."

I smacked Laurel's bun. "Can you not tell people that?"

"Uh-oh," Maxine said. "Straight girls will fuck you up."

She opened the door of 2R and we walked into a cloud of smoke. The apartment was crowded with people and food—pita bread, oily dips, waffle chips, fruit—and Laurel and I weren't ready to be social so we followed Maxine into the kitchen, where she drained the oil out of a pan of potatoes and talked about her sex life. That was the other thing about Maxine. She was sexually ravenous.

"I finally hooked up with the cabinetmaker," she said. "We went to her studio in Gowanus and I got naked and put on her tool belt. It was hot. But now she's upstate with her wife and I'm dying. I want to have sex with every butch I see on the street."

Laurel's date walked into the room and I knew it was Laurel's date because Laurel wouldn't look at her. The girl had a friendly farm-girl vibe and she obviously worked in food like Maxine because she had burn marks on her arms.

"You work at Per Se?" she said to Maxine.

"You run Holy Pie?" Maxine said to the girl.

Maxine was a meat cook and Laurel's date ran a vegan pie truck and it was suddenly clear they were meant to be.

"Go eat some spinach pies," Maxine said, in a brazen attempt to get rid of us, so Laurel and I went into the living room, where Tasha and Zinc were on the couch drinking cinnamon whiskey straight from the bottle.

"We're comparing boobs," Tasha said. "We might need to show you so you can decide." She pulled down her shirt and gave me a flashing glance at her Calvin Klein bra. "Whose are more uneven?"

"How long have you guys been drinking?" I asked.

"I had a few glasses at work," Zinc said. She tugged on her pigtails. "Every Friday we have mandatory happy hour and this week's theme was Cinderella. It was the first time I'd worn a dress in *years*."

"I thought you were going to quit your job," I said.

"I was," she said. "But then I realized I'd never find another law firm that lets me keep foster dogs under my desk."

Tasha pointed at a pair of raggedy Velcro shoes by the door.

"Whose are those?" she asked, pretending to gag.

"Mine," Maxine said.

"Throw them away now," Tasha said.

Maxine was cutting ribs with a giant knife and carrying them slab by slab over to a platter on the table ten feet away. "What? No way. I've had those shoes for years."

"Yeah, and it's time to burn them," Tasha said.

"But they're so comfortable. It's hard to find good shoes."

"I have four hundred pairs of good shoes and none of them look like that."

"C'mon." Maxine kept trying to defend her shoes. "I got them for nine ninety-nine."

"It shows," Tasha said. "If I saw a girl wearing those shoes my vagina would go dry. Dirty shoes means dirty vag."

After we lit candles, said a prayer, and tried to eat a bunch of food in the dark, including some THC-laced baked goods, Addy and Jess showed up and had nothing to say. They were just another nice lesbian couple with brown hair and glasses who looked the same.

"Eat," Maxine said, and they shook their heads. They'd already eaten.

"Drink," Tasha said, and they shook their heads again. They couldn't drink, not when they were waking up early to go upstate.

"We're renting kayaks," Jess said.

"We made a dinner reservation at that place that used to be a bank," Addy said. "Everyone has to eat in the vault."

Laurel shot me a look from across the room that said *Thank god we are single and eating pot cupcakes* and I was still nodding ferociously back when Maxine's roommate came out of nowhere and touched me on the arm.

"Hi," she said, all sweet and shy. "How have you been?"

Donna had a big moon face and watery eyes and she looked at me with such gentle abandon that I wanted to die. She was like a flower in a dainty little pot. Something pleasant that I wanted to ignore.

"I'm dating a straight girl," I said. "It's getting serious."

She handed me a card with my name on the front. I felt too high to speak or move.

"This is for you," she said. "It's just a little something."

I opened the card while Maxine, Laurel, and a bunch of other people watched. They probably all knew about the card because they were evil. They couldn't wait to see me forced to deal with unabashed tenderness.

"You did this?" I asked, holding up a watercolor picture of fauna around a pond.

Donna looked at me with the uncertainty of the gift-giver who wants to be thanked and disappear at the same time.

"I've been doing watercolors for a while," she said. "I have some more in my room, if you want to see them."

"I'd like that," I said. "Just let me go pee."

I grabbed Laurel by the arm, scooped up our coats, and dragged her out the door when no one was looking. Maxine was in the hallway with her neighbor, a man in his thirties who was gently berating her. "Outrageously inconsiderate" was the last thing we heard him say before we ran out the door to catch the bus. It actually arrived when it said it would, which felt like a miracle, and we sat in the back, where the rumbling engine and encapsulating darkness outside made it feel like we were inside the belly of a giant whale.

"What about your bike," I said, having just remembered it. "Should we go back?"

"I'll get it tomorrow."

"What if someone steals it?"

"I hope they do," Laurel said. "Then I can buy a new one without feeling guilty."

"That's how I feel about my job," I said. "I wish they would just fire me so I wouldn't have to waste so much time thinking about quitting."

She leaned her head against my shoulder and closed her eyes and I can't remember anything else about the ride because we both fell asleep.

I boarded the elevator behind Bekah, who lunged at Diana with enough intensity that I wondered if they were going to fight. "I love your lipstick! Is that Lady Danger by MAC?"

Diana squealed, "How did you know?" She touched her swollen lips. "It's my favorite. It's such a good color with our skin tones."

The women looked back at me in openmouthed confusion. They were playing the compliment game and it was my turn for empty praise, but how would that work? I hadn't worn makeup since junior prom, when I was still trying to be straight.

"I can't believe it's the numbers tonight," Bekah said, changing the topic. "I hope I don't cry."

"I already popped a zannie," Diana said.

Bekah gasped. "Do you have any extra?"

The doors opened on nineteen and they walked off together, arm in arm and happy to take drugs, while Ellie warned me about the numbers before I'd sat down.

"It's Arthur's monthly meeting for reviewing everybody's job performance. He basically goes around the room humiliating everyone."

"Sounds like fun," I said.

"It's not," she said, immune to sarcasm. "It's really intense." She bit open a bobby pin and tamped down a frizzy hair. "But don't worry." She glared into me like I was getting away with something. "Planners don't have to go."

Eight hours later I was getting ready to leave for the night, when Bekah came over to the station and said, "Ready for the meeting?" I could feel Karen and Ellie watching and sympathizing as they pretended not to hear.

"I thought it was just for managers," I said.

"It is, but I think you should go," she said. "I think it would be good for you."

I might have tumbled into full-blown despair were it not for

Madeline. We'd agreed to meet that night, and even though she was young and spoiled and totally unreliable, the anticipation of seeing her made everything else seem irrelevant. So I thanked Bekah for her warped advice and followed her to the elevators, where all the other managers in Luxury were waiting to go up while everyone else was going down.

"Awesome to be here, right?" said Tyler Petrovic, the bachelor manager on Spirits with the slicked-back hair and never-funny sense of humor. He grabbed my hand and raised it over my head. I had no idea what was happening.

"I'm trying to twirl you," he said.

"That is not going to happen," I said.

"You can twirl me," Diana said, touching her cheekbones, pin-points of rouge.

The conference room was dark because the blinds were closed and the only light was coming from the projector. Bekah, Diana, and the rest of the managers sat at the table looking glamorous and in-destructible while I stood in the back, hoping to blend in with the wall. I might have fallen into a full-blown trance staring at the dust floating in the light of the PowerPoint that was about to start, when Arthur walked in and slid the door closed hard enough to make the blinds shake.

"Let's stop wasting time," he said, which seemed odd considering he was the one who'd been late. "I just got off a call with Helen Zeller, *screaming* at me. We need double-digit growth by the end of the quar-ter or else someone's going down. Milan was not just an excuse to sit on your ass and eat tortellini."

The door opened and Tom walked in, red-faced and sweat-ing. He squeezed behind everyone's chairs to get to the last empty seat while Arthur stood frozen at the head of the table and crossed his arms so everyone could see his tanned wrists and nautical man-bracelets.

"What happened with Chanel?" Arthur went right in, gesturing at Tom's name on the screen. It was below the red line of employment security, meaning he'd sold only $50,000 worth of ad space instead of $500,000. "What did you do? Play your bagpipes for them?"

Tom smoothed his tie, rubbed his eyes, and wiped his nose. He appeared to be on the verge of a stroke. "Any day now," he said. "They're coming in."

"Bekah!" Arthur barked into the darkness. "I heard you're talking to Mezzanine. That's huge. We've been trying to get them to spend with us for years."

Bekah smiled and made a ring around her wrist, a mindless gesture that must have reminded her how skinny she was. "I have a friend who works there so . . ."

Arthur grinned into the light of the projector. His shadow burst against the wall.

"Diana, did you hear that?" He squinted at her crown of chestnut-colored hair. "Your Rolodex is officially useless."

Bekah laughed. "I don't even know what a Rolodex *is*."

"Tyler!" Another bark. "What's going on with Bacardi? I thought you were on top of those binge drinkers."

"They're rebranding—"

"Wrong." Arthur cut him off. "They're avoiding your cologne. What is that? Abercrombie and Fitch? You smell like you're on trial for sexual assault."

As soon as the meeting was over, Arthur vanished with sinister grace and the managers made forced small talk. Nobody mentioned Arthur or the spectacle of superiority he had enacted, and I understood why. His essence had left echoes in the room, and even if his body wasn't there, some part of him was surely still listening.

———

Madeline was late to the bar, and by the time I saw her coming in her tiny black skirt and clean white tennis shoes, I almost wanted to call it quits, keep my pride, and go home.

"Nice fit," she said, appraising my baggy jeans and bomber jacket. "Sorry it took me forever to get here. I was stuck in Manhattan for my evil roommate's birthday party and this devil Jennifer was there. She went to Brown with me and she's from Canada and she made a documentary about genocide that won a bunch of awards. But she's the worst. She got this impossible visa called 'extraordinary alien' and she kept talking about it. And I was right there and I have to leave in like a month."

I felt dizzy with something like abandonment. I'd forgotten Madeline was leaving. It was something I chose not to believe. "You could get a different visa," I said. "Mediocre alien."

She took off her denim jacket and revealed a white collared shirt that made her look preppy and girly and annoyingly attractive.

"Last night Cassandra and I went out with some crazy rich people from Miami," she said. "We got home at four and couldn't remember where we'd been. I need to stop putting things up my nose."

"I don't think you actually like doing drugs," I said. "I think you just like talking about them."

She plopped her leather purse on top of the bar and pulled out a beat-up copy of *A Moveable Feast*. "I know Hemingway is the worst but you should read this. It's about expats who drink too much."

"Will I be tested?"

"It's open-book."

I took her battered paperback while she looked around with a pained expression.

"This place sucks," she said. "Why are we here?"

I panicked. Madeline's moods were so changeable, sometimes I felt like I had to start juggling just to keep her from calling a car and meeting someone else.

"We can make it fun," I said. "We can play darts."

"Absolutely not. I hate throwing things."

I dragged her over to the target in the corner and gave her a handful of darts. She sighed like I was making her do something pointless, which maybe I was.

"Do it with your eyes closed," I said, knowing she would do anything as long as it involved a certain level of recklessness.

She closed her eyes and starting throwing. She hit the ceiling, the wall, and the sign that said NO BROS ALLOWED.

"See," she said. "I'm bad."

I took a turn and hit the target. She raised her eyebrows.

"Look at you," she said, reaching out to squeeze whatever arm muscle I had from typing four emails a day. "Sporty Spice."

We went back to the bar to sit and I began to feel hopeful. She took out her phone and scrolled through a stockpile of unread messages.

"My friend from RISD is a promoter at this club in Midtown and she keeps asking me to come. Do you want to go? She'll give us champagne."

I had spent the day in Midtown. I hated Midtown. I didn't want to go to Midtown.

"It sounds terrible," I said.

"I know. We should go."

She waved down the bartender and I signed for our drinks. "Cassandra's coming too," she said. "Is that okay? She's from here so she's cool."

All my fantasies about us spending the night together evaporated.

"I thought she was your evil roommate," I said.

"That's my *other* roommate. And she's not evil. She just goes off her meds and forgets to turn off the stove."

We went into a neighboring liquor store to get something for the ride and Madeline played with her hair as she surveyed the bottles. I stood beside her and felt strangely moved by our joint shopping trip, like at last we were a real couple, buying things, going places.

"This," she declared, picking up a random bottle of tequila. "This is what we want." I paid at the register and we went outside to meet Cassandra, who had shown up in a Wu-Tang T-shirt and zebra-print coat. She flung her floppy hair back and revealed a tiny teacup face with big saucer eyes and a sour little mouth.

"Can you order a car?" she said to Madeline. "I canceled all my cards so I wouldn't use them."

Madeline took out her phone. We were standing between parked cars, passing around the bottle.

"I'm actually so pissed at Matt right now." Cassandra was talking. "He said he needed to be alone to *figure things out*. Funny that he needs to be alone right when his EX is back in town." A car with a broken muffler drove by and made a horrible sound. Cassandra didn't notice. She was the human equivalent of a nail gun, a fast-talking city kid with a startling imperviousness to blinking. "It's because he's an alcoholic. He told me, which is good. Admitting it is the big thing. But he keeps doing it. He doesn't drink for months and then one day he has thirty drinks before noon."

A car pulled up and Madeline checked the plates, making sure it was the one she'd ordered and not the one belonging to the other group of girls who looked exactly like us on the other side of the street.

She opened the door and I rushed to get in next so we could sit together but I was too late. Cassandra took the middle seat, and when neither of them buckled their seat belts I had to hold back from saying something that would have made me sound like a dad.

"One time Matt was forty minutes late to a date." Cassandra was still talking. She would talk all night. "I was just sitting there, waiting for him, for like an hour."

As we crossed the Williamsburg Bridge, Madeline looked out at the skyline and I watched the side of her face in the shifting columns of streetlight. *Look at me,* I thought. *Look at me if you like me.*

"I want to trust him . . ." Cassandra turned the stud in her nostril. "But how am I supposed to trust a guy who keeps changing the lock on his phone?"

Madeline caught me staring at her and looked away like she was bored or even a little annoyed, but I think she liked it. I think she liked being adored.

The club was a gigantic and windowless tomb on Tenth Avenue. Pulsating with unearthly music, its giant marquee lit up with dire predictions:

FRIDAY—CARNAGE
SATURDAY—DADA
SUNDAY—INSOMNIA

Women teetered in heels and tight dresses. Men with goatees huddled in jeans with swirls on the butt. Nobody looked happy. Nobody was wearing coats.

"This place is a nightmare," Madeline said.

"I know," Cassandra said. "I can't wait to make fun of people."

Madeline's promoter friend came out and escorted us through a side door. She was big-haired and pretty, like Cassandra, but clearly in art school because her makeup was crazy.

"I'll touch base with you guys later," she said, a stock phrase from work that felt odd to hear in a room full of laser lights.

She dropped us off at a table in VIP and Cassandra lunged for the bucket of champagne while Madeline tucked her hair behind her ears and looked around, sullen and bored. Busboys snaked through the crowd with plastic tubs and flashlights, collecting empty glasses with the ferocity of Navy SEALs. Meanwhile the actual clubgoers were seemingly uninterested in everything but the booze. They kept touching it, spilling it, taking pictures of it, and when I finally ventured to pour some into a glass, a woman with huge druggy eyes grabbed me and said, "That's ours!"

Embarrassed, I tried again at a different table and that time it worked.

"If it's poison," I said, handing Madeline a sticky flute, "don't blame me."

"I will," she said. "I'll blame you in the hell we're already in."

We elbowed our way over to the balcony so we could look at the bathtub of bodies dancing in the pit below. Drunk and writhing, everyone appeared to be drowning.

"Isn't it weird to think all those people were once babies in diapers?" I said.

Madeline looked me up and down, taking in my boots and jeans and baseball hat. "Is it weird for you to be here with all these straight people?"

"I was about to ask you the same," I said.

Light from the disco ball shined in our eyes and I started to feel hopeful again, like we were above it all together, linked in our perpetual watching. I reached for her hand, thinking this might be the moment we'd kiss, when Cassandra came out of nowhere and stuck her big hair in Madeline's face.

"Matt's on his way," she said. "We have to leave."

Within minutes we were in a cab on the way to a different club in an even worse part of Midtown, and when the driver happened to pass the Newspaper building, I looked up at the nineteenth floor and cringed.

"So funny." Cassandra peered up at the glass. "Isn't that where you guys work?"

I shielded my eyes. "Work does not exist."

Erica Peplin

"At least you actually get paid," Madeline said.

"You could always move to my department," I said. "Start working in sales, wearing floral blouses."

"I'd rather be deported."

The second club was a sprawling red-lit dungeon filled with crystal chandeliers and people wearing glow sticks. Grimy cushions lined the walls and women were standing on them, jumping and occasionally screaming. Madeline and Cassandra found some girls they knew from school and it was too loud to talk so I just stood near them and tried not to look irrelevant.

"Cheers!" A guy in a soccer jersey handed me a glass of champagne. It tasted like melted gummy bears and I drank half of it before remembering that I was already drunk. The DJ triggered the sound of sirens and Madeline pulled me onto the dance floor. Cassandra was behind me, wooing and shaking, and Madeline was in front of me dancing with her arms up, and they took turns bumping their waists into mine, passing me between them like some kind of party trick. The song was endless, as if trying to prove a point about the eternity of every moment, and suddenly Cassandra was gone. In the bathroom, passed out, kidnapped—whatever it was, it didn't matter. Madeline was dancing with her arms around my neck, and when our eyes met, I felt gripped by forces beyond my control. Everything about her was astonishing. Her wide eyes. Her dark hair. Her wormy dancing. Her unpierced ears.

"Are you having fun?" she shouted.

"This is the best night of my life," I said, kidding but also not.

The DJ yelled into the microphone, which seemed to defeat the purpose of using a microphone, and Madeline looked intently into my eyes. Surrounded by fog and music and people with herpes, she kissed me on the lips, and it felt so right that I could have stood there all night, kissing her and swaying until we both passed out on the floor. She leaned back and looked surprised and I went in to kiss her again. I felt her waist, her arms, her neck, savoring all the parts of her

48

that had been so long forbidden, and when we finally let go of each other, there was Cassandra, pushing her way toward us in the crowd.

"We gotta go!" she said. "Matt's roommate is here."

She leaned in to Madeline's ear and said something I couldn't hear, and when they both turned to look at me, I knew they were going to leave.

"Thanks for coming out with us," Madeline shouted.

"Anytime."

"See you soon?"

"For sure."

They took a car to a third location while I did my commute all over again, but that time with a big stupid grin on my face.

november

On Monday morning, my body was still buzzing from the kiss I'd shared with Madeline. Even my morning train ride wasn't a swamp of time to wade through so much as an invitation to bask in the memory of her face.

Ellie showed up to work with her mushroom bun transformed into a shimmering waterfall of hair. She had gone from frizzy-haired dork to straight-haired office Barbie overnight and it was actually stunning.

"We're supposed to hear about the supervisor position today," she chirped. "So I woke up at five and got a blowout."

"Holy shit," Karen said. "How much did that cost?"

Diana came over and touched it, the Stepford Planners took pictures, Arthur did a double take, and Ellie soaked up their praise.

"I'm just glad all my hard work paid off," she said, sipping her tea. "I've been coming in early, staying late, helping Tyler even though he's not my manager and never will be, thank god."

"I'm glad too," I said, and it was true, though my happiness had nothing to do with her. I just wanted her to get promoted so she'd go away.

At the weekly planner meeting, there were a dozen autumnal-themed donuts on the table frosted with orange and red leaves. The Stepford Planners eyed them from a distance. Karen took two.

"Give me a second, okay, peeps?" Vanessa crawled under the table and started making squirrel sounds by our feet. "This happened once before. Just hang tight." She was trying to fix the projector, but no one moved or offered to help. We were all too well acquainted with her inability to get anything technical to work. "Time to pivot." She popped up from under the table, covered in fuzz. "I'm just gonna explain what's going on and have you guys imagine the graphics, cool?"

Ellie raised her hand. "Can we get an update on the supervisor position?"

Vanessa tugged on the bottom button of her blazer. It was hanging by a thread and, judging by the missing buttons above it, about to disappear.

"I have some not-great news about that," she said. "HR said they needed to reevaluate."

"Reevaluate?" Ellie's eyes bulged. "What about the people who already applied? Do we have to apply again?"

"I'd have to confirm with HR, but I believe that, yes, you would have to reapply."

Ellie sat back and smoothed the wrinkles of her skirt with barely concealed rage, and as soon as the meeting was over, she boarded an elevator going up, presumably on her way to HR to complain.

"Jane!" It was Vanessa. I hated it when she said my name. It meant we had to talk.

"I know it's been rough with all these changes going on." She glanced down at my notebook, where I had been drawing bugs with human faces. "I know Fashion is a lot more intense than Nonprofits so I just wanted to check in, take your temperature. . . ."

I paused, trying to figure out the best way to say, *Actually, Vanessa, I'm a dumpy dyke who belongs in a basement, sweeping cobwebs and breaking down boxes.*

"It's definitely different," I said.

Vanessa raised her fist, necessitating a bump that filled me with dread.

"You're a rock star," she said. "Good talk."

Ellie came back to the station biting her lips and started drafting a formal letter of complaint that would inevitably result in nothing.

"How much overtime have you been working?" Karen asked her.

"A lot."

"Well, stop. This company is using you. This whole department is corrupt. They only care about good-looking kids in their twenties. I've already been demoted twice. Pretty soon our jobs won't even exist anymore. You know what those guys in Tech are doing? They're figuring out how to get rid of us."

The Stepford Planners came over with sad faces they probably learned from TV.

"I can't believe you didn't get the job."

"You totally deserved it."

"Everything happens for a reason."

Ellie compulsively screwed and unscrewed the cap of her reusable water bottle.

"Actually, it doesn't," she said. "We're complex interactions of atoms and neurons responding to stimuli in an essentially meaningless void."

Diana, who was supposed to be the engineer behind Ellie's promotion as her manager, was oblivious to the slight. She sat in her cube and took cunning glimpses at her compact mirror, and when her gazpacho lunch arrived, she came over to the station to ask Ellie for a spoon.

"*Merci beaucoup*," she said, slinking away in her pearls.

Karen coughed and spat into a napkin. "She should have said something. She should've talked to HR." Her voice was righteous and hoarse, a scar that had learned to talk. "You deserved that promotion and she knows it."

Ellie fixed her collar and concentrated on her screen. "It's fine. I don't mind. It's not her fault. It's fine."

I went down to the media floor in the afternoon to see if I could run into Madeline. I hadn't seen her in the dining hall during lunch and now a muscular man in a rugby shirt was sitting at her desk.

"I have never heard of that person," he said, blinking a lot as he apologized in a gay voice that made me, once again, jealous of all the freaks, artists, and weirdos who got to work on the media floor. "I could look her up in the directory. I don't know where it is but I'm sure I could find one."

"Don't worry about it."

I went into an empty conference room and called Madeline.

"Where are you?"

"My apartment."

"What are you doing?"

"Packing for London."

"You're going to London?"

"I thought I told you."

My heart was beating fast at the thought of Madeline leaving but I couldn't think of anything more embarrassing than an honest dialogue about my separation anxiety.

"You can come over if you want," she said. "I need help getting my suitcase down from this really high shelf. I think it's stuck up there."

"I'll be there as soon as I can," I said. "We could even get dinner. If that's something you'd want."

"I have been craving hummus."

We hung up and I felt ecstatic. I took a long walk around the building and stopped somewhere between Legal and Accounting to watch a man in a navy jumpsuit painting the hallway red. The walls were already red but he was painting them again, a fresh coat of the same.

"It's the company's red," he said. "They made it. They copyrighted it. It's the Newspaper's Red." He rolled his fuzzy brush over an aluminum tray on a custodial cart that had everything he needed: rags, buckets, brushes, and a jumbo fountain soda.

"I wish we could switch places," I said, "so I could be the one painting."

He laughed like he thought I was kidding.

"Some people are nice," he said. "Some people are not so nice."

A few hours later, I was leaving early for the night when Arthur's skeletal assistant stopped me in front of the elevator doors. "Are you excited for Arthur's dinner? We're going to celebrate his leadership in style. It's going to be a truly magical soirée."

"I wasn't invited," I said, and pretended to look sad while I pressed the elevator button again.

"Bekah should have added you to the list. The whole Luxury team is going."

Ellie and Karen walked over with their coats and purses. "We can ride the train together," Ellie said. "I printed directions in case we lose service underground."

Times Square was loud and dense with tourists. More than half of them looked cold and lost and I felt sorry for them. It was getting late, they were probably hungry, and they still didn't know where to eat, what to see, or how to get there. The couples holding hands seemed to be doing so more from fear than affection, afraid of getting swept away by the crowds, hit by a garbage truck, or falling into an open cellar. Just looking at their tired faces, I could almost hear the voices in their heads thinking, *This isn't the New York we signed up for.*

"Come on." Ellie scurried down the subway steps. "I don't want to lose you."

We huddled together underground, waiting for the train, and Ellie took out her phone to share pictures of the restaurant, which wasn't a restaurant but "a Members-Only Social Club with thirteen marble fireplaces, six onyx bars, and no tips for gaining membership" because the selection process was a secret.

I despised the place instantly for its exclusivity and I knew it would hate me too, considering I hadn't washed my hair in four days and the sole of my left shoe was falling off.

"I hope they're not too fancy to accommodate my allergies," Ellie said.

"It's fucked-up," Karen said. "A bomb shelter for the one percent."

We got off the train at Fourteenth Street and found the brownstone. I led the way up the stone steps, wanting to get the night over with as soon as possible. When I reached the top, I shoved Ellie toward the door.

"You go in first," I said. "You're prettier." She looked scared. She probably thought I was hitting on her. We stepped inside and an underage model scowled at us from behind a podium.

"Hi, we're here for Arthur Truman's dinner," Ellie said.

The teenybopper blinked at us with beautiful irritation. Techno music pumped through the rococo wallpaper. "Down and to the left," she said, pointing toward a staircase at the end of the hall. We shuffled past her like country bumpkins and felt our way down the dark, narrow stairs. A tea candle flickered on every step and I wondered if this was the night we would all be burned alive.

A woman wearing a bow tie was waiting for us at the bottom of the stairs. I thought she might hand us something fun like an egg roll or one of those party favors that shoots confetti.

"Red or white?" she asked Ellie.

"Red or white?" she asked Karen.

"Red or white?" she asked me.

Why she had to ask the same question three times, I'm not sure. I guess it was her job to make people feel important.

The dining room was filled with managers and all of them were talking at the same time. Their babble was demonic. It bounced against the low ceiling and gained momentum with every gulp of wine.

"I should've known they'd beat us here," Ellie said. "They all took cars."

She left to wash the subway off her hands while I hovered beneath a medieval wall sconce and watched Tom explain Celtic rock to a woman who wasn't listening. I wanted to move around and maybe find a way to escape but I kept getting trapped behind the dining table. It was a giant slab of repurposed wood topped with exotic plants, curated place settings, and a three-tiered turntable of smoked salmon, toasted baguette, apricots, and brie. I was reaching for a hunk of bread when Diana made accidental eye contact with me and was polite enough to force herself to speak.

"How *are* you?" she said. "It's been forever."

She touched me lightly on the back and her big Botoxed eyes twitched as she seemed to realize I wasn't wearing a bra.

A dinner bell rang and Ellie waved my name card in the air.

"You're over here," she said. "Right between me and Tyler."

The walls seemed to be closing in as I took my seat and checked my phone under the table. I didn't have service and Madeline would have no idea why I wasn't coming over. Not that she would care. She might be relieved. She might go out with someone else.

"Where are you from again?" Tyler's voice boomed in my ear. He smelled like aftershave and male authority. "Wait, let me guess."

"Michigan," I said. "Detroit area."

"The Midwest! That's what I was going to say. I can tell you're not from here. You're too nice." He put his elbows on the table. "Don't tell me you're a Wolverine."

"I'm not."

"I played everything in college. Hockey, lacrosse, disc golf. Now I can barely make time for my trainer."

Bekah was sitting at the other end of the table. She hadn't acknowledged me in days and I felt certain I'd done something wrong.

"Don't worry about her," Karen said. "That's how it is with managers. They love you until you work for them. Then you're slow and lazy and you screw everything up."

Diana felt her pearls as she read the menu out loud, figuring it out like a crime that needed to be solved. "I can't decide." She looked at Tyler and blinked seductively. "Are you getting the fish or the steak?"

Karen was right; they were sleeping together, and the thought of it exhausted me. Of course the vain older woman had fallen for the oafish bachelor. It was so pathetic that I wished them well.

"I'm getting the steak," I blurted.

Diana bobbed her head, pretending to consider my choice. "A steak," she said. "Wow."

Dandelion salads arrived on silver plates handed out by the voiceless staff. The chair at the head of the table was empty.

"Do we have to wait for Arthur to eat?" I asked.

"Nope," Tyler said.

"He hasn't come to his birthday dinner in years," Diana said.

A girl with a septum piercing refilled my water. "Hi," she said.

"Hi," I said.

She went back into the kitchen and everyone looked at me.

"You know her?" Tyler asked.

My blood was rushing. I dimly remembered her. We'd shared a half-pint of whiskey on the pier, kissed passionately on a bench facing the water, and made no effort to see each other again.

"I know her from something," I said. "I can't remember what."

"Welcome to Advertising," Diana said. "Half our job is just remembering names."

"And spelling them right!" Bekah added from across the room. "This one over here"—she shook her glass of Chianti at me—"she sends an email to *Bodega* Veneta. I'm like, 'Honey, it's *Bottega* Veneta, not *Bodega*. We're not buying Doritos.'"

Everyone laughed, including the girl from the pier, who'd reappeared with some plates, and Tyler thwacked me on the back. "Cut her some slack," he said. "She just moved here from Ohio."

Everyone was still happy, talking and chewing, when the bow-tied staff doled out miniature cups of tiramisu and I slowly put on my coat.

"Karen," I said, "you want to smoke?"

She picked up her fat purse off the floor and we stomped together up the stairs.

"I didn't know you smoked," she said.

"I don't," I said. "I'm leaving."

Karen cackled. "Thatta girl."

I rode the train straight to Madeline's. She wasn't responding to my texts but I figured she was distracted, packing for her trip.

I wasn't sure which apartment to buzz but I knew her bedroom window—she'd pointed it out to me once—and I started throwing pebbles at the glass. It seemed like a romantic gesture, like something a cute boy would do in a high school movie, and when I missed her window six times in a row and started hitting other people's windows instead, I called her and left a message.

"Hi. It's me. Just calling. Call me back. Or don't. Phone calls are weird. Just don't leave without saying good-bye. I hope you're not dead. Please don't be dead."

I hung up and walked back to my place with my phone out, waiting for Madeline to text me. I walked a block. Then another. I saw nothing that was happening around me. I might as well have been on one of those moving walkways at the airport where the conveyor belt does the walking for you and you're allowed to stand with your suitcase and enter a vegetative state. All I knew was that I didn't love Madeline. If anything, I hated her. She was impulsive and inconsistent. She never offered to pay for anything. She only ever liked me so that she could have the privilege of rejecting me. And now she was gone, probably moved to London, where she'd start dating some tall, skinny boy who went to Oxford and gave her club drugs because he was actually in med school and super rich.

Laurel was lying in bed in a tie-dyed T-shirt with her pink-and-blue hair tied back in a lump. One of her model friends was sitting in the window, smoking a cigarette in slinky white overalls that probably cost five hundred dollars. I stood in the kitchen and poked my head in the door, not wanting them to see me in my frumpy work clothes.

"Are you color-blind?" Laurel asked me.

"I don't think so." I prepared myself for some kind of insult, thinking they'd gone in my room and seen the boring beige color of my hand-me-down sheets.

Laurel held up her sketch pad covered in pastel zigzags, swirls, and blobs. "Marcel said I use baby colors, but they're not baby, they're fruity."

"They're fruity candy," I said.

"Exactly. I'm fruity candy. Not baby blanket."

I agreed and felt glad to be friends with an artist. How opinionated they were allowed to be about the most trivial things.

The model lit a fresh cigarette and looked like a French New Wave movie, just sitting there, all perfect and pouty and absolutely silent.

"She works at the Newspaper," Laurel said to her friend, as if wanting to give my existence more reality, or maybe just prove I wasn't a total loser. The model looked at me and frowned like maybe she didn't speak English. She had a long face full of shadows and a tooth gap that looked preposterously sexy. "What do you do there again?" Laurel said, tossing her sketch pad onto the floor. "You make ads?"

"Something like that," I said.

The model scratched her nose and blew smoke out the window, clearly bored by the mere thought of a nine-to-five.

"I got flaked on by Madeline again," I said.

"Who?"

"My work crush."

"The straight girl?"

"She doesn't believe in labels."

Laurel did a loud yoga breath of dismay. "When was the last time you had sex?"

"Don't ask me that."

"As long as it's a choice," the model said, still gazing out the window, "celibacy can be extremely productive."

The next morning everyone in Luxury took turns going into Arthur's office to drop off thank-you notes.

"He loves thank-you notes," Ellie said. "If you haven't written one yet, I have extra stationery."

"I'll shoot him an email," I lied.

"I'm not writing shit," Karen said.

For the next few hours, I bit my nails and felt like my life was ruined. Emails piled up, asking me to do things I didn't want to do, and I couldn't fathom how I'd ended up sitting in an office, wearing a button-down shirt, and typing words like *mobile growth* onto a screen. Nobody made me become a professional woman. It was a pressure I put on myself. I thought I could live like the women I'd seen in movies who worked in an office but weren't controlled by it. Who wore nice shoes and had health insurance but whose real life happened outside of work. And yet so much of my life happened inside the office that I knew it was changing me—stunting my thoughts and calcifying certain lonely habits—and my life as a gainfully employed adult could only get worse.

Bekah clicked over to the station in stilettos the color of cheddar cheese.

"Did you change the homepage calendar?" she asked.

"I've never opened the homepage calendar in my life," I said.

Bekah sat in Ellie's empty chair and rolled up to me. "Open it," she said, her lips twisted into a new contortion of wrath. "Who has the homepage on Monday?"

Ellie came back with her oatmeal and hovered, chair-less, while

Karen dug for her cigarettes as an excuse to get away from angry Bekah.

I opened the calendar and it was immediately clear that Monday's homepage had been reserved by Diana Sands.

"Is that bad?" I asked.

Bekah swiveled with a look of despair. Tyler walked by with a protein shake and averted his eyes.

"Monday's homepage was supposed to be reserved for Mezzanine. They have stores opening across the country. You were supposed to reserve the homepage."

"Planners aren't supposed to reserve homepages," Ellie said, standing off to the side and topping her oatmeal with what appeared to be bird food. She was a sadist-perfectionist who talked incessantly about her allergies, but maybe she was good. Maybe she was nice.

Bekah got up so quickly that her chair rolled backward and smacked the window. I thought it might fall through the glass and kill someone.

"Don't touch anything," she said.

Five minutes later, Samantha messaged me from the other side of the floor.

Why is Bekah yelling at Diana?

Ellie scraped at the oats stuck to the side of her bowl. "Just an idea," she said. "But the November twenty-ninth homepage is open and if I were you, I'd reserve it for Mezzanine as a backup." She shrugged and licked her spoon. In her performance of knowing nothing, she clearly knew everything.

"Planners aren't supposed to reserve homepages," I said.

"Given that Mezzanine's plan is worth millions, I'd say the situation calls for an exception." She smiled a haughty woman's smile, which she must have learned from Diana. "I'm just saying."

The weekend was a blur. I ate Laurel's expired drunken noodles from the fridge and spent most of Saturday and Sunday sitting in the back of a coffee shop drinking bitter coffee and looking around for other impulsive, dark-haired straight girls to date. I tried to read *A Moveable Feast* but kept taking breaks to hold the spine under my nose and smell the pages for proof of Madeline. I'd never been a Hemingway fan but the simplicity of the story was comforting. I liked the way he walked in the rain, went to cafés, and wrote with a pencil over café au lait. He didn't have hot water or anything like a stable income but he was happy. He liked his bed on the floor, and the pictures he hung on the walls, and his wife, Hadley, who wore multiple sweaters and played piano.

On Monday a woman draped in Tiffany jewels sauntered across the homepage. She sat on a headline about refugees and swung her leg over the word *Starving*.

Diana Sands celebrated her homepage win by showing up to work in a flouncy pink dress with wispy wings that billowed out behind her as she walked across the long rows of gray cubes. She was circling the floor, accepting compliments from every department, and it turned the hallway into a runway of sorts that made her look like a prima ballerina aging gracefully into retirement.

"You look like you should be on a red carpet," I said when we passed each other outside the break room. She gave me a stunned look and then put her arms around me and squeezed. It felt strangely exciting to be hugged by such a beautiful woman before noon.

"You are *so* sweet," she said. "That just made my day."

She returned to her cube by the window and I watched as she carefully adjusted the many layers of her dress so as not to run over them with her rolling chair.

"Have you talked to Bekah yet?" Ellie asked me.

"No, why?"

She turned toward Arthur's office, where Bekah and Tom were sitting with their heads down. Whatever was happening in there, it didn't look good.

"I'm sure it's nothing," I said, more to myself than to Ellie, who had quietly gone back to work. "I'm sure it's fine."

A second later, the phone on my desk rang and the caller ID said *Truman*. I tried not to panic while feeling overcome with guilt. I'd left his dinner early. I hadn't written a thank-you note. And because I was a coward, as contemptuous of my job as I was terrified of losing it, I almost didn't pick up.

"Hi, Jane?"

I turned so we could see each other. He was sitting ten feet away.

"Could you come in here for a minute?"

I got up with the self-consciousness of someone being filmed and let myself into Arthur's office. I'd never been in there before and it was actually stunning. It smelled rich and leathery, like a golf club where women weren't allowed, and his antique mission lamp gave the room a deceptively calm glow. Tom and Bekah were facing Arthur, and when they didn't turn or acknowledge me, I hovered between them with my hands cupped behind my back like some kind of disgraced butler.

"I got a call from Mezzanine's CEO," Arthur said. "He says we sold their homepage to Tiffany and he wants to pull everything— all two million—so I'm trying to figure out what the fuck is going on." He paused to let the severity of the situation sink in. Tom's face was red and swollen. Bekah compulsively revolved a bangle around her wrist. They both appeared to be in a state of shock or extreme denial and neither of them was able to look at Arthur, who was staring into me.

"I called you in here to rectify some miscommunications." The razor-sharp calmness of his voice was worse than yelling. "Did you tell Diana Sands she could have today's homepage?"

It had been years since I read *The Crucible*, but standing in

Arthur's office with his big oak desk and framed magazine covers, I understood how those girls could admit to witchcraft. A part of me also wanted to lie and tell the tall, tanned prince whatever he wanted to hear.

"You're scaring her," Tom said.

"Well, this is scary." Arthur pointed at the ceiling. "Going up to the thirtieth floor and telling Helen Zeller we lost two million dollars is scary."

"I didn't know Mezzanine wanted the homepage," I said.

"I told you," Bekah said, turning to me. "I emailed you."

"Let's stop this," Tom said. "It's not a good idea."

Arthur glared at Bekah. "Planners don't reserve homepages. Don't tell me you didn't know that. How long were you a planner?"

Bekah's head fell and she started taking short breaths, trying not to cry while obviously beginning to cry.

"I have one possible idea," I said. "Mezzanine could have the homepage on the twenty-ninth. I reserved it as a backup."

"Planners aren't supposed to reserve homepages," Bekah said.

"Brilliant," Arthur said. "They can have the homepage on the twenty-ninth and we'll throw in some free banner ads. They can't say no to that." He looked at me. "You came up with this?"

My throat went dry. I thought of Ellie.

"Pretty much," I said.

Arthur slid his thick black credit card across the desk to Tom. "Buy this girl lunch," he said. "She just saved your peanut head."

I looked out the window and felt a momentary sensation of power. It was a privilege to work in an office, to have an email address, a salary, a keyboard, and a title. The river was flowing, all things were.

Laurel was gluing macaroni noodles to a pair of pants when I got home.

"Madeline's gone," I said.

"The straight girl?"

"She doesn't believe in labels."

Laurel pretended to shoot herself in the head with hot glue. She was like my bitchy therapist. "When was the last time you had sex?"

"When was the last time you left the apartment?"

"I create my own system of values and right now I have to finish this installation for the Living Gallery show and I'm not going anywhere until it's done."

I glanced at the sink, overflowing with crusty bowls and gooey paintbrushes.

"I'm going to the bodega," I said. "You want anything?"

"Wait, I'll come with you."

Laurel put on her construction boots and we walked to the bodega with dead bugs in the window where we both spent five minutes looking at the seltzer.

"I want regular water but I refuse to pay for regular water," she said.

"I know. You might as well put your head under a sink."

"Seltzer is excited water."

"Just don't get apricot. It tastes like foot."

It was dark and cold but we walked anyway, past the punk bars and Chinese takeout places and storefront churches with pretty names like Lamb of God and Never Give Up. We were cutting across Maria Hernandez Park, where some skateboarders were trying to jump over their backpacks, when Laurel started telling me about her latest hookup. Because even though she suffered from bouts of dangerously low self-esteem, it never seemed to impair her ability to date and break up with someone in the span of a week.

"I had to end it," she said. "Her second toe was bigger than her big toe."

"That means nothing."

"Until you're in bed with her and looking at her feet."

The smell of trash rose up from the curb. Pigeons scrubbed their wings in puddles of old rain.

"You know what I never do?" she said.

"What?"

"Look in the mirror. So when I do, I'm like, *What the fuck.*"

"Why?"

"Because of my face. And my hair. I'm just ugly."

I laughed. "We're all ugly."

"Do you ever look at yourself in the mirror?"

"Never," I said. "I aspire to be an orb."

Our disillusionment was endless and invigorating, and before going home, we checked on the feather boa wrapped around a telephone wire that was slowly going bald.

"In a week she'll be a string," Laurel said.

That Friday nobody did anything. Tom played loud banjo music and didn't seem to realize everyone in Luxury could hear it. Ellie printed a bunch of recipes using the good color printer and buried them in her bottom drawer with the shifty-eyed look of someone embezzling. Bekah ignored me completely, which she had been doing for weeks, and locked herself in an empty conference room to better focus on shopping for throw pillows. And Karen showed up at noon and coughed into her headset. "I hate my fucking job. Everyone around me is doing fucking nothing. I swear to god, I had two vacation days left this year and Vanessa says I have one."

The office cleared out as everyone but the planners left for the weekend and Karen had a heated phone call with her boyfriend, whose shaved head and tribal tattoos could be seen in the photo pinned over her keyboard. From what I could tell, he couldn't or wouldn't pick up their son from school so she yelled and threw her headset at the wall.

"My boyfriend is a *two-year-old*. I have to talk to him *like a two-year-old*." She went into Arthur's empty office and started opening drawers.

"I'm looking for candy," she said. "I know he's still got that bag from Halloween."

I watched in awe as she opened a leather briefcase.

"He has a prescription for Robinul in here," she said.

"What's that?" I said.

"It's for stomach problems."

She opened his closet next. Ellie was palpably nervous and trying not to look, but I was thrilled. We were kids playing spy in a house with no parents.

"Seashells, olive oil, some picture of a naked dude." She held up a framed photo that could have been a Robert Mapplethorpe. "Have you ever seen so much crap?"

Ellie looked at Karen's crates stacked in front of the window and partially blocking the view. "Never in my life."

Karen banged her fist against the glass and held up a bag of mini candy bars. "You want Snickers, Milky Way, or Kit Kat? Fuck it. I'm taking the bag."

Madeline was back from London and we'd agreed to meet for a drink. I told myself to have no expectations. To go into the night with a blasé or even uninterested attitude. Then I proceeded to play happy music, shave my legs, meticulously clean my room, and get excited over fantasy versions of our reunion. She'd take one sip of her drink, grab me by the neck, and tell me how much she'd missed me, more than she ever thought she would. I would be aloof in response, and this new indifference on my part would make her want me even more.

Don't hate me

It was Madeline, writing to me after I had just downed a preparatory shot of whiskey.

I'm sick

I think I caught something on the plane

I can't even move

My whole apartment could have burned to the ground. That's how much I didn't care about anything. Everyone at Maxine's party had been right. Dating a straight girl was a fucked-up waste.

Totally fine

Feel better soon

I lay on the floor and felt the full weight of my bleak existence pressing down on my idiotic face. I had fooled myself into thinking Madeline needed me when I never should have trusted her. She wasn't my girlfriend and she never would be. Never again would I seek out the company of another person. I would spend the night resolutely alone, training my body to need nothing from anyone so I would never be disappointed again.

"Zinc invited us over," Laurel said, sticking her head in the door. "Maxine is making tacos."

"I'm not in the mood for humanity," I said.

"And what?" She started petting my hair with her dirty boot. "You think I am?"

We took the train to Zinc's disgusting studio apartment, and as soon as we got off at Grand, Laurel recognized her model friend coming out of a deli in bell-bottoms and a big fur hat. She ran up to the girl and tried to pick her up—a joke because Laurel was short and the model was tall—while I stood by some garbage cans and watched them embrace and laugh and touch each other's hair.

"Would you mind going to the party without me?" Laurel looked back at me with a wince. "It's for the best. Zinc's place gives me anxiety."

"Because of the people?"

"No, the primary colors."

She swished down the block with her friend and I was left alone with a runny nose and a bag of chips.

"Where's Laurel?" everyone said as soon as I climbed over the baby gate that Zinc left propped eternally in her door to keep her foster dogs from running into the hall and eating the rats.

"She got stuck at work," I said.

"Liar," Zinc said, and gave me a hug. The hug loosened something in me, or maybe just reminded me that bodies were living things capable of touch, and so I went around hugging everyone, which was also a good way to get warm fast.

"Look at my family's new house in La Jolla," Zinc said, scrolling through pictures of a mansion on the water. "I want to move back."

"And live with your parents?"

"Yeah. My parents are sick. They smoke more weed than I do."

"I'm surprised they're still together," Bhumi said. A proud sociology major, she repeated some bleak statistics about divorce, and Denise, a funny broke singer who disappeared for months at a time to sing on cruise ships, sashayed into the circle to talk about her long-separated parents.

"My mom took nothing because she wanted to start over," she said, "and now, *ten years later*, she's asking me about all this shit, like this blue saucer from her grandma. I told my dad and he found the saucer and now I'm getting all these texts from her saying it's not her saucer. It's the wrong saucer."

We all agreed we would never get married, and I went into the kitchen to check on Maxine, who was fretting over whether or not the pork was done.

"It's been so long since I've had sex, real sex." She gestured wildly with the meat thermometer. "I've done other stuff, but."

"But what?"

"I haven't had a good orgasm."

"Oh."

"So I decided to trim my bush because it was getting out of control and just in case, I mean, I didn't want to bring a girl home and have her go, 'Oh, wow, your bush is a jungle.' Lo and behold, my ex calls me up that night because she needed a place to crash and I'm like, perfect. Two hours later she shows up, fresh off a skiing trip, and guess what? Bitch has two broken legs."

Someone came out of nowhere and took off my hat, which I'd been wearing as a sort of baby blanket to cover up my dirty hair and insecurities. I turned, feeling annoyed, and there was Maxine's roommate with her sad moon face wearing my hat and smiling at me with her tiny teeth in a pathetic attempt to flirt.

"You shouldn't take people's hats." I snatched it back. "They don't like it."

"They don't?"

"No," I said. "It's annoying."

I put my hat back on and fled to the backyard, where I felt like a bad person until it was time to eat tacos and the bonfire came to life. I sat huddled next to it with Zinc, Tasha, and Jess's girlfriend, Addy, while the rescue pit bull slept on her moldy dog bed, having been force-fed a Benadryl so she wouldn't jump into the flames.

"Let's play truth or truth," Zinc said.

"I'm not playing," Addy said. "I hate games." She pushed her glasses up her nose and looked cute. All dorky and resentful.

"Where's Jess?" I said.

"We broke up."

"I'm sorry."

She was wearing a red plaid coat over a thick black turtleneck and L.L.Bean boots and she didn't look cool or remotely stylish but there was something refreshing about that. She was a musician who traveled around playing shows, and maybe because of that, because of her fulfilled life as an artist, she couldn't be bothered with following trends.

"You must be writing new music," I said. "Putting all that heartbreak to use."

"Yeah, right. I sit around and do nothing."

"Nothing is still something."

She poked me with a twig. "So profound."

Zinc's tiny cement backyard had served as the backdrop of countless parties and the evidence of every one of them was still there. There was the kiddie pool left over from the Jell-O wrestling party, the projector screen zip-tied to the chain-link fence where we watched that awful biopic about Elizabeth Bishop, and there, in the corner next to the chainsaw for cutting firewood, the industrial heat lamps that somehow didn't burn down all of East Williamsburg on the night of the Christmas party when they were placed under giant flammable tents.

"I know she's still in love with me," Addy said, staring into the fire and waving away the joint Tasha was passing around. "But she's a stupid alcoholic and now she's dating an idiot who wears bow ties."

I gasped. "Anything but a dapper lesbian."

She laughed, and I could feel Zinc and Tasha watching us. I wished they would stop. Nothing ruined a good flirt like being seen.

"Your earrings," I said. "Are they heavy?"

"Not at all." Addy's hands shot up and she felt her earrings: two squares of red blown glass. "I wear them every day, so I can barely feel them. My neighbor in Maine gave them to me."

"They're . . ." I wanted to say *ugly, dorky*, even *old lady*. ". . . sincere."

Addy rubbed them protectively. "My whole family's from Maine. It's such a special place. I'm going up for Thanksgiving, but when I get back we should . . ." She paused.

"Get a drink?"

"Sorry. Yeah. I forgot what people did."

She got up to leave around midnight and I said I'd walk out with her. Then she put on her hat and gloves and I decided I was too stoned and happy to move so I told her to go without me. She gave me a jokey thumbs-down and left.

"Daaamnn." Tasha turned to me. "Denied."

"What are you talking about?"

"She wanted to boink!"

"Why are you talking like a bro?"

"It's her thing," Zinc explained. "She's a lez bro."

We laughed at Tasha, who was actually a very feminine person with long blond hair and tight designer clothes, and I might've gotten up to chase Addy down but an empty juice box fell from the sky. We looked up, totally confused, and saw the neighbor kids on their fire escape, thrilled to be up late and throwing trash at our heads. They looked like a brother and sister, maybe seven and ten. We shook our fists at them, pretending to be mad, and threw cookies in revenge.

I flew to Detroit on the morning of Thanksgiving, and as soon as I stepped out of baggage claim into the cold wind that whipped my hair into knots, my mother leapt out of her car, squeezed me tightly with her bony arms, and said, "When was the last time you showered?"

"Last night," I said. "Why?"

"Your skin looks greasy."

"It's healthy oil."

"And your hair smells bad."

"Gee, thanks."

My mother opened the trunk.

"Where's your suitcase?" she said.

"I didn't bring one."

"Then what are you going to wear this weekend?"

I looked down at my jeans. "Pretty much this."

My mother shook her head as she got in the driver's seat, sped toward the freeway, and started going over my itinerary for the weekend. There was my older brother and his wife to see, and my grandparents, and my dad, and the neighbors had been asking about me, and so had that woman Jill that I used to babysit for. As she talked in her anxious, unraveling way, I started to regret the trip. My mother was basically a grown-up version of Ellie, neurotically attached to her to-do lists and worried about everything all the time.

Out the passenger-side window, I recognized the leafy suburb that I still occasionally called home. I'd moved away at eighteen but I still knew every basketball net, bay window, and three-car garage we passed. Our town was a neatly arranged expanse of pretty green lawns and golden retrievers that concealed the most horrible things: rich housewives with pill problems, banker dads with gambling debts, society couples with DUIs, and such a preponderance of whiteness that simply consenting to be there felt racist.

"What do you think?" Mom slowed down in front of the house. "How does it look?" She did this every time I flew home, wanting to be flattered for her flower boxes, or if not that, then to be told it looked the same and wasn't that wonderful, to come home to a place that always looked the same.

"Looks great," I said.

The car inched forward. I had to go to the bathroom.

"Sometimes I think I want to move," she said in her wandering voice, "but then I see the house and I think, I can't move. I like living here. I've lived here for, what, fifteen years?"

The seat belt was tight. My bladder was being pinched.

"I bet you felt lucky," she said, "growing up in this nice house. I grew up in a ranch house so I always wanted a house with a second story—"

"MOM," I yelled at the windshield. "I HAVE TO PEE CAN YOU PLEASE STOP TALKING AND PARK THE CAR SO WE CAN GO INSIDE?"

She pulled over and glared at me. "My god," she said. "No wonder you don't have a girlfriend."

I hid in my room for the next few hours and had no idea my brother, Luke, was home until I went downstairs and found him digging around under our mother's desk in the kitchen.

"Can you move," he said. "I'm trying to fix the modem and you're blocking the light."

I went over to the counter and ate a handful of almonds. My brother was a vegetarian so he was, at all times, snacking on nuts. It was actually a form of mania. All the nuts he carried around with him and poured into little bowls.

"I got those at a new pickle store that just opened near the house," he said.

"That must be weird," I said.

"What?"

"Having a house."

Mom charged at me with her scrawny arms swinging. "There's toothpaste on that shirt. You can't wear that to dinner."

I looked down at the stain on my shirt that was no bigger than a pea.

"It's fine." I spat on my thumb and rubbed at the spot. Mom heaved with disappointment.

"Is this how you get ready for work? I feel sorry for your co-workers. You're probably one of those girls who smells bad."

She opened her purse and pulled out a magenta cardigan. "Here, wear this." She draped it over my shoulders and I recoiled in horror at the thought of wearing anything from Chico's.

"C'mon, Jane," Luke said, full of calm rationality. "Just put on a clean shirt. It's not that hard."

He volunteered to set the table while I went upstairs to change. I was still up there, looking for the weed I used to hide under my year-books, when I overheard my brother's wife straining to play the role of daughter-in-law in the kitchen.

"I forget," my mother said in the tentative, high-pitched voice she reserved for guests. "Do you have three or four more years of the PhD?"

"Five," Margaret said, "if all goes well."

I showed up in the doorway in a clean black shirt and I'd also put my hair down as a sort of peace offering. My mother rushed over and petted it. It was the most feminine thing about me.

"You're so beautiful," she said.

"Beauty is on the inside," I said.

"Well, I'm focusing on the outside."

Grandma and Grandpa barged in through the front door, already bickering, and Mom scrambled to throw away all the proof that she'd picked up our Thanksgiving dinner, fully cooked, from the grocery store down the street.

"Where are the tongs?" My mother was opening drawers. "Jane, did you move the tongs?"

We piled our plates with lukewarm food and sat bunched around the dining room table that went unused every day of the year except for this one.

"Doug's coming over later," my mother said, with such trepidation in her voice that she suddenly seemed sixteen again, telling her parents about a boy from school.

"Doug who?" Grandma said.

"It's Doug!" Grandpa shouted at her. Not because he was mad. He just always shouted at Grandma. "You know Doug. Big Doug."

My mother threw down her fork. "Dad! You can't say that. He's lost a lot of weight."

Grandma waved her wineglass under my nose. "You want to try Grandma's wine? You'll like it. It's pinot."

Doug showed up after dinner with a pan of bread pudding. He doled out heaping chunks of it while my mother went around giving everyone scoops of fat-free vanilla ice cream on the side.

"It tastes the same," she said, preemptively defending her lifelong diet, and Doug sweetly agreed. A round, friendly man who dressed like a history teacher in khaki pants and cable-knit sweaters, his presence in the house was strangely comforting, especially because he seemed to genuinely adore my mother.

We moved into the living room and played a game called Password that involved knowing a secret word and trying to get other people to guess it. Grandpa struggled to read the word on his card so my mother had to whisper it into his ear, which turned out to be difficult because he couldn't hear.

"Popsicle!" she shout-whispered.

"We heard that," I said.

She tried again while we covered our ears and sang *"Lalalalala"* and that was more or less how the night ended, with all of us singing as we tried not to hear.

A few more days of forced family togetherness passed before my brother and his wife drove back to Pennsylvania to reunite with their cats while I got shuttled over to my dad's house for one of his strange "appetizer dinners" composed exclusively of reheated food from Costco. That night, after showing me the new birdhouse he'd made out of PVC pipes, we went into the kitchen to check on the tofu he was grilling on the stove.

"It's more of an experiment," he said, looking jolly in his worn-out slippers. "It's supposed to be stir-fried but I'm mixing it with pesto."

"Are we just having tofu for dinner or is there something else?" I asked, and at the sound of my slight disappointment, my stepmother scratched my dad's back with her long fingernails and cooed into his ear.

"Smells great, honey," she said. "I love it when you cook."

It was barely five when we sat down for dinner, and Nancy launched into a long talk about her volunteer work, which made it impossible to hate her or the cloying perfume in which she had once again doused herself.

"My clients at the shelter, they're good people, they've just fallen on hard times. And you know, big corporations, they don't want to hire people like my clients. People who might have a criminal record or an unstable home environment, and it's really too bad because they deserve a second chance. I gave Debra a few of our old patio chairs and you should've seen her. She burst into tears."

I picked apart a crab cake, trying to decide whether a shred of orange was cheese or potato.

"That's why you're lucky to have your fancy job," Dad said, buttering another piece of bread. "A stable income, benefits—those are things you can't take for granted."

"Not in this economy," my stepmother chimed in.

"Don't worry," I said, popping the entire crab cake into my mouth, mystery orange and all. "I'll work there until my skin falls off."

"What does that mean?" Nancy said, her eyes on the tartar sauce I was spilling down my chin.

"It means I'm slowly going to die in the office building where I work."

"Oh." She nodded. "Well."

"We all die someday," Dad said, reaching for one last crust of bread.

My flight was at six in the morning and I set two alarms, just to be safe, but there was no point. My mother barged in around four, opened the blinds, and turned on the overhead light.

"You're still in bed?" she said. "I thought you'd be showered and out the door by now." She dragged a suitcase into my room. She'd clearly been up all night, washing and folding my old clothes, and now here they were, packed and ready to go, along with some paper lanterns and muffin trays she no longer needed at the house. I should have been grateful for the warm clothes and suitcase. Instead I was mad about the muffin trays.

"Unbelievable," I said. "You think I have time to bake?"

"When I was your age, I used to find it comforting. It's really just following directions, measuring out ingredients."

"I hate baking. I hate muffins. I'm not you."

"I'm not saying you're me. I'm just saying it might be fun to have a hobby. Something to do when you get home from work."

I put on a dirty sweatshirt and grabbed my backpack off the floor.

"I don't think you realize how little you know about my life," I said. "I'm actually sad. I'm actually going through a lot."

I went downstairs to chug coffee and call a car. My mother followed me in her purple robe.

"I know you get lonely out there," she said. "Have you ever tried meeting someone? I mean, I just feel like if you opened your heart up to something like that, you might surprise yourself."

"Barf," I said. "Don't quote your self-help podcast at me."

"I just think if you were a little more vulnerable, or a little less hard on yourself, you might start attracting the people you're meant to meet."

"I'm open!" I was screaming. "I'm vulnerable!"

She wiped up the coffee I'd spilled on the counter.

"Well, I'm sorry," she said in her low voice, full of martyrdom. "You never tell me anything about your life, so how would I know?"

At the sound of a car pulling up, I rushed out the door.

"Car's here," I said. "Gotta go."

She followed me down to the street in her robe and stood by the curb with her eyes full of tears.

"Just give it some time!" she called after me. "I'm sure you'll meet the one!"

I rolled down the window and shouted, "I don't believe in the one!" but I don't think she heard me. She'd already turned around.

I took another car to get to the office by ten, and when the elevator doors opened on nineteen, I was immediately met with Tom and Bekah standing in the hallway and gaping at that day's paper.

"This is not good," Tom said.

"Fucking disaster," Bekah said.

They showed me the dime-sized puddle of red ink in the middle of Mezzanine's centerspread. It was comically tragic. A million-dollar mistake.

"It's a stain from the other side," Tom said. He turned the page and revealed a story about gang violence featuring a photo of bleeding calves.

"Fuck, fuck, fuck."

Bekah kept repeating herself while the elevator doors opened behind us, continually delivering new people onto the stage of Bekah's latest misfortune.

"Can we call the factory?" Bekah said.

"It's too late for reprints," Tom said.

"They need fifty copies. I can't show them this."

Diana walked past in a slinky wrap dress and took a perfunctory glance at the stain. "Use a pencil eraser," she said. "Works for me."

Five minutes later, Tom and I were standing over a conference room table, erasing the red stain off a stack of fifty papers and letting our fingers blister.

"Make sure you brush all the shavings off," Bekah commanded as she closed all the blinds so we wouldn't be seen through the glass. "Can we get that other girl in here," she said, "the one who kind of looks like you?"

Offended, I went to get Ellie, who looked nothing like me. We both just happened to be pale.

"Bekah needs us to erase a stain in the big conference room," I said.

Ellie was stirring chia seeds into her oatmeal. She didn't look up.

"I heard about your big win," she said. "The backup homepage and all."

"I think they just got us confused," I said.

"Huh."

I returned to the conference room and Bekah glared at me.

"She's on her way," I said.

"Good."

The three of us erased ink stains for the next twenty minutes, and when the papers were ready, Tom got Alvin from the mail room so he could deliver them to Mezzanine.

"Not Alvin!" Bekah screamed, when Alvin was standing in the doorway behind her. "He's too special-needs. Jane should take them. She's not doing anything."

I went to the station to get my coat.

"Heading out?" Karen asked. She was cheerful and oblivious and I wondered how stress couldn't travel through walls.

"I have to deliver fifty newspapers for Bekah," I said.

"Goddamn it, Bekah," Karen said. "She used to be so sweet."

I walked east on Forty-Second with a tote bag full of newspapers and a vision of leaving everything behind. It wasn't impossible. I could leave the office, the subway, and all the flashing crosswalk signals saying when to stop and when to go. Life was so much bigger than Sephora and Foot Locker and every other garbage chain store in Times Square. Life had nothing to do with shopping, or even work. It was closer to something my mother had been trying to say. Something about the surprises that brought about change.

"Jane?"

Someone tugged at my sleeve. I thought it might've been a crazy person so my body did what it does during every emergency, which is freeze.

"What are you doing here?"

The voice that came around to meet me belonged to Addy. A very not-crazy person in her now-familiar red plaid coat.

"I work around here," I said. "Unfortunately."

"That's cool. I almost never come up here. So it always feels really special when I do, you know?"

I blinked and said nothing because I had no idea what it was like to feel like Midtown was special. Every street, every storefront, every suit, every pair of heels—it was all the same proof of consumerist misery to me.

"I had to get something from my label," she said. "Technically they're on Thirty-Fourth but I came up here to walk around. That's one of the best things about living in New York. Just the ability to walk around and see so much." She looked down at my bag. "What's in there? It looks heavy."

"Newspapers," I said.

Addy looked confused.

"You deliver papers?"

"Sometimes."

Times Square honked at us and I felt oppressed by the noise, but Addy didn't seem to mind. She looked around, checking the street signs, and then pointed at a big, shiny bakery that looked like the entrance to an airport.

"I was about to get a donut," she said. "You want to come?"

I followed Addy into a giant bakery with a forever-long line. It smelled like Karen. I started talking about Karen.

"She's kind of my hero," I said. "Her teeth are yellow and she swears a lot but she's actually fun to be around."

"She sounds like my grandma."

"The one you just saw in Maine?"

Addy took the tote bag from me, insisting it was her turn to carry some of that weight, and by the time we got to the ordering screen, I'd completely forgotten it existed. The weight was gone. We sat and ate donuts dipped in mint and butterscotch.

"I'm having a hard time wanting to go out with anyone," Addy said. "And it's not because I miss Jess. I'm good at being alone. It's just that the more time I spend alone, the harder it becomes to want to see people."

"Vicious cycle."

"Exactly."

A woman carrying lots of shopping bags almost tripped. She caught herself just in time and smiled at us, mildly embarrassed, and we smiled back. It was such a sweet moment, shared between us and this middle-aged woman who was probably a tourist from some faraway place, that I almost didn't notice what the woman had tripped over.

"Shit." I grabbed the papers, apologized to Addy, and rushed to the headquarters of Mezzanine only to show up there, panting and helpless, long after the papers were due.

I gave them to the security guard, who appeared to be the only employee in the dimly lit bamboo-walled lobby that was also playing rainforest sounds.

"I don't know who these are for," he said.

"They're for Mezzanine," I said.

"I don't know anything about that."

"Can I leave them here?"

"If you want."

I ran back to the office—it was faster than taking a cab—and when Bekah emerged from the private room for nursing mothers with a broken, teary-eyed face, I thought she might be mad at me. I thought she might fire me, right there on the spot.

"Thanks so much for doing that." She put her hand on my shoulder and gave it a rub. "I appreciate everything you're doing around here."

"It's nothing."

"It's not nothing. You're staying late. You're running errands. You're doing a lot. I'm sorry if I've been distracted. It's just . . ." She closed her eyes and sharply inhaled. "My mom's in town this week and we were supposed to go out for dinner but now I can't because of Arthur and this stupid Mezzanine fiasco, and I'm just so sad about it. I feel like I never get to see my mom."

"Where does she live?"

"Boston."

She pulled on her earring, stretching the lobe. "Every time something good happens, I think, *This is it. This is what I've been waiting for.* But then people are so intense and things get so messed up."

"Your job is hard."

"It really is," she said. "Nobody understands."

december

BEKAH WASN'T AT HER DESK THE NEXT MORNING AND I WAS GLAD. I assumed she was working from home, which meant she wouldn't be working at all and she wouldn't ask me to do anything. I read a long article about Mary Shelley and went for a walk around the building. When I got back to the station, Karen was waiting for me with big, gossipy eyes.

"Have you seen Bekah?" she said.

"Nope."

"Has she called you?"

"Not yet."

"So you haven't heard from her?"

"She disappears."

Ellie looked nervous. She kept touching her hair and fake-typing.

"Can we not gossip?" she said.

"Sure," Karen said. "We'll wait until you go to the bathroom."

Tom called me into his office and asked me to close the door. My hands started to sweat as I sealed us into what could only be a cave of bad news.

"Bekah's trial period ended and they decided not to keep her." He sat back and rolled up his sleeves. "These things happen. She made a few mistakes. It's sad for Bekah. It's sad for us. But it's for the best and until we find someone for her position, you can start working with me directly."

He scratched the backs of his knuckles and seemed remarkably calm. Maybe that was the perk of working in the same industry for twenty years. You got used to all the flippant decisions made by powerful people—abrupt, unsparing, and cruel.

"Don't say anything to them." He gestured toward Karen and Ellie. "They'll find out. They'll talk. But for now." He didn't go on, but I nodded to let him know that I understood.

Ellie and Karen stared at me as I left Tom's office, passed the managers' cubes, and sat in my chair.

"So." Karen picked a piece of dry skin off her lips. "Where's Bekah?"

"No idea," I said. "She didn't come up."

I went to the bathroom and made coffee, and when I got back to the station, they knew.

"I bet Jane doesn't know," Karen said to Ellie.

They looked at me.

"I know," I said. "Tom told me not to talk about it."

They looked disappointed and we talked for a while in a stunned way about how sudden it was, and not entirely unexpected.

"I wonder where she is right now," I said, unable to say Bekah's name because it had begun to feel like a curse, like all you had to do was say it and your elevator cord would snap. "I almost miss her."

"I don't," Ellie said. "Her emails had too many exclamation points."

"I liked them," I said, suddenly defensive. "They were reassuring."

Ellie raised her pointy index finger. "One," she said. "One is enough."

And then, as if she knew she was being talked about, an email arrived from Bekah. She had forwarded me a message from a client and included a note.

Deal with this please. I no longer work at the Paper.
Sent from my iPhone.

It was thrilling to read, like getting an email from a ghost.

"The old guard's next," Karen said. "People like me and Sue and Tom—we get treated like shit. I bet they hope we get Alzheimer's and start going to the old building."

The rest of the day proceeded like normal and I'm not sure whether it was out of respect or fear. Everything about Bekah had gone through the shredder—her skirts, her smells, her snippy commands—and now that she'd been torn to shreds, everyone was focused back on their screens and it was freaking me out. I felt shaken by forces beyond my control. There was no security in life. We were born fragile and searching and we spent the rest of our lives that way. Would Bekah sneak into the office at night to get her things? Did her badge still work? Would I ever see her again?

Arthur strolled into work around noon, sat in his cushy chair, and looked at his phone. I waited for him to make some kind of announcement, but there was nothing—no updates, no speeches, not even an email. It struck me as the tactic of a corrupt regime, executing dissidents in the middle of the night and then acting like it never happened.

It was the Stepford Planners, of all people, whose unrepentant gossip made the office feel normal again, or at least more human.

"Did she cry?"

"Did she steal?"

"Who told her?"

"Was it Helen?"

I ate my sandwich, the solace of sameness in the midst of change, and told them I didn't know anything. "She was here and then she was gone," I said. That's when it dawned on me that getting fired was like dying except worse because nobody gave you a gravestone.

"I so feel bad for her."

"Just awful."

"What's she gonna do?"

The Stepford Planners gazed into their soup.

"She'll bounce back," I said. "She's rich."

I had just turned my computer off for the night when Ellie asked me if I wanted to pitch in for flowers.

"Flowers?" I asked.

"For Bekah," she said.

I wanted to say no. Bekah was mean. She laughed at the woman in the dining hall who had facial hair. She called Alvin a tard. She said, "You really should know this," and "I can't believe nobody taught you that," and "You really need to start listening when people talk." The last thing I wanted to do was give her flowers. Then Karen pulled out her fat purse, Ellie clicked open her hard-shelled wallet, and I took out my backpack and fished for ones.

"Of course," I said.

"We should," Ellie said.

"How much?" Karen asked.

Laurel had been working late in Red Hook, prepping sculptures for her boss's upcoming show, so I was surprised when she wrote to me after work to see if I wanted to meet her at the Chobani store in SoHo because she was craving yogurt. I rode the train down there and found her standing on the corner in her raggedy purple Carhartt with duct tape over the sleeves, smoking a joint and frowning because she'd changed her mind. She didn't want yogurt anymore. She wanted McDonald's. So we walked to the McDonald's on West Third, ordered a bunch of food, and sat in a booth.

"I don't know what to do about Nina," she said.

"Who's Nina?"

"That girl I'm sleeping with. She's nice but she has ugly tattoos."

"A girl can have ugly tattoos," I said, "as long as she regrets them."

"Well, this chick doesn't and I am *not* turned on by the rosemary sprig on her butt."

Laurel dipped a nugget into tangy barbecue sauce and let the goo get on her fingers.

"What happened to the butcher?" I asked.

"They're hot but their room smells like pepperoni."

"So does yours."

"Yeah, but it's *my* pepperoni."

The air outside was dark and the city looked especially gloomy. Accordion buses made tragic gasping sounds, as if wishing they could roll into a junkyard and die, while bikers trying to pedal home in the wind took turns pounding on the hood of an SUV double-parked in the bike lane.

Laurel raised her empty nugget cup and dumped the fry crumbs into her mouth.

"I need to stop chasing people I don't like and go back to the same crush I've had for years," she said.

"Who's that?"

"My therapist."

I laughed but Laurel didn't. She was the funniest person I knew but she didn't seem to realize it.

"At least you're making art," I said.

Laurel took the lid off her Diet Coke and started un-poking the bubbles so she could, I knew, poke them again.

"Art's a joke," she said. "The whole system is jacked." She looked out the window at a FOR SALE BY ZEUS sign attached to a renovated redbrick building across the street. "You know those Zeus signs you see everywhere? That's my boss's mom's company. She's like this New York real estate billionaire."

"At least she raised an artist."

"Yeah, who could rent his own gallery and start showing his work at twenty-two."

"That's fucked-up."

We put our heads down on the disgusting table and made loud wailing sounds. Then we raised them and started talking about girls again.

"I'm done with Madeline," I said. "Done. Over it. No more Madeline. If you see me texting her, take my phone and throw it in a well."

"What did she do?"

"Nothing. She just makes me miserable. I texted her one simple question—*Are you still sick?*—and she ignored me for a week."

"Is she still sick?"

"I don't know! She won't text me back! She's useless. Totally inert. Totally uninspiring. She cares so much about how people see her. Her name isn't even Madeline. It's Magdalena."

Laurel shuddered. "Watch out for church girls," she said. "They've got that Catholic guilt."

We unstuck our butts from the booth and walked in the blistering wind to the Rusty Knot, a nautical gay bar in the West Village that decorated every drink with lusty plastic mermaids. After shoving our coats under a bamboo table, we got drunk off piña coladas and tried to touch the fish in the fish tank. I went first and panicked at the thought of touching something slimy. Laurel went next and got her hand halfway into the water, when the bouncer shouted at us and we fled to the pool table in the back. Our laughter was loud and maniacal, but that was one good thing about being heartsick. It made us giddy enough to think that being miserable was the same as being alive.

The next day Bekah's cube was still filled with her stuff. Lipstick cases, expense reports, an old smoothie the color of swamp. It felt like a warning, intended for me, so I went into Tom's office determined to be good.

A zitty teenage boy was sitting in Tom's chair. He didn't look at me because he was busy wrapping his fingers in Scotch tape.

"Is Tom here?" I said.

"He was."

I checked the school photo on the wall and confirmed that the boy was Tom's son. It felt exciting to meet a coworker's kid, like one of those moments in a sitcom when a character from one show appears in another.

"So," I said, trying to sound nonchalant so the teenager would like me, "is Tom a good dad?"

The boy ripped the tape off his hands. A bright and painful sound. "He's all right."

His indifference made me feel old for the first time in my life, and

I saw myself the way he must have seen me: an adult, a finished thing, trapped in an office, just like his dad.

"Most bosses are mean," I said, "but your dad's really nice. Everybody likes him. He's really down-to-earth."

The boy took out his phone and blinked at me. His cheeks were volcanic. "What's your number?"

Tom walked in scratching his stubble and wearing Karen's leopard-print bifocals. "I can sell a centerspread for a hundred K but it's not good enough for President Truman. Apparently I'm useless if I can't sell a banner ad on the internet."

The boy got up and Tom sat back in his chair, ignoring us both to better focus on his desktop covered in folders that led to more folders that led to more folders. His entire working life seemed to be an endless process of fielding damage, catching up, looping people in, circling back, and I wanted to help him and become some sort of asexual office wife as much as I wanted to leave the building, burn my blazers, and never come back.

He opened a tin of mints and popped a handful in his mouth. "I talked to Valerie. She said you're the expert in digital." He chewed the mints like candy, chomping into them with his teeth. His son banged his forehead against the wall.

"I think you mean Vanessa," I said.

"I'm starving," the boy said. "Can we *go*?"

"I'm not saying we don't need ads on the internet." Tom leaned back in his chair and I noticed his paunch, stretching the buttons of his starched white shirt and exposing the undershirt beneath. "I'm just saying Arthur can't expect me to sell a sponsorship with a one-mil price tag overnight."

God, I hated it when people used nicknames for money. "Bucks" and "K" and "thou" and "mil." It made money seem like a bunch of frat bros, hooting and chugging and whacking each other's butts with lacrosse sticks.

The boy walked out and Tom followed. "I have to drop my kid off at his alcoholic mother's house. Just hang tight. I'll send you the details about Prada at a red light."

Addy was in Laurel's room when I got home. I didn't think they were friends so I was surprised to see her.

"I'm getting a painting," she said.

I looked at Laurel. "You're selling your work?"

She picked at some rubber cement stuck to her thumb.

"I always try to buy my friends' work," Addy jumped in. "I just know how hard it is, to be an artist. I mean, I remember when I was first getting started—"

"Sorry," I cut her off. "My pants are tight and I'm gonna go take them off."

"Will you come back?"

"Sure."

I changed into baggy jeans, and Addy was standing by the door in her red plaid coat.

"This might sound weird, but I'm never in Bushwick and I was just wondering if you might want to get that drink."

"Let's do it."

I put my coat back on and we went to the cocktail bar around the corner. I'd been there once with Madeline, but this time it felt different. I sat and ordered a whiskey and felt completely at ease.

"I'll have the fries," she said, handing her card to the bartender to open a tab.

"I thought we were drinking," I said.

She pushed up the sleeves of her thick wool sweater. "I don't actually like drinking that much. I almost never go to bars. They're so loud and the music's always bad and no matter where you put your coat it always ends up on the floor."

"You sound like a mom."

"I like being home at night. Is that such a bad thing?"

She pulled a lens cleaner out of her Strand tote bag and wiped her glasses clean.

"I didn't go to college," she went on. "I stayed home and taught myself how to play guitar. So I never really had those drinking and partying years, and I'm not mad about it. It was definitely depressing, but that's where the music comes from, so I can't hate it."

The bartender dropped off a basket of fries, and after dousing them in ketchup, Addy ate them quickly, one after another, and I liked watching her do it. She had a nice full mouth with freckles around it.

"So what's it like to be a rock star?" I said. "Having fans and playing shows and all that?"

She shrugged and ate another fry. "It becomes a job. I'm definitely grateful, don't get me wrong, but I'm an introvert. And playing shows, being on the road, it takes something out of me."

I asked her some more questions about her career. How long are your tours? Where do you sleep? It was standard small talk, but as long as she was talking I was happy. I didn't want to have to be clever and self-revealing. I just wanted to sit and listen to her talk about the checkpoints in Arizona, the impossibility of finding parking in Amsterdam, and the night in Omaha when her drummer locked both sets of keys in the van, which didn't even seem possible.

"What about you?" she said. "Do you like what you do?"

"It doesn't matter," I said.

"I still want to know." She smashed her last fry into the bottom of the basket and dragged it around, collecting the salt.

"There's nothing to say about what I do," I said. "I sit and stare at a screen."

"Are you going to do this every time I ask you a question?"

"Do what?"

"Deflect."

The bartender picked up my empty glass and I signaled for another.

"Advertising is hell," I said. "But I like some of the people."

"What are they like?"

"You really want to know?"

Addy nodded and looked at me so sincerely that I started telling her about Tom quoting Yeats and Diana misspelling *committee* and Ellie's allergies to everything but beans.

"Cubicles are called cubes," I said. "The dining hall charges for cups of hot water but not cups of cold. And when confronted with a big talker in the hallway, you can always end the conversation by walking slowly backwards."

Addy laughed with the confidence of someone who knows they'll never have to work in an office.

"Must be nice," I said. "Waking up every day with nothing to do and nowhere to be."

"It feels like floating," she said.

"Sounds peaceful."

She shook her head so violently that some of her hair got in her mouth. "It's not like that at all. It's like floating in space with nothing to hold on to, no security, no guarantees. My job isn't easy. Every day there's some new girl with a guitar."

"I still don't feel sorry for you."

Her wild eyebrows got twisted and I could tell she was mad.

"You're judging me, aren't you?"

"I know you don't have to work in an office," I said. "I know that."

The bartender dropped off my second drink and I suddenly wished I hadn't ordered it.

"I'm not just some rich kid who fell into music." She tugged on the collar of her sweater to release some of the tension that was building up under there. "I was raised on a shitty Air Force base in Arizona.

I wanted to take karate but my parents couldn't afford it. They got divorced and my mom moved us to Maine, where I was basically depressed for five years."

"I didn't mean to offend you."

"You didn't offend me. You just . . ." She sputtered a little as she tried to speak. "You just don't seem to see me the way that I see myself, and that's one of my biggest fears in life. Not being understood."

I felt my phone vibrating in my pocket and I wanted to check it but I didn't want to be rude, especially not in front of someone as intense as Addy.

"I'm gonna go to the bathroom," I said.

"Of course! Sorry! I've been talking your ear off."

I got up and went to the back and found a bunch of texts from Madeline.

Hey

It's Cassandra's birthday

We're at Three Diamond Door

She wants you to come

I didn't want to go. I wanted to be cool and distant and apologize a month later for not responding. But the bar was literally a block away. What forces of the universe were conspiring to bring us together, I wasn't sure, but it felt compelling, so I went back to the bar, put on my coat, and told Addy it was time for me to call it a night.

"I liked talking to you," I said.

"I liked talking to you too."

She signaled for the check and pulled her hat over her ears.

"I'll text you," I said.

"Will you?"

I gave her one last friendly nod. "Yep. I'll be in touch."

We hugged and I walked slowly out the door, only to start running as soon as Addy couldn't see me. Overcome with masochistic elation, I couldn't wait to see Madeline. I'd missed her so much. It suddenly didn't matter if she made me want to dig a ditch and bury myself in the dirt. Madeline was back. She was better. She wanted to see me. I wondered if we'd kiss.

Madeline was in the back, drunk and pretending to be moody. "You kept me waiting," she said, sipping a glass of mostly ice. "Was your date mad that you left?"

"She was pissed."

I looked at her face and loved it. I loved her thin eyebrows and her delicate nose and the neat middle part that separated the two halves of her perfectly straight black hair.

"What about you," I said. "How were all your dates in London?"

"Marvelous." She smiled a little, her devious grin. "Why? Are you jealous?"

"I'm seething."

Cassandra came over with her floppy hair swinging and put her hands on my face, either trying to warm me up or simply doing something a lot of drunk people did.

"You're coming home with us!" She grinned and looked at Madeline, and for a second, I was freaked out. I thought she was talking about a threesome.

"It's my *birthday*," she said. "And I am *not* going home alone."

She stumbled back to her friends on the dance floor, letting the hem of her dress get dragged through multiple pools of beer, and Madeline pulled me over to a table covered in coats. Semiconcealed behind a mound of hoods, hats, and sleeves, she gripped me tightly by the wrist and brought her face close to mine. "I saw that movie about those girls in Turkey who get locked in their house for hanging out with boys. That's what my life in Guatemala was like. Especially the virginity stuff. I cried when I saw it. I think we should run away."

"Where to?"

"London."

"Absolutely not. You just want to be able to tell people you live in a *flat*."

"Fine," she said. "We can go to Berlin. I have a friend who lives there and she says it's pretty like Paris but cheaper and nobody has real jobs and the clubs stay open all night."

A pudgy white guy in a Brooklyn Nets shirt sat next to us and said, "So how do you two know each other?" He gripped his drink and smiled all fake-friendly and I could tell he wanted us to out ourselves so he could make some enlightened comment about how much he supported girls kissing.

"We're friends," I said.

"Old friends." Madeline put her arm around me.

Cassandra pushed the boy out of the way and dragged Madeline to the dance floor so they could shout-sing along to a pop song that played in delis. As soon as it was over, Madeline found me and sighed defeatedly into my ear: "Now you've seen the real me."

Seeing her jump around to Ariana Grande hardly counted as self-revealing, but the gambit worked. I loved hearing her sing. I loved seeing her dance. I loved standing near her in the dark with our mouths close together.

"I wonder which one of my parents is perverted," she said.

"How would I know? You never talk about them."

"You never ask."

"Forgive me. Who are the people that made you and how can I properly thank them?"

"My dad's boring. He's a lawyer and he wears a suit every day, but my mom's cool. She has a funny accent and she uses the blow-dryer on the dog."

"Where was your school? Did you play any sports? Did you have a boyfriend?"

"I went to the beach. I went to church. I still remember my first communion. I wore a white dress and my whole family was there, watching me drink wine."

Cassandra came over and leaned against the coats because she could no longer stand. "*Lez* go," she said, spilling scarves onto the floor.

Madeline turned to me with a pouty look. "Are you coming or what?"

"Do you want me to?"

"Kind of."

I had spent half the night praying she would say something like that and it made me think of Alvin. How he always said we would all be blessed.

"I'll call a car," I said.

"My hero."

We piled into the backseat and it felt like old times when Cassandra took the middle seat and neither of them buckled up. The driver sped toward their place, less than a mile away, and Cassandra held out her hand like she wanted me to hold it.

"Your phone," she said. "I need your phone to look at Matt's pictures."

"What's wrong with your phone?" I said.

"Nothing. I just blocked him so I can't see his pictures."

The driver dropped us off at the opera house and Madeline got out first, opening the gate and going inside while Cassandra clung to my arm and showed me a string of texts she'd sent Matt over the course of the night.

What's up?

I think I like beer now.

Birthday sex?

I mean why not.

Omg I can't believe I asked.

"He hasn't written back yet," she said. "Is that bad?"

It was worse than bad, but I would never tell her that. The whole point of being in love was living with illusions.

"I bet his phone died," I said, helping her up the stairs. "You're so smart and cute, he'd be crazy not to like you."

Madeline opened their apartment door. It was unlocked and all the lights were on and so was the TV.

"The point is that he's *sketchy*," Cassandra said, overenunciating as she held on to me. "The point is that he's . . ." She paused, forgetting the word.

"Sketchy?"

"NO," Cassandra said. "The point is that he's *shady*."

She opened a kitchen cupboard filled with jars while Madeline poured herself a glass of water. I desperately wanted some but I would never ask. I didn't want to seem needy.

"He thinks he can get away with it," Cassandra said, pouring Kashi into a mug. "He thinks I don't know."

She sat cross-legged on the rug in the living room and ate her cereal like a toddler, hyper-concentrated on each bite while spilling milk all over the floor. Madeline wiped it up with fifty sheets of paper towel and it was cute.

"That's the most domestic thing I've ever seen you do," I said.

She curtsied and went into her room, leaving the wet paper towels in a ball next to Cassandra's butt.

Madeline was moving things around in her room and I wasn't sure if I was supposed to follow her in there. Maybe she was getting something and coming back. Maybe she was changing her clothes.

"Stop being weird," she said. "Come and see my pink lights."

I stepped into her room, small and plain with bare yellow walls and clothes all over the floor. Her bed was a mattress covered in bunched-up blankets and the only noteworthy piece of furniture was a large wooden dresser that probably came with the room.

"I'd say don't judge me but I know you already are," she said.

She got on her knees and plugged in her pink flamingo lights, which made the room feel like a seedy nail salon. Then she sat on her bed and leaned against her limp gray pillows, content with her one accomplishment for the day. I stood over her with my hands in my pockets. I probably looked like I was waiting for the bus.

"Am I supposed to sit?" I asked.

"That's what a normal person would do."

A crash came from the kitchen.

"Is she gonna be okay?" I said.

"Yeah," Madeline said.

"She's really drunk."

"That's what we do when we hang out. We get really drunk."

I sat on the bed next to Madeline and she leaned over me and picked up an open bottle of wine off the floor. Her shirt was cropped so I could see her stomach. We took turns sipping the wine. It tasted sour and bad but we drank it anyway.

"I was in love once," she said. "We went to Paris and it was really romantic, but when we got back to school, he acted like nothing happened."

"How could anyone do that to you?"

"I know."

She took a drink of wine. I took a drink of wine. Neither of us swallowed because we had both been pretending.

"Have you ever been in love with a straight girl?"

"Only you."

She shoved me and I loved it.

"I take it back," I said. "You're different."

"How am I different?"

My mind went blank. I had no idea how to describe her contradictions without ruining them. How she went binge drinking with a copy of *The Woman Destroyed*. How she judged trendy bars while wearing trendy clothes. How she mistrusted the wisdom of others while constantly seeking advice. I kept my mouth shut and waited for some other part of my body to answer.

"I want to kiss you," I said.

"Why don't you?"

She closed her eyes, and when I kissed her lightly on the lips, she seemed checked-out but also anxious to keep going. Breathing unevenly, she put her arms around my neck and pulled me closer. I kissed her slowly, not wanting to rush her into accepting something she didn't actually want, and when she turned sideways and landed on her back, it suddenly seemed perfectly natural to be on top of her, holding myself up with one arm and fixing her hair with the other.

"Not that I don't want to eat your hair," I said.

She closed her eyes and smiled. A small, embarrassed smile.

"I'm nervous," she said.

I leaned back. Her eyes were still closed and her face looked vulnerable. I didn't want to say the wrong thing or make her feel small.

"I'm not going to make you do anything," I said. "I just want to be close to you."

She stuck her hands up my shirt and started rubbing my sides. I wasn't expecting that. How fast things were moving. How suddenly gay she seemed to want to be.

"Are you sure this is—" I started in a low and possibly inaudible voice, and before I finished, she rolled over and took off her skirt, an arduous and time-consuming effort that involved lots of wiggling and grunting.

"Stop looking at me," she said, struggling to get her tights past her knees.

"Never."

"It's embarrassing."

"It's not."

I climbed on top of her as a motorcycle backfired, a dog barked, and someone, somewhere, flushed a toilet.

"I've been thinking about this," she said.

"Don't lie."

"I'm not."

Her hair fell in front of her eyes and I moved it back, lightly touching her ears.

"Please," she whispered into my ear and shifted beneath me so that my leg was between her thighs. "Please." A word she must've picked up from somewhere, like a sexual talisman or verbal toy—I wasn't sure where it came from, and I didn't care. I slipped my hand under the waistband of her stringy black underwear and ran my fingertips along her waist.

"Jane," she whispered, and I felt so overcome with want that I stuck my arm between her legs and up around the base of her back and held it there, just to feel her warmth. She opened her mouth and raised herself up. Slowly, I felt her rubbing up against my wrist. It created in me such a dizzying feeling that I felt like I was falling even though I was the one on top of her, holding her down.

I rode the train to work in a state of shock. It felt like a low-level form of perversion to be riding the train, looking normal on the outside, while remembering the way I'd bitten Madeline's ribs and tasted her sweat.

"Make it new" was all Tom said about the plans he needed for Prada, Armani, and Dolce & Gabbana, whose demands were technically impossible but Tom would never tell them that. It was the endless job of the salesman to perform peerless optimism, and yet when he did bring in some money from Chanel, he was too busy to sign the contract.

"Orchestra or mezzanine?" He leaned in to his screen, picking out seats for a show at Radio City. "One of them is better and I can't remember which."

I held out the contract. "All I need is your name."

The sun vanished behind dark clouds while people were still

eating lunch and Ellie seemed to take morbid glee in announcing that it was the shortest day of the year. I'd spent most of it thinking about Madeline. She was fickle and unpredictable and yet I couldn't wait to see her again. I had even started fantasizing about surprising her with gifts, like more pink string lights or some new black thing to wear.

Laurel was drilling holes into pennies when I got home. I didn't ask why. I just sat on the metal folding chair covered in dried paint and waited for her to be done making noise so we could talk.

"I think something's wrong with me," I said. "I'm obsessed with Madeline."

"I thought she was getting deported."

"She is."

"So what's the problem?"

"I don't want her to go."

Laurel touched the mustard stain on my shirt and I could tell she liked it. The shape. The color. Something like that.

"Relationships are dumb," she said.

"A lot of people like them."

"Yeah, and those people suck. Relationships are just expressions of a selfish desire for possession and control." She bent over and tried to touch her toes. Wobbly from chain-smoking and filled with Cheetos, she couldn't get past her knees. "Calling someone 'babe.' Cooking lasagna. Going on hikes—it's all so boring. Everybody knows gender is a performance, but I think relationships are too. It's accepting physical comfort in place of self-discovery. So I think we're lucky."

"Why?"

"We're lucky because we're single and we can experience the world as fully as possible." She lay on her bed and mumbled into her dirty sheets. "Now sit on my back. It's really sore and I want to feel like I'm being smashed."

At the weekly planner meeting, Ellie appointed herself organizer of the planners-only holiday party, and by the time we got back to the station, she was hyperventilating with stress.

"Where should we go?" she asked. "What do people like? Should we go bowling? It's too cold to rent a boat."

"A bar," Karen said. "We should go to a bar."

"Just drinking is okay?"

Karen suggested an Irish bar near Penn Station, and suddenly it was decided. We were going to Karen's pub with the good macaroni.

"You're coming, right?" Ellie asked, looking at me.

"Of course," I lied. "Wouldn't miss it for the world."

Madeline wrote to me in the late afternoon.

> Hi
>
> Miss u
>
> Meet me tonight?

The more truncated her messages, the more riveting they became, imbued with mysterious coyness and clipped romance. She was getting kicked out of the country in less than a month but I was still burning with a desire for her so irrational that it bordered on pubescent. I wrote her back with over-the-top affection to conceal my over-the-top affection.

> That is all I want
>
> It is my reason for being
>
> Please let me buy you a drink
>
> And listen to you complain

The rest of the day meant nothing and in some ways it didn't even happen. It was just empty time, a plastic-nothing space that I had to pass through until the sun went down, the rats came out, and I could meet Madeline at some trashy bar where nothing respectable happened. The only snag was my mother. She called me three times in a row, and the fourth time, I picked up.

"There you are," she said. "I thought you'd been kidnapped."

"Not kidnapped," I said.

"I'm at JFK. We just got off our flight from Amsterdam, me and Doug, and there was some kind of mix-up. Our flight home isn't until midnight, so I figured we'd pop by the office and you could show us around."

I covered my face and tried to suppress the feeling of vertigo that was making me want to fall out of my chair. The last person I wanted to bring to the office was my chatty midwestern mother.

"I'm swamped," I said. "Can you come closer to eight?"

She screeched into the phone, "Eight? That's too late! We'll be there at five."

My mother texted me from the lobby at 4:45.

Here!!!

I pulled out my ponytail so she would think I wore my hair down and walked over to the elevators as slowly as possible because I wanted more people to leave.

"You forgot to turn off your computer!" Ellie called after me.

"I'm coming back."

"Oh." She looked disappointed. "Well, you left it on last night."

I circled the floor just to kill some more time, and when I finally rode down to the lobby, I spotted my mother immediately. Surrounded by stylish New Yorkers in long black coats and patent leather shoes, she stuck out in her dorky purple pea coat and matching earmuffs. Her boyfriend, Doug, was standing close to her and looked equally out of place with his hearty midwestern girth and history-teacher clothes.

"They're with me," I told Mike and Bart, the security guards who'd once told me they used to work at Rikers, and they happily buzzed them through, these two innocuous boomers who posed no threat to anyone but me.

"Honey!" My mother sprinted through the turnstiles and wrapped her wiry arms around me. "I still can't believe you work here."

"Lots of people do," I said.

She let go of me and gave me the usual up-and-down, I'm-making-sure-you-don't-have-any-tattoos-or-weird-piercings look.

"You sure took your time getting down here though," she said. "I hope you don't do that to people you work with. Make them wait like that."

"Only you," I said.

She ignored me and danced her way into an open elevator, clutching Doug's arm.

"This building's still pretty new," she told him. "It was designed by that famous architect. . . ."

Seeing her with Doug reminded me that things would be different. She wasn't the mom I could still sometimes talk to about life and love and work. She was here with Doug. She was Doug's girlfriend.

The doors opened on the Stepford Planners, who gawked at us in their billowy blouses, having recognized a parent.

"Show me around, babycakes!" My mother pinched me on the arm as we shuffled past them.

"Can you be a little quieter?" I said. "People are trying to work."

"I birthed you. I raised you. Can't a mother be proud of her daughter?"

Karen had gone home for the night but Ellie was still at her desk, working late for Diana, and Mom delighted in meeting her, this clean-cut, squeaky-voiced, straight version of me.

"Where are you from? Where's your boyfriend from? What's his name?" She interrogated Ellie for ten minutes, and when she was done, she gazed out the window and labored to identify every building in sight.

"And that's Penn Station?"

"Yep."

"And that's New Jersey?"

"Yep."

"And that's north?"

"No, it's the other way."

"Are you sure?"

"Yes."

"I feel like it's this way."

"It's not."

Doug didn't seem to mind my mother's constant talking. His charm, at least for me, seemed to lie in his ability to follow her around, listen to her digressive monologues about how much she loved New York City and had always wanted to move here, and then agree with her when she stressed repeatedly how amazing it was when that pilot landed on the Hudson and nobody died.

"My coworker Karen saw it," I said.

My mother was flabbergasted.

"I could never. My *god*. Land a plane? On water? No. I'd panic." She turned to Doug. "What about you? Could you land a plane?"

We put on our coats and went down to the street and I thought we might be able to call it a night, but my mother insisted on dinner. There was an Italian place nearby, she said; she'd already looked up the menu online.

"You're not coming home for Christmas," she said. "Getting a bite with us is the least you can do."

We walked to the restaurant, but before going inside, my mother took a travel-sized brush out of her purse and ran it through her wispy gray-blond hair. It reminded me of all the times I'd seen her doing just that in front of the bathroom sink at movie theaters and restaurants. Then she held the brush out to me and I remembered another part of the scene. The part I'd chosen to forget.

"Your hair's all snarled in the back," she said. "Let me get out the knots."

I ducked to avoid her arm and opened the restaurant door.

"No time," I said. "We gotta eat."

The restaurant turned out to be nice. It had homemade focaccia bread and ivy-covered walls and the sort of farm-to-table food I would never want to pay for myself.

"It was great to meet your friend at work," my mother said.

"She's not my friend," I said.

"That reminds me. Do you have any, you know, special friends you might want to tell us about?"

"You can just say 'girlfriend,' and no, I don't have one."

"What about dates? I feel like some nice lady would love to take you out."

"Nice lady?" I gagged. "She sounds like a pedophile."

"But isn't that what you want? A nice person to date?"

"No. I don't want anything like that. I don't want some normal boring life like yours."

The waiter dropped off more bread, which put me in a better mood, so I asked about their trip to Amsterdam and Doug put his hand over my mother's as they talked about the wind and the rain.

"And everybody there looks Dutch," my mother said.

"What do Dutch people look like?" I asked.

"Dutch people look Dutch." She made a circular motion around her face. "You know, Dutch."

We walked to Broadway after dinner and hugged good-bye outside their subway stop. They were going back to JFK and I was walking to the L a block away. I dug into my backpack to look for my headphones. My mother and Doug watched me search.

"You don't have to wait," I said.

"We don't mind," she said.

I was halfway to my stop when I heard a shriek. My mother was running after me.

"Jane!" Her purse banged against her hip. "Right after you walked away, Doug said that women are ten times more likely to get attacked if they're wearing headphones."

"Good to know." I pretended to put away my headphones. She leaned in to hug me and burped.

"Did you just burp in my face?" I said.

"I did," she said, smiling a little, as if surprised at her own power to make such a sound. We laughed and went our separate ways, and it wasn't until I got on the train and sat on the bench and remembered how to exist that I realized I had forgotten to tell her how much I loved her and cared about her and appreciated her deeply.

Madeline was waiting for me outside the Jefferson stop even though it was cold and she immediately threw a fit.

"My ears are frozen," she said.

"You could always wear a hat," I said.

"Never," she gasped. "I look so bad in hats."

She tucked her short braids into the collar of her fuzzy black coat and walked ahead of me as if trying to prove a point. I caught up with her at the light on Willoughby, where the traffic was going in five different directions and the whole world smelled like gasoline.

"Sorry," she said. "I'm in a weird mood. I talked to my friend from home today and I feel so bad for her, I don't even want to talk about it." She blew on her fingers, numb from the cold. "She married some guy and they have a kid and they're living in a shitty condo in Florida and her husband goes to school while she stays at home with the baby."

"A lot of people live like that."

"I know. Isn't it awful?"

"Did she tell you she was unhappy?"

"No, we don't talk like that. She would never say, 'Madeline, I'm unhappy,' just like I would never say, 'My internship at the Paper was boring and I hated it.'"

"You should," I said. "You shouldn't hide who you are."

"You're the one who never has me over," she said.

"Is that what you want?"

Madeline looked confused. It was possible she couldn't hear me over the traffic and I might have shouted but it suddenly seemed pointless, the whole effort to be understood.

"My mom was here," I said. "It was really embarrassing."

"You have a mom?"

"Yeah, we got dinner."

"I wish I could've met her."

"You're lying."

"I'm not."

We went into Bossa Nova Civic Club, a tropical techno bar with fake palm trees that was hell on weekends but kind of fun on weeknights. There was a short line out front and we waited in the icy wind while the bouncer checked our IDs. It took a while because his gloves kept covering our faces, birthdays, or expiration dates, and when he finally stamped our wrists with goofy smiling faces that were the opposite of his own, I led the way down a dark hallway and Madeline clung to my arm.

"Are you going to murder me?" she said.

"No, but I might walk us into a wall."

The hallway led to another hallway that led to a room filled with fog. The music was electronic and droning. The walls were covered in mirrors. I got us drinks and it felt good to be there because it felt like no place on earth.

"You shouldn't have taken me here," she said. "I never want to leave."

She snuggled up to me under a plastic leaf, and just like that, the night turned warm and full.

"I think I'm moving to Berlin," she said.

"When?"

"Soon."

We moved to the back room, where there were eight people dancing with their eyes closed. We joined them and bobbed along to an endless song with no lyrics until a girl with a British accent gave us poppers. Then we took turns sniffing the cap and feeling perfect but also like we might fall over.

"I have to . . ." She leaned into me.

"You have to what?"

"I have to puke."

I was glad. I thought she was going to say she had to leave.

"Here, come with me, it's over here."

She held on to my arm as I led the way to the bathroom and opened the door.

"I'll be right here," I said. "Unless you want me to go in there and hold your hair."

She ignored me and went in there to puke, which she did in such absolute silence that I wondered if she'd been lying and she just wanted to text. Then she came out and looked so defeated that I knew the puke was real.

"Sorry I'm gross," she said.

"I have mouthwash," I said.

"You do?"

I gave her the mini bottle of Listerine that I took with me on all my dates. She took a big swig of it, spit it back into the bottle, and handed it to me.

"Thanks," she said. "I feel better."

I closed our tab while Madeline picked up a stranger's black coat and started putting it on. "Not yours," I said, twirling her out of it.

"It's not?"

"Nope."

It felt shocking to rediscover the outside world and realize that it was pouring rain. Big plunking drops flew sideways through the streetlight. Potholes and warehouses shimmered in the wet.

"I'm calling a car," Madeline said, bunched up next to me and using my body as a shield.

"You could always come over."

She went on calling her car and a part of me was relieved. My apartment was small. My bed was broken. And I couldn't imagine introducing Madeline to Laurel, who had recently called her a bicurious waste of time.

"I wish I didn't have to fly home for Christmas," she said.

"When do you leave?"

"Tomorrow."

I unzipped my jacket and she huddled into my side.

"It's just for a few weeks," she said. "I'll be back before the new year."

I looked down at her face, so delicate and painfully close to mine.

"I want to kiss you," I said.

"I just puked," she said. "You still want to kiss me?"

"More than anything."

She gave a little nod and we kissed under the awning, with our bodies pressed together inside my coat, and when she leaned back, she looked dumbstruck and I'm sure I did too.

"It makes you look like a kid," she said, touching the dimple on my cheek.

I wanted to go back to kissing but her car was waiting, and before I could say anything, she ran to catch it in the rain.

The next morning the elevators were broken, so people were standing around the lobby with heavy coats and frozen faces, waiting for the brokenness to go away. It was exactly how I felt about Madeline. She was in Guatemala for the next two weeks and her absence was like a broken elevator stuck in my chest, this empty box going nowhere.

Tom was waiting for me at the station, sitting in my chair with a puffy, stressed-out face. There were dozens of plans to build and all of them were due weeks ago.

"Where's the first plan you made for Versace?" He rubbed his eyes until his forehead turned into a giant wrinkle. "Go back to that one. They liked that one better."

All of my thoughts about Madeline disappeared as I slumped in my chair and moved around decimal points while Tom and Karen talked loudly over my head.

"Kyle's a good kid," he said. "B student. Teachers like him. I'm only a little worried. I raised him on William Carlos Williams and Charlie Parker and now he says he wants to work in finance. He says he wants to be like DiCaprio in that Wall Street movie."

They were old friends and drinking buddies, and the longer they talked about their kids, cavities, and commutes, the more I wanted to tell them to stop. Madeline was gone and everything was supposed to stop until the moment she came back.

Laurel was packing for LA with Missy Elliott playing out of her beat-up laptop speaker.

"It's probably good that I'm going home," she said. "I forget what my parents look like."

"You must be excited to see them."

"I'm more excited to see the dog."

"What's wrong with your parents?"

"Nothing. My mom just talks and doesn't listen."

I sat in the paint-splattered folding chair that I secretly considered mine.

"My mom does the same," I said. "She's always giving me the most demented professional advice. Like she thinks I'll get hired as a writer if I talk to people on the elevator."

"My mom tells me to talk to people on elevators too," Laurel said. "And escalators. Then we get in a fight and I tell her she's bipolar."

"Is she?"

"No, I just say that."

Laurel's paintings were stacked against the wall. They were pink and purple with loops and squiggles and one of them had a ball of gunk smashed into the top right corner.

"Is that gum?" I said.

"Yep." We both looked at the dried-up wad of orange. "I was done with it and had nowhere else to put it."

"You're very original."

"Probably just dumb."

Laurel picked at the clay in her hair and I felt inspired. She could be moody and pessimistic, but her work, with its bright colors and blobby forms, always pointed toward something else.

It rained for the rest of the week and I showed up to work in soggy pants because I was too self-hating to buy an umbrella. They were like paper towel holders, dryer sheets, and houseplants—benchmarks of an adulthood that I didn't deserve.

You sticking around for the holidays? A text from Addy came through as I got to my desk. A terrible time to send a text—Addy should have known better. Morning texts carried a whiff of desperation, an embarrassing sense of need, and I avoided responding to her simple question mostly because I was already late to the office and Ellie's beady eyes were staring me down.

"It was the train," I said.

"Wow," she said, rubbing lotion into every pore of her hands. "The train was two hours late?"

"Someone jumped on the tracks," I said. "We had to wait until the guys with shovels came to pick up the limbs."

"At least you made it." Ellie scooted up next to me. "Let's go over the plan for Dolce & Gabbana. I know it has lots of bits and pieces, and I'm happy to help."

Happy to help. Anytime. Thank you so much. They were all lines from a script invented by invisible power structures to keep us docile wage-earning citizens.

"I got it," I said curtly, warding off her mousiness as if it might be contagious.

"You sure?"

"Yeah."

The rain mixed with sleet and snow and dripped down the window-panes, making the office feel like a wet cocoon, and when all the planners started leaving for the holiday party, I pretended to be writing an email to a made-up woman named Barb.

"Go without me," I said. "I'll meet you there."

Twenty minutes later, Ellie called. "Are you coming or not? We're all waiting for you."

I knew she was lying, trying to guilt-trip me into joining her gulag of forced drinking, but then I heard Samantha and the other Stepford Planners in the background.

"Is that Jane?"

"Jane!"

"Where are you!"

"We miss you!"

Moved by the sound of any girl calling out my name, I hung up the phone and immediately rushed over to the bar, a sticky-floored Irish pub filled with sports flags and beer logos. It was the sort of bar I'd passed a million times on my way home from work, clumped as they were around places of mass transit like Penn Station and Port Authority so that miserable office people could get drunk before heading home to pass out and do it again the next day.

V-necked waitresses shuffled behind the bar, and when one of them saw me looking lost, she led me to a room in the back where Ellie was threatening a busboy with a lawsuit unless he took away the mixed nuts. The Stepford Planners stood nearby, discussing their rising signs, while the rest of the planners talked about work, all of them fine and diligent specimens who would get promoted, get married, have kids, and die.

"Is Vanessa coming?" Samantha said. "I'll get one drink but I'm not getting any more unless the company's paying."

The Stepford Planners crossed their arms, united in disappointment.

"The company pays for everyone's else's holiday parties."

"It's not fair."

"They should pay for ours."

Vanessa walked in with her company card in the air. "On the Paper!" she shouted, and suddenly the mood turned ecstatic. Within a few minutes everyone was drunk and telling secrets.

"It's from Old Navy," Samantha whispered in my ear as she swayed in a red dress while sucking down gin through a straw. "But we're not telling Arthur that, are we?"

The other Stepford Planners put their hair in pretty buns so they could eat the celery off the platter of chicken wings without getting their hair in the blue cheese. I was about to join them when Ellie cornered me over the quesadillas.

"The founder of North Face saved a million acres of land in South America and I want to do something like that for the environment but I don't know what." She was so well-intentioned that I couldn't escape. "I posted some pictures of a hike I went on with my boyfriend in Cold Spring last week and I included a bunch of information about deforestation, but I don't know how many people saw it."

"I'm sure some people saw it."

"You're right. It got a few likes."

Multiple TV screens played a never-ending stream of music videos including "Livin' La Vida Loca," "Heart of Glass," and a mash-up cover of "All I Want for Christmas Is You" featuring Justin Bieber and Target logos, and everyone danced, song after song, until I lost my hair tie and people started moving around chairs just to help me look for it. Samantha turned on her flashlight, Ellie looked under the grimy couch cushions, and Vanessa offered me the hair tie she always kept around her wrist. "It's shitty but you can have it," she said. Everyone was being so nice that I wanted to cry.

"You guys are the most awesome people in this business right now." Vanessa raised a glass as one of the V-necked waitresses handed out shots. "You should all be proud of yourselves."

It was a gross exaggeration. We were low-level number crunchers in an office building that was identical to every other office building in every major city, but maybe there was something to be said for being in that office at that time with those people. Maybe we really were doing something that mattered.

"CHEERS!" everyone shouted, and suddenly Karen was wasted and no one knew what to do about it. She had gone from tipsy to trashed in thirty seconds, dancing and singing along to the music but also flailing wildly from person to person and holding on to their shoulders for support. Then she grabbed me by the elbow and shouted at Vanessa: "Jane's quiet but she's *the best*. She's just *the best*." She leaned in to my face like she wanted to kiss me and that's when her glasses fell off her face. She bent over to pick them up, lost her balance, and banged her head against the table. It made a horrible *thump*, and when she pulled herself up, she was so embarrassed that she could only look at the floor. Ellie brought her a glass of water but she didn't want it. She wanted to keep dancing, and for a while we let her float around in a state of unsupportable drunkenness. Then she went outside with Vanessa, who came back twenty minutes later and said, "She's in a cab to Jersey."

The next morning, the plastic, buzzing atmosphere of the office felt strange. Whatever conviviality had been shared beneath the music videos and twinkle lights had been replaced by the stark reality of cubes and screens.

"I hope Karen's okay," I said, looking at her empty chair. "She must have passed out in the cab."

Ellie agreed. "She'll be sick all day."

"She needs to rest."

"Poor thing."

Karen plowed toward the station with a bag of donuts. "I woke up *drunk*," she said. "I spent half the morning looking for things. My boyfriend left me alone to get dressed, and when he came back I was on the floor with a pair of leggings on backwards and no top."

She clicked on her monitor and snapped on her headset. "I sent him a cute text this morning on the ride here, you know, a little romantic. A couple minutes goes by and he doesn't write back. Then I check my phone, and guess what? I sent it to my kid's bus driver."

Before we could react, her voice changed. "Sue? Guess what happened this morning. . . ." She went on to tell the same story, and I wondered what my life would be like if I married someone like Karen. Her constitution was amazing, capable of surmounting insults, illnesses, and inebriation. Maybe it would be nice to ditch a dandelion like Madeline and embrace some kind of loudmouthed single mom who could cuss out her grandmother and fix a flat tire.

A box arrived from Michigan, coffin-shaped and twenty pounds. I carried it upstairs, cut it open with one of Laurel's X-Actos, and was distressed to find a vacuum cleaner with fifty different pieces and parts.

"An early Christmas gift," Dad explained over the phone. "You wouldn't believe the sale."

"It's nice," I said, lacking the heart to tell him that I lived in an apartment with wooden floors and no spare room in which to store things like vacuum cleaners. It wasn't his fault he had no idea what my life looked like. He'd never been to New York.

"Do you think you might ever, I don't know, come and visit?"

Dad scratched his beard. It made a sound like sandpaper through the phone.

"We're not big on the whole airport thing."

"The flight's ninety minutes," I said.

"We like it here. We're not the type to want to pack up and go."

"You're homebodies."

"I guess you could say that."

"There's a lot you're missing out on."

"We don't think so."

On the morning of December 23, the trains were filled with suitcases, duffel bags, and neck pillows. Everyone was packed and ready for their long holiday breaks, off to Newark, LaGuardia, JFK, and Grand Central Station, the whole city a galaxy of departure points that were useless to me because I never went anywhere.

Luxury was deserted. The managers had ditched their desktops in exchange for their loving families' homemade cinnamon rolls and functioning radiators, and I responded to emails in a blank state of frustration, mad at Karen's loud phone calls and Ellie's weird lotion smells and the flashing LED billboards out the window touting the glory of Bank of America, Verizon Wireless, and Heineken beer to the swarm of bodies below.

Karen took a two-hour lunch, and when she got back, her face was flushed and she spent an hour talking to the air in front of her screen.

"In your head, you never get older."

"I miss the old building."

"Did I ever tell you about my old boss, Kurt? He was such a dumbass. He used to ask me for an *alpha david*."

Tom called me into his office and I went in there to find him in a radiant mood. He was playing Count Basie and sitting with his feet on his desk.

"Gucci, Prada, Chanel . . ." He drummed his fingers against his desk. "We need to review everyone's spend. Get screenshots, budgets, recaps, click reports."

My eyes went up to the ceiling. It was the same look of annoyance that Bekah had made months ago and I hadn't meant to do it, but now that I had, it felt crushing, like life was a matter of stepping into roles created long, long ago, every part having been played a million times before.

Tom leaned back and gnawed on a fountain pen that I felt certain belonged to Ellie.

"By the way," he said, "what're your plans for Christmas?"

"I don't have any."

"You're not going home?"

"I can't. I have to be here on the twenty-sixth."

He looked appalled. "You have to be here the day after Christmas?"

"All the planners do."

Back at the station, Ellie sprayed her desk with some kind of bleachy-smelling disinfectant that I longed to swallow. More than anything, I missed Madeline. I missed her soft black hair and clothes on the floor. I missed her bad manners and boozy breath. I missed the night we danced to sirens and the way she seemed sad all the time, like this lost little girl who never knew what to do.

Karen got back from a smoke and said Sue had found a photo of Arthur that we needed to see. We rolled over to her screen and there was Arthur, posing like a porn star in thigh-high leather boots in a sexy Santa costume. Ellie was aghast.

"Doesn't he have a partner?"

"Of course he has an apartment!" Karen said, mishearing her. "Did you think he was homeless?"

I was putting on my coat to leave when Tom waved me into his office.

"Celine called," he said. "It'll be quick."

I took off my coat, picked up my notebook, and went into Tom's office. He was on the phone.

"I gotta go, honey," he said. "I know. *I know.* I'll be home in an hour. Love you too."

He hung up and moved some papers around, as if trying to remember what our job was and how it worked.

"Celine," I said.

He frowned. "Let's deal with that next week."

I turned to leave, so annoyed with Tom's absentmindedness that I wasn't going to bother saying good-bye.

"Wait! I talked to my fiancée. We don't like the idea of you spending Christmas alone so we wanted to invite you over. We're on the Upper West Side. It shouldn't be too hard for you to get there from . . ." He paused. "Wherever you live."

I rode the train to Eighty-Sixth Street with a pumpkin pie from the grocery store—it was the only thing Tom had told me to bring—and spent most of the trip imagining the sumptuous apartment where I would be having my first fancy uptown dinner. Crown molding, granite countertops, one of those fireplaces you could turn on and off with a switch—I could only assume Tom would have all of these things and more.

"I'm here for Christmas dinner with Tom Hagerty and his fiancée," I said in a shaky voice to the doorman, who escorted me into a once-impressive elevator and yanked the cage door shut. "E," he said with a drowned look as he let me off on the third floor.

Tom's fiancée, Irina, answered the door. She was a petite middle-aged woman with long dark hair and discriminating eyes, and I developed a crush on her instantly. But a playful one that made me feel closer to Tom.

"It's a little cluttered," she said, stepping gingerly through the hallway filled with boxes, baskets, plant pots, and mail. I hung my jacket over a mound of other coats hanging on the wall and followed Irina into the living room, where we made the hurried small talk of two people trying to get to know each other very fast.

"You work in advertising?"

"For now."

"You don't like it?"

"Not really."

The apartment was small with a low ceiling, musty furniture, and a huge rickety table covered in frantic and colorful scraps.

"I used to write poetry"—Irina motioned toward the table—"but then I thought, I'm tired of words. I want color. I want images. I want to make something that I can hold."

"I'm about to change!" Tom called out from the little kitchen, where he was chopping squash in a T-shirt with holes. "Or not."

Irina's mother was sitting in a faded armchair, her birdlike body swallowed up by the cushions. I asked her if it was true what Tom had said, that she had been a professor of women's studies, and she responded by pushing up her tiny glasses and launching into her life story.

"My mother was from Poland and my father from Mexico and they met at an anti-fascist rally in Guadalajara."

Irina's daughter, Zoe, watched us from the end of the couch. She was a junior in high school with braces, combat boots, and a passion for marching band, which she interrupted her grandmother to tell me about.

"I'm the section leader for the woodwinds," she said. "We're trained in the high step. It's pretty intense. I go to a high school in the Bronx that's the twenty-fifth-best high school in the nation."

Dinner was served on mismatched plates. We sat shoulder to shoulder at a deeply scarred wooden table, passing around bowls of brussels sprouts, turkey breast, and sweet potatoes with walnuts that would've made Ellie die.

Tom's son with the erupting cheeks and ill-fitting khaki pants sat across from me, swirling the single glass of red wine he'd been allowed for the night and sharing random facts from the internet.

"It's physically impossible for pigs to look up."

"Every year two hundred people are killed by coconuts."

"They grow fruit in artificial molds in China. They have Buddha pears, star-shaped cucumbers—"

"It's a novelty," Zoe interrupted him.

"It's not a novelty! They're in grocery stores!"

Tom washed the dishes after dinner. He rubbed our plates with soap bubbles that went up to his elbows and tossed them roughly onto the drying rack so they clashed and clanged.

"I can help," I offered from the table.

"I got it," Tom said. "I'm fast." And he was. I saw him suddenly, the same as he was at work. Calm, happy, and nonstop busy. I should have known his apartment wouldn't have bay windows or a Nespresso machine. He was a bohemian dad who blew his nose on deli napkins and answered the phone by shouting "YELLO."

We moved into the tiny living room to eat dessert and Irina sat on Tom's lap. The teenagers argued about journalism and terrorism and it was obvious that neither one of them knew what they were talking about. Then Irina's mother's partner showed up in a baggy sweater and rubber-soled shoes. She said she was a poet and spoke to me calmly as if from a great distance. "You have to read Rebecca Brown and Jeanette Winterson," she said, and I nodded, feeling how you're supposed to feel on a holiday—warm and held by generous strangers who are suddenly your family.

"Tom, quick question," I said. "Does the Paper ever hire people not from the United States?"

"There's a process," he said. "A little lengthy. A little tedious. But nothing impossible. My last assistant was from Estonia. She was great. Too bad they had to let her go."

"Because she was from Estonia?"

"No. Arthur just decided I wasn't important enough to have an assistant."

"I think I know someone, that's all. She used to be an intern and I think she'd be good in our department."

"Send me her résumé."

"Really?"

"Of course."

My mind did somersaults over a drunken and dreamy vision of the future with Madeline back at the Paper and me leaning over her desk, teaching her how to use some arcane software program before sneaking in a forbidden kiss.

"Where did you say this pie was from?" Tom was now bent over the coffee table, divvying up slices of fruitcake and pie.

"The grocery store," I said.

"In Brooklyn?"

I nodded.

"Irina!" Tom called out to his fiancée, gathering forks in the kitchen. "This pie came all the way from Brooklyn!"

january

A WEEK INTO JANUARY EVERYONE AT WORK WAS STILL TALKING ABOUT their New Year's resolutions, taunting me with the absence of anything new. I knew every stain in the carpeting. I knew the bathroom stall with the broken lock. I knew the elevator car with the scratch on the door. I knew about the candy bowl in Legal. I knew the smell of Ellie's lavender lotion. I knew the lip-smacking sound of Karen cleaning her teeth of donut glaze. And I knew that routine and repetition were necessary and useful aspects of any life, but I still didn't understand why life couldn't have repeated the good parts. Like the night I tied Madeline's shoelaces, damp and grimy in the cold, or the moment in her room when she took off her shirt the sexy way, crossing her arms at her waist before raising them over her head, or that one day last summer when I called in sick to work and met Laurel at the Frick, where we got shushed for making fun of the Whistlers, or even the morning this past Thanksgiving when I woke up in my childhood room with its peach-colored walls and shitty movie posters and felt, for a minute, like a kid again, with no past and no future and nothing to lose.

A thick cloud of smog hung over Port Authority and I was about to hide in an empty conference room and nap when Tom waved me into his office and told me to bring a pen because he didn't have one. "Write these addresses down and send them the new issue of *Chic*," he said, scrolling through a list of foreign street names with accents and umlauts and seemingly no separation between the end of one address and the beginning of another.

"Why don't we print the list?" I said.

"Print?" Tom looked confused. "I haven't been connected to a printer in years."

Alvin was on his knees in the mail room, picking up Styrofoam peanuts someone else had probably spilled and left.

"Hello, Miss Jane. How was your New Year?"

His face was so open and childlike, I wanted to flick him on the forehead, if only to teach him not to trust.

"Fan-fucking-tastic," I said. "How was yours?"

I slid magazines into giant envelopes and thought about Madeline. Night after night, she appeared in my dreams. We kissed. We climbed mountains. We got haircuts.

"My faith has made me well," Alvin said. "Like the prophet Jeremiah, formed in his mother's womb. He was called to be a prophet and he had to put his faith in God, who made that life for him. That's the defining moment of our lives, accepting God's love."

Listening to Alvin repeat himself about God and prophets and oceans of love, I wondered if religious people were just like me but instead of thinking about a girl all the time they thought about God. It seemed boring, really, to spend all that time obsessing about an entity whose face you couldn't even see.

Meanwhile Karen clucked at anyone who passed the station, because she had pressing gossip about the weather. "Temps are goin' down twenty degrees," she said. "Mother Nature's a bitch. If I look extra fat tomorrow, it's cuz I'm wearing two pairs of pants."

Laurel was blow-drying M&M's to one of her old paintings. It was either *Weenie 3* or *A Hole*, two of my favorites because they had both been, at some point, left out in the rain.

"I MISS MADELINE." I had to shout over the hair dryer so she could hear me. It made me feel like I was making a desperate confession, which I guess I was. "She's not back for another week."

Laurel turned off the hair dryer by ripping the plug out of the wall and unfolded an ironing board attached to the inside of her closet.

"Smell it," she said.

I smelled the ironing board and it smelled like nothing. Then I smelled it again and it was bad. Musty and burnt.

"It's bad," I said.

"But it's *interesting*."

"You're right," I said. "I want to smell it again."

"See?" Laurel turned off the overhead light, jumped into bed, and covered herself with a mildewy quilt. "Life is full of interesting people and smells and there's no point in missing anyone who doesn't miss you back." She made room for me under the blanket and we huddled there to watch TV on Laurel's crusty laptop perched precariously on her knees. *Long Island Medium, How It's Made,* and then a biopic starring Juliette Binoche as the sculptor Camille Claudel, trapped in a beautiful insane asylum in the South of France, where she clearly doesn't belong and is forbidden from making art. She leaves the stone edifice one afternoon to walk with the mentally handicapped women up a mountain. Later she weeps in the doctor's office, her eyes hollow with grief. *I'm here without knowing why. Is this joke going to last long? Will it be much longer?* She watches the floor as if it might come up to get her and wipes away her snot with the back of her hand. *I cannot resist the sorrow that overwhelms me.*

Tears formed in my eyes and I wasn't sure why. I just knew the movie had made me think about the office and how Vanessa told everyone during planner meetings, "We want you to be you!" She said it a lot. "Be you! Be you!" As if we all wanted to become people who sold ad space on the internet.

The next morning it was six degrees and Karen came into work wearing black gloves with the fingers cut off. She looked like one of the bad guys from *Home Alone.*

"I dropped my kid off at school this morning and his eyes wouldn't open. I thought he was tired, but no, he said they were frozen shut." She blew on her nicotine fingertips. "I don't care if it's global warming or what. It's ruining my smokes."

Tyler, having overheard the sound of women in distress, stood up in his cube and suggested we all buy his gloves, which he had gotten from a winter clothing company known for animal abuse. "Water-resistant nylon, polyurethane shell, goatskin leather palm . . ." He listed their virtues and looked into Arthur's office, probably hoping the baron of Luxury was listening. It was a lost cause, considering Arthur was one of those New Yorkers who disappeared as soon as the thermometer over Central Park dropped below thirty. The city was the center of his universe and yet he refused to live there for certain months of the year.

"'Already snow submerges an iron year,'" Tom said, unable to keep silent anytime we passed each other in the halls. He raised the end of the overlong scarf Irina had knitted for him, filled with knots and snags, and which he let drag along the floor every time he went to the bathroom. "I don't actually mind the cold," he said. "It's training my body for Aspen. If all goes well, I'll be there next week. Did I tell you about the time Arthur called me in the Rioja valley? I was in the middle of a vineyard, just me and Irina. Two hours later, I'm on a flight to Paris to meet with Chanel. Needless to say, Irina hates him."

I let him talk while I held a cup of hot water, the consumption of boiling liquid being the only thing that kept my insides from crystallizing.

"Did you have a chance to look at my friend's résumé?" I said. "I know Tyler is looking for a planner."

He slapped himself on the forehead.

"Can you resend it?" He walked off with scarf still half-coiled at my feet. "I think it got lost in the shuffle."

The only other two people who didn't seem bothered by the cold were Ellie, who bragged about her ten different layers and made a habit of counting them in the morning ("camisole, Oxford, cardigan, blazer . . ."), and Diana, who refused to take off her parka, a sleek, black, floor-length, feather-down thing. She typed with her parka on, ate lunch with her parka on, went to meetings with her parka on, and around three in the afternoon when the sun started going down, she opened her purse and put on a cashmere scarf.

"I like your coat!" Ellie shouted her compliment over the partition, and Diana looked pleased.

"You should get one!" she said, all happy and failing to realize that a coat like hers cost an eighth of our annual salary.

Sunday was the most abysmal day of the week, not a period of time so much as a nihilistic headspace I still hadn't learned to withstand. After walking past Madeline's building and looking up at her window, which had become my routine, I went to the coffee shop that sold skateboards and hated everyone there. The guy typing on a laptop. The girl looking for the bathroom. The couple holding shopping bags. *Fuck you*, I thought. *Fuck you*. And *Fuck you*.

Outside the wind blew my hair in vicious circles and after stepping over a pool of what appeared to be urine, I got stuck waiting for the light to change next to a man clipping his fingernails with repugnant delight. *Clip! Clip! Clip!* The sound of it followed me all the way into the Dollar General, where I overheard a white man with a handlebar mustache talking with his girlfriend in Ugg boots.

"This'll be good to have," the girlfriend said, picking out a bag of frozen shrimp.

"For dinner or something," the boyfriend said.

"Yeah, next time I call you and we're like, 'What do you want for dinner,' we can—"

"I can grill or something—"

"Yeah."

I felt claustrophobic. Then the boyfriend noticed the frozen vegetables.

"I don't understand how poor people can, like, complain about not being able to eat healthy."

"I think it's more about access," the girlfriend said.

"I don't get it," he said, shaking his head.

The line to check out was long and I somehow got stuck in front of the boyfriend, who was having a fit. One register was open and two employees were helping the clerk, a middle-aged woman in a polo shirt with glasses on the tip of her nose.

"Three people and only one register," he said loudly, so everyone could hear. "This happens *every time* we're here, *every time.*"

The girlfriend shrank.

"That's what we get for a five-dollar bag of shrimp," she said.

Laurel wrote to me on my walk home, telling me I had to meet her at a certain bar in Williamsburg because she had a surprise.

I hate surprises, I texted back.

You won't hate this one, Laurel wrote. She's cute and she wants to see you.

My mood was foul but I rode the train to Williamsburg anyway, captivated by the thought that any woman would want to see me and darkly determined to prove her wrong. She probably had me mixed up with someone else. Or maybe Laurel was lying. Maybe I'd show up and the woman would turn out to be a taco Laurel had bought on the street and named Tiffany.

The bar was a ritzy place on Grand with all-black walls and almost no one inside. The only person there seemed to be Laurel, whose messy bun I could see bouncing over the top of a big round booth in the back.

"Look who it is," Laurel said. "Perfect timing. We were just talking about toilets."

I slid into the booth next to Addy, the nice musician I'd neglected to text for no good reason.

"I forget," Laurel said, draping her arm around Yaritza, a handsome actor whose dreamy-eyed resemblance to James Dean was so uncanny as to be offensive. "Have you met Yaritza? Addy and Yaritza are old friends. Isn't that funny? How everyone knows each other?"

Addy said nothing. She just stared at me with her squinty eyes and pushed around her half-empty glass of what appeared to be whiskey.

"I thought you didn't like to drink," I said.

She kept staring at me and it felt like an accusation. My presence made her so miserable that she had no choice but to turn to booze.

"Anyway, toilets," Laurel said, turning to Yaritza. "Do you think you could die from getting a swirly?"

"You could drown," Yaritza said.

"Or get your skull cracked," Laurel said.

"Or ingest bacteria."

"Or get pinkeye."

"That's the same thing."

"No it's not!"

Their faces kept getting closer and closer and right when I thought they might kiss, Yaritza unraveled a pack of cigarettes from the sleeve of her crisp white T-shirt and they traipsed out the door, bumping elbows and talking over each other as they went.

"I saw your friend in that show on Broadway last year," I said. "Is that still playing? I don't normally go to shows but I got a free ticket through my job."

Addy scooted over to me at the edge of the booth and stuck her nose in my face. She had dramatically wide nostrils and thick, unplucked eyebrows and her mouth was small and adorably plump.

"I'm mad at you," she said.

"Why's that?"

"Don't play dumb."

I shrugged and looked down at her shirt. She was wearing a Stevie Nicks T-shirt, soft and loose.

"Is that real vintage?" I said.

"Don't deflect."

"Sorry, it's just. That's a valuable shirt."

"You said you wanted to go out again," she said. "You said you'd 'be in touch' or whatever. Then you disappeared."

"I didn't know we were supposed to do anything."

"You're probably still seeing that girl."

"Which girl?"

"The straight girl."

I looked at the door, half expecting Madeline to walk in.

"She's gone," I said. "She moved away."

Addy relaxed her shoulders and sat back against the booth.

"It's real, by the way," she said. "The shirt. It used to be my mom's."

Laurel and Yaritza came back, everybody signed their checks, and as we put on our coats and headed into the cold it felt vaguely like a double date but an absolutely failed one, considering one couple was happy and the other was not.

"Well, have fun, you two," Laurel said.

"Stay out of trouble," Yaritza said.

They walked away laughing and left me alone with Addy, whose dorky hat was pulled so low over her head all I could see were her angry little eyes.

"So," I said. "Do you live around here?"

I thought we might have a normal conversation, part on good terms, maybe even hug.

"I can't believe you're not going to apologize." She stood on her toes and got in my face. "I was really mad when you didn't write to me. I felt really tricked."

I took a step back. She took a step forward. It was like a dance. A modern one with bitter wind and angry faces.

"I thought we had a good time," she went on, "but you clearly aren't ready to be real with people and I respect myself too much to have any tolerance for games." She went on about the value of her time and the nature of her life's priorities and my blatant disregard for both of those things, and suddenly her face was so close to mine that I got the feeling she wanted to kiss. It made no sense. She was actively angry with me. But still, I sensed something else beneath the shield of her hurt.

I leaned forward, just a little, and like a trap, she fell for it. She leaned in and kissed me, her lips moving hard and fast. It wasn't a good kiss but I didn't hold it against her. Maybe she hadn't kissed anyone in a while. Maybe being with Jess for so long had meant she'd forgotten how to kiss. When I pulled back, I looked over at Laurel and Yaritza, watching us enact this little disaster from up the block. I waved at them. They waved back. Addy exhaled in annoyance and took out her phone to call a car.

"I wish you hadn't done that," she said.

"Waved at them?"

"No. Kissed me."

"You're the one who kissed me."

She went over to the curb as if wanting to get as far away from me as possible.

"I didn't mean to," she said, kind of grumbling.

Her car pulled up, and after getting in the backseat and slamming the door, she took one last look at me and I could've sworn I saw her middle finger rising up in the glass.

Madeline wrote to me a week later, inviting me to a movie at Lincoln Center. It was about aging Mexican prostitutes and the twin dwarf luchadores whose prize money they planned to steal. The obscure nature of the film—foreign, black-and-white, low-budget—appealed to me because it seemed to say something about the oddity of our own pairing. How wrong it looked on the surface but how right it felt from within.

I got to the theater early, bought our tickets, claimed the two best seats in the middle of auditorium, and then tested the armrests to make sure they folded up in case we wanted to make out. Then I watched the back of an old man's head as he fussed and frowned over the Sunday crossword puzzle. A few more geezers came into the theater, almost all of them alone, and when the lights dimmed and the old man in front of me was still stuck on the same clue, I knew Madeline wasn't coming. It had been wrong to hope, wrong to care, wrong to want anything at all. Stout women wailed onscreen, expressing precisely the spiritual dereliction I was feeling after having been stood up, when a door opened in the back of the theater and Madeline appeared at the end of my row. She sat close to the aisle in her fuzzy black coat and I wondered if she had seen me, if she knew I was there. I unscrewed the cap of my water bottle and threw it at her. It bounced off of her knee and rolled across the floor. She looked at me with scorn. *Did you just throw something at me?* I berated myself internally for being a toddler until she came over and we sat beside each other like colleagues, with our hands in our laps.

"I thought you weren't coming," I whispered.

"I got lost."

"You should've texted me."

"That's embarrassing."

Madeline kept her eyes on the screen but she kept fidgeting with the armrest, moving her legs around, and touching her hair. I wanted to put my arm around her and tell her everything would be all right, but it suddenly seemed impossible. We suffered from the same uncertainty. I just knew how to hide it.

"It was short," was all Madeline managed to say after the lights came up, and I agreed, feeling equally speechless and strange.

"What should we do now," she said.

"We could sit."

"And then what?"

"And then nothing."

We wandered into the plaza and sat at the edge of the fountain. The water formed a rising waterfall behind our backs, and after a moment of silence, spent listening to the water ascending and landing back on itself, Madeline leaned her head against my shoulder and I put my arm around her waist. All of the nervousness we'd been holding on to during the movie was gone. We looked at each other while the fountain sprayed a mist over our heads and people floated by, posing for pictures with *Playbills* tucked under their arms. If I were alone, I would have wanted to watch them, to study their faces and make guesses about where they were from and what their lives looked like back home, but with Madeline, I only wanted to look at her. It was remarkable to be so self-centered, to feel like we were the only two people in the city. I had the urge to tell her that I loved her. It was an indulgent and clichéd thing to say, but I was tired of feeling small. I opened my mouth and waited for the words to come.

"How was Guatemala?" I said.

"Boring," she said. "There was nothing to do so I came back early. New Year's was good though. I did Molly and went to that club Verboten." She reached for the zipper on my coat, pulling it up and down so it made a shriek.

"You've been here since New Year's?"

"Something like that."

My chest felt hollow. I'd sat awake in bed at night, composing messages to her in my head—*let's move in together, let's make a documentary, let's fly to Peru*—and all that time she'd been passed out in a bed nine blocks away.

"I forget," I said. "When do you leave again?"

She let go of my zipper and winced in the wind.

"Soon." She turned away from me, or maybe just the cold, and tried to raise the flimsy collar of her coat.

"I'm moving into my friend's place in Berlin," she said. "It's right next to this big park that used to be an airfield and she said people throw big parties there in the summer with sausages grilling and people on Rollerblades, just, like, high and rolling around."

The nonchalance with which Madeline was describing her new life overseas made me want to hurt her. Not physically. I just wanted her to feel what I felt. This internal, abysmal, spiraling hurt.

"What about money," I said. "How are you going to live."

She perked up and said, "I can't believe I didn't tell you. I got hired to work on a movie set. I'm gonna be the assistant to some famous German actor."

"But you don't speak German."

"She speaks English."

"The actor's a woman?"

"Yeah, and she's super hot."

"How exciting," I said. "I'm happy for you."

Madeline seemed to have no grasp of the rings of hell I'd gone through in order to get to know her. And now that she was leaving, she was blasé. It was insulting. To love someone so unabashedly for months on end only to realize on a winter night that they were wrapped up in their own life and brazenly moving on.

I took out my phone and started writing to Addy.

"Who are you texting?"

"A friend," I said. "A musician."

It took Madeline a second to process this information. This subtle reminder that I was an adult in New York City who knew real people with real artistic careers.

"What kind of music?"

"Um." I still hadn't heard Addy's music. I'd been meaning to listen to it; I'd just been lazy and kept forgetting to look it up. "It's pretty genre-less."

I hopped off the rim of the fountain in fortuitous unison with a stream of water, shooting up behind Madeline's back.

"Well," I said. "It was good to see you."

"Good to see you too."

Her mirroring me signaled a sort of frailty on her part, and it gave me sick pleasure to see her fumbling for words at the moment of my departure.

"See ya!" I said as I headed toward the train. A deliberately clipped and even barbaric form of good-bye; I knew my victory was certain.

Temperatures dropped below zero on Monday morning and I buried myself beneath so many layers that I forgot I had a body. It was better that way. A body was a soft and porous thing that came with so many needs. To be touched, to be held, to be seen, to be heard. It seemed better to surrender to complete isolation and just give in, once and for all, to being a blob.

I was on my way to the break room to drink more boiling water when the Stepford Planners waved me over to their station so I could meet the new girl, a tall redhead in gladiator bracelets.

"This is Robin Myles," Samantha said, gesturing toward the mannequin smiling at me like a school photo. "Isn't she cute?"

Her eyes were glowing, her skin was clear, and I felt like I knew her entire life. She would buy a house in Connecticut. She would host parties. She would name her son Linden. She would make pies.

The new girl leaned over and hugged me with her strong spin-class arms. She was Amazonian in stature and she smelled amazing, like oranges and clean.

"I heard you're the planner I should to talk to if I ever have questions," she said.

"That's Ellie," I said. "I'm the other one."

"Which one?"

"I don't know," I said. "The gay one who bites her nails."

Tyler appeared with a foam football. He tossed it between his hands in a mock performance of juggling and then pretended to chuck it at the Stepford Planners' heads, winding up and then freezing at the moment he should have let go.

"*Staaahhp iiit,*" the Stepford Planners sang, like birds about to get run over.

Tyler walked away laughing and the Stepford Planners shook their heads in playful disapproval.

"That's Tyler."

"He's your manager."

"Nobody likes him."

It snowed for the rest of the day, and when I left for the night, the glass awning over the revolving doors was blanketed in a sheet of ice with long, cone-shaped stalactites hanging over the edges. Feeling sentimental and slow in the head, I stopped to admire how beautiful they looked, these frozen missiles dripping water onto everyone's heads, and I was about to pass through a gap in the spears when a man with a shovel came out and began to whack them down.

Madeline was moving to Berlin any day now, but I made no effort to see her and wrote to Addy instead. A test to see if she'd write back.

> Hey it's your least favorite person
> Blue Velvet is playing tonight at Film Forum
> Do you like David Lynch?

She wrote back right away.

> I love David Lynch
> Are you asking me out or just being weird?

I rode the train straight to the theater after work without bothering to change out of my work clothes. It just didn't occur to me. Addy wasn't someone I was trying to impress. But I did get nervous when I saw how crowded the lobby was, and I felt even worse when I overheard someone say the eight o'clock screening was sold out. *Great*, I thought. Now we'd have to see the stupid nature documentary about migrating butterflies that started at nine.

"I wasn't sure what you liked." Addy walked toward me holding two tickets and a bag of jelly beans. She was wearing a red-and-white baseball tee tucked into soft gray pants and she looked comfortable but also confident in her big brown glasses and L.L.Bean boots.

"Jelly beans are fine," I said.

She looked down at her giant bag of candy. "Oh," she said. "You think I'm sharing?"

I laughed, and she rushed to say that she was just kidding and she was actually really generous, so generous, in fact, that it was problem.

"I know," I said.

"You know I have problems?"

"No. I know that you're nice."

We wasted so much time chitchatting in the lobby that when we got into the theater the only two seats left were in the very back row. I wanted to complain but Addy didn't seem to mind. She opened her bag of jelly beans and offered me any flavor but pear.

"If you get a pear," she said, "you have to give it to me."

"What if it's already in my mouth?"

"Spit it out."

"For you?"

"On principle."

A bespectacled film critic stood behind a podium to introduce the film. He said all the things I'd expected him to say about *Blue Velvet*, a film that "still shocked" after all these years, and I didn't like his dry, old-man way of talking in clichés, but then the movie started and I forgot all about him and our seats in the back because *Blue Velvet* really was transfixing. It was also longer and more perverted than I remembered, so I kept looking over at Addy, checking to see if she was all right, or bored, or asleep.

"What?" she hissed at me in dark.

"Nothing," I said, turning back to the screen.

Sadomasochism, voyeurism, exhibitionism—all the different isms played out onscreen, and I felt oddly comforted by Addy's presence beside me. Her calm way of sitting with her legs crossed and slowly eating candy while being careful not to let the bag rustle made me feel more grounded, turning the surreal and violent world of the film into something more dreamlike and enjoyable.

"I'm impressed," I said when the lights came up. "You sat very still, and you didn't fidget or seem bored."

"Why would I be bored?" she said. "Do you think I have no attention span just because I didn't go to college?"

She buttoned herself into her red plaid coat.

"I couldn't care less about you not going to college," I said. "I went to college, and I promise, I'm extremely stupid."

"You shouldn't say that about yourself."

"But it's true. Sometimes I look around New York City and I'm like, *How are all these buildings not falling down?* I genuinely don't understand."

She wrapped a fluffy scarf around her neck and took a tube of Burt's Bees out of her Strand tote bag.

"It's cold," she said, "but I'd love to walk. If that's something you're okay with."

"Or we could get a drink," I said.

She rubbed her lips together—I could smell the peppermint oil—and shook her head. "I'd prefer to just walk, if that's okay."

Through the lobby, out the double doors, and up to Bleecker we walked at a steady pace, and I was impressed with Addy's legs, shorter than mine but fast and strong.

"Every time I see *Blue Velvet* I appreciate something new," she said. "This time it was the chip in Isabella Rossellini's front tooth."

"You noticed that?"

We crossed Bowery and walked into the East Village, where it was easy to see into all the apartments, illuminated on the inside and starkly visible from the street.

"I don't understand people who use overhead lights," Addy said. She looked into the next apartment. "Who would paint their living room orange?" And the next. "God, look at that light fixture. It's absolutely horrendous."

She talked like talking was easy and had so many opinions to share. It was like she was an expert in everything, and maybe she was. She was an artist. She lived alone. She'd had a relationship—a long and healthy one—that had ended peacefully, from what I could tell.

"What did you want to be when you grew up?" she said.

"A baseball player."

"I wanted to be a police lady."

"We were so gay."

"I know," she said. "How did our parents not know?"

We went underground at Essex and Delancey. Her train was on one side of the station. Mine was on the other.

"Thanks for walking with me," she said.

"I liked it."

"Me too."

We were standing under a bright light that made our faces look sickly, and it was also hard to hear because of the trains, but Addy seemed unfazed. She was focused on me.

"I need you to be honest with me," she said. "How many girls are you dating right now?"

Her question was so unexpected that I laughed.

"I don't know what you're talking about."

"That girl who moved away. Are you still talking to her?"

"No."

"What about other girls, like, girls from the internet?"

"Stop being paranoid. I'm single and miserable. Like everyone else."

She looked at me suspiciously. I think we both knew I was lying.

"What are you doing this Friday night?" I said.

"Nothing," she said. "I don't do anything."

"Come with me to the Morgan Library. It's nothing crazy. It's just a museum with a bunch of books. Actually, now that I think about it, we probably shouldn't go. You might not like it."

"Because you think I don't like books?"

"I just think you might get bored."

"That's offensive."

We agreed to meet at the museum at seven, and before going our separate ways, I warned her that I'd be wearing my stupid work clothes again.

"Why would you warn me about that?" She reached out and fixed my collar so it wasn't stuck under my coat. "I like your work clothes. But you need a scarf."

The new girl moved into her desk next to Karen's and made a point of repeatedly bumping into Karen's crates.

"Whose crates are these?" she asked, knowing exactly whose they were.

"Sorry about that," Karen said. "I've been meaning to go through those."

"They're kind of an eyesore," Robin said. "I keep running into them."

Karen fidgeted with her headset and bobbed her head up and down and I hated seeing her like that, subservient to the new girl with the big, pretty face. "I'll go through 'em," she said. "I'll go through 'em today."

Next the man-boys from Telesales came over to "check out the view," a bogus errand that segued into asking Robin whether or not she went out, which was code for *Do you have a boyfriend?*

"I used to go out a lot," she said, "but now I mostly hang out with Dylan." The man-boys nodded at the sound of a boyfriend and left, never to return.

Then Brad from IT came up to fix Robin's computer.

"There's nothing really wrong with it," she said. "It's just really slow."

They laughed together, and Karen and Ellie and I looked at each other, dumbfounded. The guys in IT were the meanest people in the building, vengeful nerds who stood over you and snapped at how you should really just hit restart.

"No worries," he said. "I just ordered you a new hard drive."

Robin gushed, "Can I take you home?"

Tyler must have overheard the opposing lion's roar because he abruptly came over to the station, jaunty and whistling.

"We should get lunch." He shook the back of Robin's chair. "I know a decent drinking hole on Ninth. I'm tight with the bartenders. They'll hook us up."

Robin pushed her thick red hair away from her face and touched her neck, a surefire sign that she was about to lie. "That sounds amazing."

He lumbered back to his cube to get his coat, and Robin's voice dropped an octave. "I know he's the worst, but if I put in the effort now, I shouldn't be stuck working for him for much longer."

"Don't count on it," Ellie said. "It takes years to get promoted around here."

"Or demoted," Karen said.

Robin talked through the morning and into the afternoon about how much she loved cooking, loved her boyfriend, and loved her job. She spoke with a very particular type of baby voice—not sexy baby, like the voice a girl might use in a beer commercial, but happy baby, with the bouncy vowels and bright naïveté of someone whose life was going really well for them. Everything was "wonderful," "lovely," or "beautiful," and within a short amount of time, I started to hate her.

It snowed all night and massive snowbanks had formed around the building, making the relatively short distance between the subway and the revolving doors treacherous with slush that changed color throughout the day: coffee brown in the morning, dog-pee yellow in the afternoon, and black with car exhaust by six. I monitored them throughout the week, and on Friday, when they were mostly gone, the mood of the office had transformed. The fact of the coming weekend cast a mystical light over everything we did.

"Great," Karen groaned at the sound of Robin crushing dried banana chips into her overnight oats. "You're healthy too?"

"For all your lack of nutrition," Ellie said, "you actually look really young."

Karen gave Ellie a sharp look over the partition. "How old do you think I am?"

After a pause, when it became clear that no one was going to tell a middle-aged woman that she looked middle-aged, Karen said, "I'm forty-one," and we were all politely stunned.

"Your skin is so tight."

"I thought you were thirty-six, tops."

"And you've never had work done?"

Karen touched her forehead lightly. Even in the middle of winter, her face really was as tight as leather.

"You know what Tom says to me?" she said, smiling a little. "He says when I die, he's gonna donate my body to Louis Vuitton."

A few hours later, when it was just me and Karen at the station, she looked at me with a mournful face and said, "I lied. I'm forty-nine." Why she admitted that to me and why it mattered, I don't know, but it gave meaning to that stupid phrase "Happy Friday."

I walked to the Morgan Library after work and was waiting out front, leaning against the handrail and trying to look cool, when Addy walked past me and proceeded up the block. I had to chase her down, which wasn't as demeaning as I thought it would be, and tap her on the back at Thirty-Seventh.

"I didn't see you," she said. "I left my glasses at home."

"Is that bad?"

"It's really bad."

I tried to hide my disappointment. It seemed only natural that our date would be over before it had even begun.

"If you need to go home, that's fine," I said. "We can go out another time."

"No, no." Addy was insistent. "I'll be fine. You might just need to help me get around."

I led us up the stone steps of the museum, guiding her gently with my hand on her arm, and it occurred to me that she might've been lying. She might've left her glasses at home on purpose just to be able to seem adorable and disadvantaged.

"Tell me the truth," she said. "How many girls have you brought here?"

"Only you."

"I know you're lying, but okay."

She took off her coat and I couldn't think anymore because she looked good. She was wearing faded blue jeans, soft leather boots, and a light-red T-shirt that said *ADY* across the front.

"It's a merch shirt that got misspelled," she said. "I've been wearing it for years."

"I feel like you wear a lot of old clothes," I said.

"I do," she said. "I definitely hate shopping. But I also try to wear clothes that have some kind of meaning for me, because otherwise, I don't know, it's just posing, you know? Like girls who buy jeans with holes already in them. That's such a joke."

"Totally." I nodded and walked ahead, anxiously trying to suppress the memory of a certain pair of Madeline's jeans. "I'm bad at shopping too. I just wear the same thing every day."

"As you should." She tugged on my sleeve. "You always look good."

We opened our bags for the security guard, who nodded at our gum and tampons, and then we hovered between large marble pillars in the lobby, where gray-haired friends were drinking tea and a string quartet was playing Vivaldi. The atmosphere of the museum was stuffy and decidedly unsexy and I had to the urge to apologize to Addy for bringing her to such a prim and proper place.

"I can't believe I've never been here before," she said.

"So you like it?"

"Of course I like it."

We went into a gallery on the second floor that was showing some of Andy Warhol's handmade books. They were little paper things, like zines from the sixties, full of colorful drawings of strawberries, snakes, and frolicking cherubs.

"I would hate to be a cherub," I said. "All they do is dance in circles." I could hear myself talking nervously. I seemed unable to stop. "This panel says he had twenty-four cats and they were all named Sam." "Look at this print he did of Goethe. Did you ever read *The Sorrows of Young Werther*?"

I rushed us into the library next, a gloomy room full of old books with a big glass case that contained, among other things, a cigarette-stained letter by Tennessee Williams, some handwritten notes from Zora Neale Hurston, and an early draft of *Jane Eyre* made extra remarkable by Charlotte Brontë's infinitesimally small handwriting.

"I came here really high once and got teary-eyed in front of this." I motioned toward the Gutenberg Bible, crispy and charred.

"You're into the Bible?"

"I'm into the Gutenberg Bible. It's the first book printed in

Europe with movable type so it kind of marks the dawn of Western lit, and I guess I just think it's awesome that it ended up here where a random dyke from Michigan could come and see it."

"You sound like you're high right now."

"I'm not."

"Good. I get really annoyed when I'm around high people."

"Noted."

She looked up at the vaulted ceiling, painted with a detailed mural of centaurs, zodiac symbols, and white men from world history.

"Is that an animal?" she asked.

"It's Plato," I said.

She pointed at Michelangelo. "And that's a dragon?"

"You lied," I said. "You can't see anything."

After some hesitation she admitted she needed her glasses and without them, she was both legally blind and getting a headache.

"Come to my place," she said. "I'll get them and we can go back out."

"Where do you live?"

"Park Slope."

I was momentarily horrified. Park Slope was an oppressively suburban neighborhood full of liberal married people and their Starbucks-drinking teens. It was also far from Bushwick, with no direct train line or bus connecting the two, so if I went to Addy's place, I was liable to get stuck.

"I'll go with you," I said. "But we have to go back out."

"We will. We can go wherever you want."

We walked to the nearest F train, and after I asked her a few polite questions about her family, she talked in giddy run-on sentences about her sister, who was engaged to her high school boyfriend; her gay younger brother, who worked in a lab that processed urine samples; and her mother, a sweet, angelic woman who baked whoopie pies and was married to a piece-of-shit alcoholic shipbuilder on the coast.

She was so eager to share her life with me and talk about whatever people were supposed to talk about on a date that I couldn't decide whether I felt oppressed or relieved.

"You're making me do all the talking," she said. "Will you talk? It's your turn."

"It must be weird living in Park Slope."

"It's actually beautiful."

"But the strollers."

We got off the train with a bunch of respectable-looking people carrying yoga mats and reusable grocery bags.

"That's where I get bagels," Addy said, walking ahead of me and pointing at all the cute storefronts that lined her avenue. "That's where I get pizza. That's where I pick up my prescriptions. And that's a new Peruvian place that just opened up."

She turned onto her tree-lined block, and I gazed up at all the prewar brownstones with fancy doorbells and wood-paneled garbage bins that all the moneyed homeowners knew how to conceal.

"Are you rich?" I said.

"I just got lucky." She opened a wrought iron gate and skipped up the steps of a four-story building with period details carved into the twin French doors. "The landlord's nice. He gave me a deal."

I followed her up to the fourth floor, and when she disappeared into her room, I stood in the kitchen and looked around. Saucepans dangled over the stove. Cookbooks were stacked on the fridge. A fruit bowl on the counter overflowed with apples, oranges, and limes. Her life was so settled, so domestic and clean, I almost didn't trust it.

"Why are you standing in the dark," she said. "Come here and see my room."

"Are you sure? It seems kind of soon. Seeing someone's room is like seeing them naked."

She stuck her head in the doorway and I saw that she was wearing her glasses, which she had found suspiciously quickly.

"Don't worry," she said. "I'm not naked."

I went into her room and looked around, taking in her queen-sized bed, voluminous white comforter, potted plants, and twenty framed photographs of friends, family members, and other seemingly random loved ones spread across her dresser and hung on all the walls.

"Your room's cute," I said.

"It's not *cute*," she said. "I'm not some little girl."

"C'mon." I gestured toward the photos. "You have a shrine."

"It's not a shrine. It's just all the people I love."

She went around the room and introduced me to Grandma Dot, Auntie Lynn, Uncle Theo, her brother, her sister, her best friend, her other best friend, and her young and beautiful parents in 1988, before they got divorced.

"My mom and dad were super in love." She sat on her bed, getting comfortable. "They used to kiss in front of us and we'd run away screaming. But now I think it's adorable." She repositioned herself against her plush throw pillows and patted her all-white comforter that I was suddenly afraid to touch. I didn't want to pollute it with my triple-worn work pants.

"Stop being weird," she said. "Sit."

I sat on the edge of the bed, three feet away from her.

"I thought we were going out," I said.

"We will."

She scooted closer to me so that I could feel the warmth of her leg as it bumped against my back.

"What are you thinking about?" she said.

Offended by the question, I wasn't sure what to say. I thought the whole point of having thoughts was not having to share them.

"Nothing," I said. "I have no interesting or original thoughts."

She looked annoyed and I was glad. What did she expect? The eloquent unfolding of my inner life?

A draft blew in through the cracked-open window and made the sheer white curtains shake. Her room was cozy. Her life was pretty. I had no idea what I was doing anywhere near it.

"You need to talk to me," she said. "Or else this is never going to work."

I looked out at the pretty branches that I couldn't believe were there. Nobody I knew in Brooklyn had a view of trees. We all faced brick walls or air shafts or metal security bars covered in spiderwebs and dirt.

I could feel her watching the side of my face, and it should have been endearing. She was showing her persistence, her interest, her open need. Instead, I felt trapped. She cooked and cleaned and bought hand soap with olive oil. What did she want from me?

I got off the bed and rubbed my face, feeling like Tom stressed out in his office.

"It's getting late," I said, glancing up at the clock that assured me it was not.

Addy hopped off the bed and stood in the doorway.

"You're not leaving yet," she said.

"I'm not?"

"You came all this way."

She felt the collar of her shirt and I looked at her neck. I knew I was supposed to start kissing her. To do all the slow and erotic things two people in a quiet room were supposed to do. But my body felt inert, like a lifeless thing, and when I did lean over to kiss Addy lightly on the lips, I thought, improbably, of Madeline. I hated her so much. Her selfishness. Her caginess. Our obvious incompatibility. And it was maddening to be thinking about her again, against my will, when I was trying to kiss someone else.

"I need to be honest with you about something," I said, pulling back. "I'm not feeling very sexy tonight. It's been a long week. My body's kind of tired."

She let go of her shirt. "I get it. That's fine. That's totally fine."

Nervousness flickered across her face as she moved out of the way and into the kitchen.

"What about next week," I said, following her. "Are you around next week?"

She turned on the overhead light and opened the door to the hallway.

"I'm going upstate to work on music."

"Okay, so after that."

"Maybe."

We hugged good night and I walked to the train, passing the big old trees and the shadows they cast in the street.

I invited Laurel to the office for lunch and she showed up in sweatpants and clogs. Her streaky pink-and-blue hair and duct-taped coat got stares in the elevator, but she didn't care.

"Bright in here" was all she said about the dining hall with its floor-to-ceiling windows and spectacular view of Manhattan. She put on her orange-tinted sunglasses and plopped a piece of fried chicken onto her cardboard tray.

"I bet all these normies are into you," Laurel said, lowering her chin to peek at the women around us in pantsuits and heels. "You're lucky you're an LHB. That's high-demand."

"LHB?"

"Long-haired butch."

"What does that make you?"

"Nothing special," she said. "I'm just a classic crazy bitch."

We passed the Stepford Planners sitting at their usual table and I could feel their eyes narrowing in on Laurel's arm, perhaps trying to read the tattoo that said *FAG*.

"Who's your friend?" Robin said, and I cringed, not wanting

Laurel to think I had anything to do with four hyper-straight girls with pink iPhone cases.

"Sit with us," Samantha said. "We have room."

Laurel, who was clueless, sat and started eating.

"So how do you two know each other?" Robin said, surveying Laurel's tray, smothered in fried chicken, curry noodles, veggie carnitas, and other random food from the salad bar that went together not at all. "Jane won't tell us anything." She leaned into Laurel's elbows, firmly planted on the table. "What's her type?"

"I don't know." Laurel shrugged. "Long pubes?"

I poured more hot sauce into my sandwich to give it a painful sort of flavor and thought of Madeline. I knew I should banish her from my mind, yet I had grown to like the pain of missing her, to depend on it and maybe even crave it.

"Is *The Bachelor* still on?" I blurted. "He must be down to two or three roses by now."

I escorted Laurel down to the lobby when lunch was over but I wasn't ready to say good-bye. So I emailed Tom some bogus line about "personal business" and went with Laurel to the Dave & Buster's on Forty-Second, where we ordered a goblet of merlot and spent thirty dollars on an arcade game that involved throwing germy beanbags at creepy smiling clowns.

"The thing about dating girls is this," Laurel rambled as I knocked another clown into oblivion. "The sane girls are boring . . ."

The clowns, having all been destroyed, popped back to life and grinned with gigantic menace, looking not unlike Robin in the hall.

". . . and the interesting girls are nuts."

Flimsy paper tickets shot out of the machine and assured us both we were talented and successful people with prosperous, inspired futures.

"We need to come here more often," I said.

Laurel snatched up the tickets and added them to the pile spilling out of her back pocket.

"You should do this for a living," she said.

"Work at an arcade?"

"No." She waved our goblet in the air. "Throw balls."

We killed enough clowns to win five vanilla Tootsie Rolls, two candy necklaces, and a set of plastic vampire teeth that glowed in the dark. We took turns wearing the teeth on the escalator ride back down to the street.

"I *shink* you are *shpecial*," I said to Laurel, and handed her the teeth.

"I *shink* you are *shmart and shweet*," she said.

We hugged outside the Applebee's and I shuddered at the thought of having to go back to work.

"I should quit right now," I said. "All I want to do is go home with you."

Laurel looked at me seriously as Spider-Man waved at us, a shih tzu rolled by in a stroller, and a crust punk sat on the curb and changed his shoes.

"Your job isn't perfect but it's fine," she said. "It's a good job and it won't last forever. You have a paycheck. You have a chair. And you get to eat lunch with people."

I put the vampire teeth in my mouth. "*Shank* you," I said.

"You're welcome," she said, and then she went down the subway steps to the beat of a toothless man pounding the drums.

Cruise ships docked along the Hudson in the morning and made triumphant departures in the afternoon. I took masochistic pleasure in watching them glide through the icy river, these glittering palaces bound for Costa Rica with frozen yogurt machines and quesadilla bars and meet-and-greets with friendly bikini-snatching dolphins. Karen pointed at them and shrieked, "The cruise ships are going by! Wave to all the assholes!"

The sky clouded over at six and Robin tucked in her chair and followed Diana, Tyler, and the rest of the managers into the elevator going up while Ellie straightened her pens, picked lint off her cardigan, and tucked loose hairs into her bun, unable to keep still in the shadow of Robin's blatant social climbing.

"I can't believe she's going to the numbers meeting," she said. "Arthur doesn't even know who she is."

Karen zipped her fat purse and shrugged. "Now he will."

I was having one of those Saturday nights where no matter how much I drank I never got drunk. I just got dizzy and tired and annoyed at all the people wearing top hats and leather bras. The party was at a warehouse in Bushwick a few blocks from our place. Laurel had dragged me there because she didn't want to go alone and then instantly disappeared, having recognized people more important than me.

I went out to the street and sat on a cement ledge near some rat poison and dumpsters. I sat there for a while, just counting the potholes and feeling blah, when I saw Madeline on the other side of the street. She was walking quickly in her white tennis shoes, and something about her skinny legs and aloneness made her seem extra vulnerable.

"Are you following me?" I called out to her, and she spun around.

"You texted me," she said, crossing the street. "Did you forget?"

She sat beside me as if nothing was the matter and I wasn't sure what to do. Touch her, kiss her, or leave her alone.

"How was the party?" she said. "Did it have a line long?"

"A line long?"

"A LONG. LINE."

Drunk—she was drunk. It made sense.

"It doesn't matter," I said. "I'm going home."

"You can't leave yet," she said. "I want to see it." She got up and yanked on my arm. "I want to see what it's like."

I paid her cover and led us into the roomful of half-naked bodies painted in glitter and dry-humping under disco lights. Madeline said nothing and started dancing, swaying from left to right with her hands in the air, like a scarf stuck to a fence.

When the sweat was dripping into my eyes and it became hard to tell apart the shoving from the dancing, I told Madeline I was leaving.

"It's not fair," she said, wrapping one of her spidery arms around my neck. "I've still never seen where you live."

"And you probably never will," I said.

Madeline looked surprised. She tucked her hair behind her ears.

"You're not letting me come over? Not even if I ask?"

She followed me out to the street, where Laurel was smoking with some uniquely unattractive people in long tweed coats. Laurel looked at me and then at Madeline and then back at me.

"Having fun?" she said, taking a drag off someone's menthol she'd bummed.

"I'm leaving," I said.

"We both are," Madeline said, struggling to zip her coat. It was the fuzzy black one, and it suddenly looked stupid on her, basic and try-hard.

I started walking home and Madeline followed.

"Who was that?" she said. "Someone you're sleeping with?"

"It doesn't matter."

"It matters to me."

The sidewalk was covered in black ice and half-melted snow, so we slid along the cracks and bumps while the atmosphere of Bushwick turned increasingly depressing. Tipsy girls in tight dresses leapt over snowbanks next to skater boys eating burritos, and baby-faced NYU undergrads huddled together for warmth and group identity as they waited for the cars that would take them back to their dorms across the river.

Madeline stopped in the middle of the sidewalk. Her coat was hanging open and she must have been cold. She had no hat, no gloves, no scarf. Nothing but her tiny black skirt and white collared shirt that made her look like a schoolgirl, underage and out past curfew.

"Do you hate me?" she said.

"Why would I hate you?"

"Then let me come over," she said.

"Another time."

"There won't be another time. I leave tomorrow."

Knowing that she'd come shit-faced to a party and then wanted to spend her last night with me forced me to realize that I might have been wrong. Madeline wasn't cool or popular or even that confident. She was just another young person who didn't want to be alone.

"I was kidding," I said. "Of course you can come over. Did you think I'd just abandon you in the cold?"

"Yes," Madeline said, and then she held on to my arm and followed me home. Up the deformed stairs of my building, past the dirty dishes piled in the sink, and into my big, drafty room, where she immediately threw off her coat, got under the covers, and closed her eyes. I went to the bathroom to splash water on my face, and when I got back, she hadn't moved. I touched the covers. She opened her eyes.

"Do you want a T-shirt or something?" I said.

She nodded and I gave her one of my black T-shirts. She swiveled around to put it on so I wouldn't see her chest.

"Your church girl is coming out," I said.

"Sorry. I forgot you're you."

I turned off the lamp and got in bed next to her. I didn't expect anything to happen. I thought we might go to sleep. Then she scooted in to my side and slipped off the shirt I'd only just given her.

"Okay," I said, "so we're not a church girl."

She brought her lips up to mine and gave me a warm, conciliatory sort of kiss that felt like a first.

"Was that okay?" she said.

I could no longer speak. Her kiss had already done something to me. Something melty and potentially not good.

"It's just dangerous."

"Why?"

"You know why."

We kissed again, and all of my longing for her came back with unprecedented force. I wanted her tongue in my mouth. I wanted to slowly embrace her. I wanted us both to surrender to whatever fucked-up situation we were entering in my embarrassing period-stained sheets.

"It's weird when you're in a room with someone," she said, "and it's like that's all there is."

"No world outside."

"Yeah."

I kissed her tenderly, and for once she didn't seem to be enduring my passion so much as experiencing it with me. She closed her eyes as I moved down to her neck and it didn't bother me. I liked being the only one who could see. It made me feel like I was her guide, taking her someplace new.

february

IT WAS ANOTHER BULLSHIT DAY AT THE OFFICE. EXCEPT ELLIE'S DESK was covered in flowers, Robin's chair had been tied with heart-shaped balloons, and Karen was eating from a box of chocolate.

"Happy Valentine's Day," she said to me so sweetly that I almost felt loved. "I bet you gotta buncha cuties."

"Only you," I said, and she laughed so hard that I actually blushed.

Robin's bouquet arrived next, and after placing it on top of an empty shoebox so that everyone in Luxury could see it, she gave me one of the yellow roses.

"You can keep it," she said, "if you ask someone out."

"I'm not asking anyone out on Valentine's Day."

"You're too shy."

"I'm not shy," I said. "Just hopeless."

I read over the frantic, five-word-long emails Tom had sent to me at one in the morning while Robin and Ellie discussed whether it was too soon to move in with their long-term boyfriends.

"You don't have a drawer at his place?" Robin said. "That's weird. How often do you sleep there?"

"Three nights a week," Ellie said. "How often do you sleep at Dylan's?"

"He sleeps at mine five or six times a week but he works on Wall Street so it's not like we're making dinner. He just comes over at ten, and we talk and go to bed."

"How big is your bed?"

"Queen. Yours?"

"Full."

"That's okay because you're small. Dylan and I are big. We create so much body heat we can't even touch. We just hold hands."

"We hold hands too."

"Actually," Robin said, "we link pinkies."

I went to the bathroom to sit in a stall and think about Madeline. She'd been gone for weeks, and we hadn't been talking but I kept seeing her in every dark-haired girl I passed on the street.

"Jane?" It was Ellie's squeaky voice, coming to get me because I was more or less asleep in a bathroom stall with my head against the toilet paper. "Are you in here? I think something's wrong. Tom's looking for you."

I rushed into his office and found him listening to cacophonous jazz and bobbing his head to a drum solo.

"I thought you were supposed to be in Aspen," I said.

"Delayed," he said. "I need a plan for Armani with full-page ads in Main News."

Arthur's voice rang clear in my head. Print was dead. The future was digital.

"What if we offered them something digital?"

Trumpets launched into a warring duet.

"They like print," he said. "Offer them print."

I might've started working on the plan but it was time for lunch and Robin joined us in the dining hall with nothing but a giant water bottle. The Stepford Planners asked if she was getting ready for a wedding, and Robin said no, it was just her army diet.

"I can't eat breakfast or lunch so I basically starve all day. It gives me headaches and hunger pains, but then at eight I can eat a hot dog and a bowl of ice cream."

The Stepford Planners were amazed.

"With the bun?"

"What kind of ice cream?"

"Is it the best thing you've ever tasted?"

Robin paused. She was like a guru. "I always eat the hot dog with the bun," she said, "but sometimes I'm so out of it I don't even want the ice cream."

Back at the station, Alvin showed up with a giant purple medicine ball and rolled it into Diana's cube. When Karen got back from lunch and saw it, she laughed herself into a coughing fit.

"It's my stability ball," Diana said. "You want to try it?"

Karen threw off her headset and went to sit on Diana's ball. She bounced and laughed and then got up abruptly, a little cross-eyed.

"I can't keep doing that," she said. "I drank wine at lunch."

Ellie didn't eat until two, opening a Tupperware bowl filled with sprouts and beans because, as she declared, she'd decided to quit gluten.

"I've been meaning to for a while," she said. "It's been giving me stomachaches."

"What does that leave you," Karen said, "onions and wood chips?"

"But you never eat bread," Robin said.

"I had couscous the other day."

"Isn't that rice?" I asked.

"It's wheat," Ellie said, and once again I felt amazed by her knowledge of grain products. She dipped a spoon into her bowl and paused, looking pensive over the fiber. "I also need to quit dairy."

It was snowing in all directions when I left for the night and saw Rudy in the lobby. I had never seen him out of the archive before and it felt momentous, like seeing a teacher at the pool. Passing through the turnstiles, I wished him a good night.

"I can't remember the last time I had a good night," he said. "Yesterday my doctor told me I have sleep apnea, and this morning I went to the good deli on Sixty-Third and left a bag of bagels on the counter."

"It's hard to be a person," I said.

Rudy nodded, big and wise, and we walked together into the windy dark.

The bathtub was purple when I got home. I went into Laurel's room and found her lying in bed in basketball shorts with a towel wrapped around her newly dyed hair. A mopey Joanna Newsom song was playing through her laptop speaker and she looked comfortable but also miserable.

"It's been a hard week. Month. Forever."

I dragged my folding chair over to the bed and put my hand on her prickly knee. Purple hair dye dripped down her pillow.

"At least your hair looks good," I said.

She reached across the bed and picked up a painting of blobby colorful objects in a room.

"I keep neglecting red," she said. "Marcel told me at our workshop. He thinks he can talk down to me just because he sold some chairs and got mentioned in *Artforum*. I know furniture sells, but I make what I make and I can't change that."

"Don't change."

"I won't. I can't. But I still feel like I should."

She threw the painting across the room, knocking over an easel and spilling ashes across the floor.

"Now distract me," she said, holding up the ends of her hair and studying the wet. "What happened to your girl?"

"She went to Berlin, but she's such a flake, she's probably still here."

"You're better off. Who even is she? Like, what is her life?"

It hurt to hear Laurel being so harsh, but I knew she was right. I needed to move on. Find a hobby. And spend more time besmirching Madeline's name in a healthy, cathartic way.

"I bet she's gonna meet some rich guy in Berlin, fall in love, and get married within the next year," I said.

"And they'll probably talk about you."

"Her lesbian fling."

I picked up some broken crayons off the rug and started reading their names. Piggy pink. Tumbleweed. Atomic tangerine. The space heater was on full blast and it made the room feel like an infernal art supply closet.

"You should go out with girls from the internet," she said. "That was my New Year's resolution."

"To online-date?"

"No," she said. "To be slutty."

"Let's both be slutty."

"Yeah, and start composting."

Over the course of the next week, while the Stepford Planners executed crash diets and Tom pitched a million-dollar print campaign to Armani, I went out with girls from the internet.

The first was an alarmingly pale nursing student who showed up to the bar with a bag full of needles and asked if she could draw my blood. "I need to practice and I can tell you'd be easy because your veins are super bulgy."

"Another time," I said.

"What about the bartender?" she said, craning her neck. "I really need to practice, and you're of no help."

The next girl was a squirrelly graphic designer with tiny teeth who ordered a vodka martini and said she hated it when people talked about politics.

"It just creates tension, you know? It's like, can we just not talk about it? It's drama, you know? It's like, what's the point?"

"It's like, kind of important," I said.

"Kind of," she said. "But also not."

Next was a big-boned sportswriter with a sprained ankle who wanted to play Jenga. We took turns pulling away the pieces and not talking, as if the vibration of a single whisper would have made the tower fall, and when it did collapse, tumbling bricks across the tea candles and cocktail napkins, I knew the date was over.

"We should have a rematch sometime," the sportswriter said, and I agreed, having sincerely enjoyed being on a date without any talking.

Then there was the frail kindergarten teacher with the slight pug nose who told me about the kids she had to deal with, except she didn't use the phrase "deal with" because she actually loved kids.

"What's your favorite color?" she asked me, and I laughed because I thought she was kidding.

"Blue," I said. "Because I'm the same as everyone else."

"Mine's sage green," she said with great self-satisfaction, as if it had taken her years to come up with such a clever response.

Rather than flee the date then and there, I began to think something was wrong with me. Because this person, like all the others I'd gone out with, was not unattractive, unintelligent, or unkind, yet I felt, at nearly every point in our date, like I might as well have been talking to a cousin. And not a close cousin or a cool cousin but a random one, met once at a wedding and never again.

"So what's home for you?" the kindergarten teacher asked me, and I stared at her face. It was small and pretty, like a nice piece of toast, and her eyes kept darting around the room as if she was amazed at everything even though it was just a bar in Williamsburg and there was nothing amazing about it.

"Well, that's a tricky question." I guzzled down the rest of my drink. "Home isn't really a place, is it? Existence being more like a perpetual feeling of displacement relieved by periods of relative solace found primarily through other people, but whether or not that sense of security is truth or illusion remains unknown, so we may seek out a home our whole lives without ever really finding such a place. Does that make sense?"

"I'm from Denver," the teacher said. "But my sister lives in Jersey."

The last girl I went out with was an artist named Amanda Heck and the only reason I know her full name is because I read it on a trophy in her room while she was in the bathroom. We met at Happyfun Hideaway, a grungy gay bar in Bushwick with three-dollar corn dogs and genderqueer bartenders who sometimes took off their shirts.

I got there late and didn't apologize because I didn't actually care about being late. If anything, I thought the world should just accommodate my lateness because there was nothing that I nor anyone else on the face of the earth needed to rush toward, except for maybe witnessing the birth a child. But even that, I don't know. Was one birth really all that different from the next?

"They're playing *Beetlejuice*." I pointed at the fuzzy TV in the corner. "I love *Beetlejuice*."

I took a seat next to Amanda and she looked startled, but I think that might've just been her face. She had an angular face with nervous eyes and long brown hair tied back in a braid that went halfway down her back.

"They're about to go into the netherworld," I said, unable to stop looking up at the screen, "where all the dead people are stuck in a waiting room and hell is an office full of skeletons typing."

She looked at me like I was nuts and I wondered what would happen if I kept talking about *Beetlejuice*. Would she get up and leave?

"My mom says *Beetlejuice* was my first word, but I know she's lying. It's not possible on multiple levels. But I can't prove her wrong. I wasn't there. I wasn't cogent."

Amanda took off her duffle coat and revealed a surprisingly sexy ribbed tank top beneath it.

"It's an amusing lie," she said. "You should let her keep it."

I looked at her narrow shoulders and tried not to think about Madeline.

"So you're an artist," I said, swiftly changing the topic. "What's that like?"

For the next hour she talked about the white painter bros in her program at Columbia and I told her about my coworker Samantha, who once brazenly told me she "didn't like art."

"Did you see the Chris Burden show?" "The Kara Walker?" "The Mike Kelley?" We talked about artists and exhibitions for so long that I forgot I was on a date.

"Where should we go?" Amanda said, when we finally went outside. It was after one in the morning and the snowplows were scraping down the street.

"I don't know," I said. "That way?"

We passed the falling-apart Victorian mansions that lined Bushwick Ave. and then some weedy lots filled with mounds of kibble that lonely people poured out for the street cats with chewed-up ears, and after turning down a side street, we were suddenly at the beat-up door to Lone Wolf, a crummy dive under the J train with snakes painted on the walls and macho dudes behind the bar.

"What do you want?" I said.

"Anything," she said.

I ordered us whiskey drinks over ice, and when those were gone I ordered some more. Women with thick, happy bodies danced in front of the DJ with bloodshot eyes.

"Are DJs tragic or enlightened?" I said, absolutely shit-faced. "They're curating the mood of the room, which makes them powerful, but they're also alone, essentially apart."

It was after three in the morning when I walked her home. She lived in Bed-Stuy on one of those long avenues with fast cars and a few naked trees. We stood outside her door and she took out her keys.

"You want to come up?"

"I shouldn't," I said.

"You sure?"

"Yeah."

She opened her door and I followed her up. She had a small dog named Pear and I was relieved when she didn't talk to him in a baby voice. She unfolded a white mat and we both watched in silence as the dog pooped on it. Then she picked up the poop with toilet paper, flushed it down the toilet, refolded the mat, and placed it above the toilet.

"I enjoyed watching that," I said.

"It definitely beats going out in the cold."

We lay on her bed and she opened her laptop and turned on *The X-Files*. Five minutes into the show, after pointing out all the chunky cell phones and nineties pantsuits, she touched my leg and I touched her arm and we started to kiss. We kissed slowly and then quickly and then she shoved her hands down my pants. It made the whole existence of pants feel pointless. I took mine off and she took off hers and sex felt easy. I kissed her full mouth, her pale neck, her mushy ears, and her dorky, dangling earrings, tasting her in all her specificity while knowing, perversely, that I didn't know her at all.

"Is this okay?" she said, curling into my side after we'd collapsed onto our backs.

I told her it was, and after closing my eyes for three seconds and experiencing a profound sense of rest, I opened them and it was morning. My skin was dry. A cactus sat on the windowsill. A jean jacket was draped over a chair. It was strange to be in someone else's room, and I looked at her stuff for a long time, wondering what to say, what to think, and how soon I might be able to leave.

I leaned over the bed to sift through my clothes on the floor. She sat up in her rumpled tank top and watched. Her face looked different without glasses, thin and pale.

"What you are doing today?" I said.

"What am I actually doing today?"

"Yeah."

"I'm going to my studio to buff this one piece that's almost done. Then I have to dip some metal magnets. It's hard because it's expensive and you're supposed to immerse them but I can't. I have to paint it on."

My boots were tied but I wasn't going anywhere. I sat on the floor and listened to her talk.

"I have a crit Monday, then another on Tuesday, and then group crit on Wednesday. I'll probably sleep at the studio tonight."

Her pillowcase had slipped and she was lying on the raw yellow insides.

"This Wednesday's crit has seven people and it's two hours long and my program leader doesn't like me. When I first applied, I was wait-listed, and I know it was her fault. She doesn't like my art. So that's hard."

I stood and put on my coat. "I should get going."

She sat up and reached for her glasses.

"Stay where you are," I said. "Should I close this door behind me?"

"That's fine."

"I'll text you."

I walked home in an oddly good mood and saw the city through new eyes. The sidewalks glittered with ice. Pigeons munched on arroz con pollo. And on Broadway I saw a bus driver stopped at a red light, looking into her side mirror and primping the most glorious hairstyle stacked above her head, and when the light turned green, she didn't move right away. She was making a mirror face, still fixing her hair. Then she noticed me looking at her as she pressed on the gas and we smiled and waved at each other like loving neighbors who would never actually meet.

It was sunny and beautiful on Monday morning and Karen was mad. "Sucks to be back in this hellhole," she said. "I'm gonna quit. I'm gonna fucking do it. I got three managers and nobody knows what's going on. Nobody listens. And Vanessa's useless. You should've seen me last night. I drank a bottle of wine, ate a bag of Chinese food, and sat in front of my laptop crying."

She left for lunch with Sue, and when she got back, the sound of a small engine erupted from her desk. *Ch-ch-ch-ch-ch!* It was an old-fashioned, mechanical sound, like a turn-of-the-century cash register about to implode. *Ch-ch-ch-ch-ch!* I looked over the partition and saw a calculator as big as a cabbage with lots of chunky buttons and a roll of receipt paper at the top instead of a screen. Karen banged it with her fist. "What the frick? I think my adding machine broke." She picked up the heavy thing and shook it. "C'mon! Don't do this to me!"

Ten minutes later, she was shouting into her headset, clearly talking to a robot. "Pay bills," she said. "No, I don't want to change my plan. Paaaaay billlzzz. . . . Prepaid lines?! No! PAY! BILLS!"

Ellie lowered her head, mourning whatever silence her life had once contained, while Robin looked at me with big eyes and pretended to drink from her thumb.

I couldn't be bothered to react because Amanda Heck, the sculptor with the tiny pooping dog, had sent me a text, asking if I wanted to come over for dinner. Feeling suffocated by the mere thought of sober conversation, I told her I had "a lot going on" and she backed off. Girls in New York are smart like that. As soon as they catch on that you're not for real, they move on and find someone else.

When HR called me the next morning, I felt certain they were going to fire me. I was an impostor in business clothes, playacting the role of loyal assistant while never truly helping anyone, and they could no longer fathom keeping someone like me on the payroll. Someone who took walks around the building and stole cups from the cafeteria and read long articles about serial killers on the internet.

"Hello, Jane." An efficient-looking woman with a clipboard ushered me into her curiously empty office. "It's good to see you. I hope you're well."

She slid the door closed, situated herself behind her desk, and opened some kind of FBI folder while I crossed my legs, uncrossed them, and crossed them again, unable to decide what kind of woman to be.

"I called you in here to ask about a sensitive matter. We're going to need your discretion. I hope you can understand."

My hands were getting warm. I tried to swallow but I lacked the spit.

"It's about one of your colleagues. Karen Vitelio."

The woman paused to search my face for clues.

"Miss Vitelio is a longtime employee, but we've received more complaints than usual from an anonymous party about possible alcohol consumption during work hours and routinely disruptive behavior. I'm sure you can understand that we can't have employees reaching a level of intoxication that inhibits their ability to work."

My hands were no longer hands at that point but burning slabs of meat forming sweat puddles on my thighs.

"Would you say that Miss Vitelio is ever loud or disruptive?"

"She can definitely be talkative," I said.

"Specifically, after lunch. Have you ever heard her talk about alcohol or has she seemed under the influence of, say, wine? Or margaritas?"

The sunlight banged across my back like some kind of punishment from the gods, but I felt no qualms about lying. Karen swore and smelled like cigarettes and recited entire plotlines of *American Horror Story*, but I couldn't imagine going to work without her.

"Karen works hard," I said. "She's never seemed drunk. I don't have any complaints."

"Thanks for coming up." The woman stood and opened the door, a sliding motion that was my permission to leave. "We appreciate everything you do for this company."

I took the stairs back down to nineteen to have some extra time alone, and as soon as I got back to the station, Karen screamed, "It works!"

I looked over the partition and saw her pressing buttons on her adding machine. It printed a short receipt and she held it in the air, thrilled with her friend Lazarus and his paper tongue.

"You know what it was? I sprayed it with Fantastik."

She snapped on her headset and called Sue. "It works! My adding machine! I told you that would happen."

I studied Ellie's and Robin's faces, trying to decide if either had reported Karen for drinking.

"My boyfriend loses everything." Karen was still on the phone. "Today it's his sunglasses. He calls me and tells me about it and I'm like, 'What am I supposed to do? Comb the streets of Manhattan for your fuckin' sunglasses?'"

Ellie and Robin looked the same, engrossed in their screens with gently frowning faces, as if copying numbers into spreadsheets required the utmost concentration, and I decided it didn't matter who had complained about Karen. The office was full of eyes, policing screens, snooping through drawers, measuring the length of lunch breaks, yet Karen had gotten away with a small victory and it gave me hope.

march

I WAS ALONE IN THE KITCHEN, ATTEMPTING TO LOCATE THE ORIGIN OF the rancid smell behind the fridge, when a new lease got slipped under the door by our landlord, an unseen but all-powerful force in our lives who delivered ominous letters about rodent problems and beer cans left on the roof. I skimmed the new lease and was ready to sign it until I noticed in fine print at the very bottom that our rent was nearly doubling. The apartment itself wasn't going to change. The ceilings would still leak, the radiators would continue to have nervous breakdowns, and bugs would remain camped out under the stove; we would just be paying an additional $1,200.

Laurel got home after midnight with a girl who stomped. She stomped up the stairs and into the kitchen, and when she stomped into the bathroom, I went into Laurel's room and showed her the lease.

"Let's fight it," Laurel said.

"Can we?"

"Marcel sued his landlord and turned their legal correspondence into meatballs. He served them in a gallery with blood."

"Real or fake?"

"I can't remember."

Laurel's date appeared in the doorway. She was small but sinister-looking, given her green army pants and clumpy mascara.

"You can't fight this," she said, looking over Laurel's shoulder. "It's legal."

"How do you know?" Laurel said.

"I'm a lawyer."

Laurel carried the vile piece of paper over to her heat sealer. It was basically a twenty-pound ray gun with the power to melt cats.

"Wait!" I grabbed the lease. "Let's give it a night. We need to think."

"There's nothing to think about," Laurel said. "The gentrifier gets gentrified. That's just the way it goes."

Robin and the five hundred pairs of shoes she kept under her desk disappeared overnight and I assumed she'd been moved. The company moved people all the time, with little warning, and when I passed her in the hall, I pretended to look sad.

"Where'd you end up?" I said. "Not facing the SpongeBob billboard, I hope."

She tossed her hair over her shoulders and beamed. "Nobody told you? I got promoted. I'm a manager now. I took over the role in Tech."

I mumbled some kind of congratulations and got a fresh box of Kleenex for Ellie, who was likely going to be sobbing or stabbing herself with a fountain pen.

She was typing and she looked suspiciously normal. Karen and I made eye contact over the partition. Ellie must have sensed it.

"I'm fine," she said. Her voice was low and her face expressionless. "Robin's good at her job. She worked hard. It's not her fault that nobody in this building likes me. And it's not like she passed off my ideas as her own."

"It was for the good of the company," I said.

"Oh, please," Ellie said. "Since when do you care about the company?"

Alvin came over with a grow-at-home herb kit and Ellie, who normally rejoiced at the arrival of packages, kicked it under her desk. Alvin should have walked away, but having sensed another's pain, he couldn't resist the opportunity to preach.

"When Jesus walked from Galilee and he saw the man on the side of the road, he could not go on."

He was looking wistfully out the window, talking to himself and whatever else was out there, and it was sort of pathetic. We all knew success was a matter of pedigree and popularity, but he hadn't caught up yet. He was still looking for answers in the clouds, which nobody had told him were just giant clumps of future rain.

The next morning Arthur perched outside his office in a beautiful pair of plaid slacks and made an impromptu speech nobody wanted to hear.

"Style is the perfection of a point of view. Your mission here is to sell. It's what we pay you to be good at. And Tom—that old bagpipe—Tom is a great example of what *not* to do. Armani wanted to reach young people, and what did he do? He pitched a million dollars' worth of print ads. Now Helen says they're talking to the *Wall Shit Journal* about a spend in digital. We cannot afford these mistakes."

Everybody in Luxury looked at me. As the representative of Tom's shabby ethos, his public shaming was clearly my fault.

"You have to push for things," Ellie whispered.

"Yeah," Karen added in her gravelly voice. "It's good to push."

I sat motionless and unthinking, my response to pressure a kind of shutting down. I didn't know how to tell them that I didn't want to push, I didn't like to push, and if I started to push, I would push the wrong thing and it would break.

A vaporous sadness came over me when I left for the night and passed a butcher shop on Eighth Avenue. Monuments of bloody heads and severed legs hung proudly in the window. Death was something a jowly man with a knife liked to put on display. I wasn't a vegetarian and didn't plan on becoming one, but in that moment the disembodied limbs of those pigs were making me sick. I wished I could put them back together, revive their hearts, and usher them out the front door, a stampede of ecstatic pigs rushing toward the river.

I called Madeline as soon as I got home because I had nothing to hold on to, which felt like the same as having nothing to lose.

"Do you miss me?" she said. Her voice was bright and sharp, girlier than I remembered.

"I can't eat. I can't sleep. I walk past your old building just to look at your window."

She made a smug little hum. "My new room has a chandelier. It's big and there's a couch and the carpeting is full of cigarette burns."

"That's perfect for you," I said. "Decadent and dissolute."

"How's your new girlfriend?"

"I don't have one."

"I don't believe you."

I pushed aside the beach towel that covered my window and looked at the moon. *Madeline*, I wanted to say, *do you see the moon?*

"You should move here," she said. "It's like Brooklyn but cheaper and everybody's queer and everybody speaks English."

"I'll think about it."

"Don't think about it. Just come. You can stay with me."

Days became other days and I thought about Madeline. Our conversation had been so filled with promise that I wanted it to stay like that forever, a perfect opportunity never to be realized. At the same time, I obsessed over what it would be like to leave. Not for a vacation or some kind of company-sanctioned sabbatical but to turn off my computer and disappear for good.

Vanessa cornered me in the elevator with her mom haircut sticking up so she looked both stressed and slightly electrocuted. "I wanted to touch base," she said. "Check in. Take your temperature." She touched the zit on her chin. She always had a zit on her chin but it wasn't the same zit. It was a new one that grew and shrank and grew again somewhere else. "I know you're killing it in Fashion right now, but how would you feel about helping Tyler Petrovic on Spirits? It would only be temporary, just until we find a new planner to replace Robin." I opened my mouth to say no, I would rather herd rats, and Vanessa raised her fist for an insufferable bump.

"You're an incredible human. A rock star. Thank you *so* much."

A bitter feeling of déjà vu came over me as I realized this gradual manipulation, this convoluted meritocracy, would slowly colonize my life until one day I'd wake up a middle-aged woman with a crick in her neck, complaining about her kid's college loans and the ever-present threat of a layoff.

Tyler was waiting for me at the station with chest hair poking out of his shirt. He asked if I could "hop in" on a brainstorm for Ketel One, and for a full minute I said nothing. I just followed his muscular back down the hallway and watched as he took over the nearest empty conference room and circled the table. It struck me as a business tactic, like some primal gesture he'd picked up to appear more domineering.

"I don't know if Vanessa told you this, but we do things differently on Spirits. You can be creative with me, share ideas, be yourself." He outlined the campaign goals for a new line of flavored vodka aimed at "youthful drinkers," and I went into a blackout state when he suggested a "virtual reality drinking contest."

"So what do you think?" he said, spinning a pen between his meaty fingers. "Do you have any top-line ideas?"

"I'll think about it," I lied. If I had any creativity inside me, it wasn't going to be wasted on strawberry vodka.

For the rest of the day, thoughts of leaving came and went and I responded to emails with triple exclamations points as a vehicle for my rage. *Thanks a trillion!!! Wow, you're the best!!! Hurraaayyyyyy!!!* I got up to make coffee and envied the machine because it felt nothing. I went to the bathroom and took it personally when the motion sensor faucets didn't work. Nobody wanted to see me, not even the sink.

On my walk from the train to our treeless block in Bushwick, I counted all the new stores that had materialized overnight. There was a dog salon, an ethical jewelry store, a vegan Ethiopian restaurant, a vintage clothing store with occult symbols in the window, and another ramen place with backless concrete chairs.

I went into Laurel's room to ask her for advice. She had traveled more than me, not only to South Korea, where she had aunts and uncles, but also to Zurich and Warsaw and Split, a city in Croatia that didn't even sound real. I sat in my folding chair and waited for her to notice me, but she was too busy drawing circles on a piece of graph paper.

"I want to move somewhere and start over but I feel like I can't," I said. "My whole life is here. My friends. My job. My apartment."

"Apartment's a bust." Laurel turned toward me with her notebook propped up against her knee.

"And I refuse to become another twentysomething 'figuring herself out' in the middle of nowhere."

Her eyes were glazed over and I could tell she was drawing me.

"And I'm afraid if I go all the way to some cool city in Europe like, I don't know, Berlin, I won't want to come back. Plus it's expensive. With the exchange rate and everything. Will you tell me what to do? I'm tired of making choices. I want someone else to tell me what to do."

"You're overreacting," she said.

"What if I'm not?"

"Just go to Berlin. Who cares? And you can see Madeline."

"How did you know she was there?"

"You told me, doofus."

I got up and Laurel ordered me back.

"Sit," she said. "Put your hands where they were."

I sat in the same position so Laurel could finish her drawing, and in her toxic-smelling room with my hands in my lap, still and careful in the service of art, I started to wonder if Madeline was my Hadley, Hemingway's first wife. They broke up and he married other women, but years later, when they met again in Paris, he told her that he'd never stopped loving her and they both knew it was true.

Over a week had gone by since Robin's promotion and Ellie remained quietly devastated. She searched for split ends and angry-stapled things together.

"Someone stole my scissors," she announced. "Who would steal left-handed scissors?"

She got on her knees to look for them under her desk while Karen and I made eye contact over the partition. All we could do was let her be. Whatever she might have needed to cut wasn't nearly as important as catching a thief, a body to blame, and punishing them mercilessly for all the bad things she didn't deserve.

Madeline sent me pictures of contemporary art at the Kunst-Werke and I couldn't stop looking at them. The fact that she had sent me anything at all struck me as further proof that her invitation wasn't a bluff. She wanted me to come to Berlin, to stay with her, to be with her. I stared at the sculptures and memorized the angles, the light, the colors. Then I studied the people in the background, wondering which ones, if any, she might be sleeping with.

Laurel wasn't home so I paced around the apartment and called my mother.

"We're setting up my new Fitbit," she said. "Can I call you back?"

"I have important news."

"Can it wait? Doug and I want to start counting our steps."

I had the impulse to hang up and never talk to her again.

"I'm quitting my job," I said. "I thought you should know."

Considerable time passed as she shifted the phone around, took a deep breath, and said, "And then what are you going to do?"

"Go somewhere."

"And do what?"

"Something else."

"Well, do let me know when you've figured out how to pay for your apartment, your food, your phone, your health insurance—"

"Can I talk?"

"—and you really need to be putting money into your IRA."

"CAN I TALK?"

"Doug just found out he has to get a tooth pulled."

"I'm hanging up."

"Grandpa had his job at Ford for thirty-seven years."

I lowered the phone without hanging up and looked at the picture Madeline had sent me of a lemon tree in her courtyard. *Are you coming or not?* she wrote in a lighthearted tone that in no way reflected the gravity of the situation. I went into the kitchen to heat up some leftovers and left my phone on the pillow, thinking my mother, miles away, might appreciate that touch of comfort while she talked herself into a fit.

Being a manager gave Robin the right to speak to us differently, to "visit us," as she put it, as if she'd moved to a foreign planet and not just a cube fifteen feet away.

"Hi, friends," she said, strolling over in a long cotton dress that made her legs look like they went on forever. "Dylan surprised me with a trip to Newport. It's this cute little town with a bunch of old mansions and I thought Taylor Swift has a house there but I was wrong. It's actually in Westerley." She shared a picture of herself on the back of a Vespa with her arms around a chunky white boy with a blandly smiling nonface.

Ellie said, "Do you think he would ever?"

She didn't go on and I knew why. Women weren't supposed to talk about proposals, or even say the word.

"Don't ask me that. I don't know what's going on. What about you? Do you think your boyfriend would ever?"

"He showed me a picture of his grandmother's ring. It's a petite trellis solitaire and it's gorgeous but I don't think we're ready. He still lives with his twin and it's hard for them to be apart."

"My boyfriend would never propose to me," Karen said. "He knows I'd laugh in his face."

Ellie and Robin and Karen looked at me—the token single person.

"What about you?" Robin said. "Been on any good dates recently?"

The women were still staring at me, eager for some kind of soul-crushing update or, if not that, then some wacky anecdote about a girl from the internet who identified as a Viking or drank too much and fell on her face or spent an hour talking about herself and waited, until the very end of the date, to say she was actually moving to LA.

"Robin, I'm going to be honest with you." I picked up a paper clip and bent it into something sharp and useless. "Dating is fun. Falling in love is fun. But it ends. It can't last. Nothing lasts. And when it's gone, what you're really left with is the appalling nature of your own idiotic hope. And that's just the way it is. Because no one is good enough. People mess up. Everything dies."

Karen slapped her cigarettes against the edge of her desk. "Gee-zus Christ."

"Not to be a total downer," Ellie spoke up, "but pair bonding is pretty unrealistic, at least from a biological standpoint."

"See?" I dug the paper clip into my palm. "There's no point, Robin. No point."

Laurel was in the kitchen flattening cardboard boxes by jumping on them. I asked her if she had any ideas about how not to lose our apartment and she was blasé.

"I'm over it," she said. "I found a room in Sunset Park."

"What am I supposed to do?"

She stopped jumping and looked at me sideways. "I thought you were moving to Berlin."

Rain fell in horizontal sheets and made darting lines across the office windowpanes. It made the building feel like it was wrapped in gauze, and nobody seemed to notice or care when I locked myself in a conference room and called Madeline. She'd said it was important and I was hopeful. I thought she might say that she loved me; she'd loved me all along.

"I just realized I have fifty euro left to live off of for the next week," she said. "I don't know how I'm going to survive."

"You just have to budget," I said, trying to be rational. "Maybe you could stop buying lattes and taking cars everywhere."

She sighed loudly into the phone, managing to seem both poor and profligate at the same time.

"That's not a budget," she said. "It's just *no* money."

"If you really need it," I said, "I could help you out."

"You could?"

"I could send you a deposit for letting me sleep on your couch."

"That would be amazing, and don't worry, you're not gonna sleep on the couch."

"I'm not?"

"No, it's too small. You can sleep on the floor."

She laughed, which made me laugh, and then I sent her some money and prayed for the bed.

The gray sky dissolved into black and I was packing my bag to leave for the night when Karen unraveled the sweatpants she'd been wearing around her neck to say that Rudy got the boot.

"He took the buyout," she said. "Thirty-three years doesn't mean shit to this place. He's got two kids and a bunch of cats. Used to have five but they kept gettin' sick. I swear to god one of them ate a sock and died."

"What's a buyout?"

"Buyouts are just the company's bullshit way of saying laid off," she said. "They give you some money and kick you out. For young people, maybe it's okay, but god forbid you're over forty. You'll be scrubbin' toilets."

"Nobody's ever really secure," Ellie said. "We think we are but we're not."

We looked out at the rain, so dense it seemed to swallow the building whole.

"At least he got a severance," Karen said, and it sounded scary when she said it, like something a person might get for losing a limb.

Laurel and I went out for dinner at the new Ethiopian place, where we dipped spongy bread into spicy mashed-up peas and she listed the pros of moving to Europe while I listed the cons.

"Cheap rent, total freedom, hot queer people with accents."

"No income, no purpose, no friends."

I was glad when she started complaining about Yaritza, a topic that was, for Laurel, never not of interest.

"I get that she's focused on her career and part of that involves sleeping with her costars or whatever, and it's not like I'm not also sleeping with other people, but I still feel like we could've had something, like a real relationship."

"I thought you said relationships were dumb."

"I was just trying that on."

I waited until the end of the day to go down to the archive, and even then I didn't want to go. Rudy's barrel chest looked withered beneath the overhead light. His shoulders went up in a defeated sigh when he saw me coming, and we both shook our heads at how terrible life could be.

"I thought it would have stopped snowing by now but it never stops," he said. "I was born in Bay Ridge, lived all my life in this city, and it never gets easier, these winters."

He gripped his gnarled armrests and looked around. The filing cabinets seemed more than ever like his personal possessions, the weight of history on his shoulders.

"They've got guys coming down to put all this on the internet. They think it'll take two weeks." He laughed, a shadowy bellow of hurt. "More like years." He dumped a mug of highlighters onto his desk and started going through them, tossing away the ones with missing caps and dried-out tips.

"I told my wife we're headed for the poorhouse. I'll be buried in a potter's field. She says it's okay. We've still got our trip to Niagara. The girls are happy. They're excited about the mall."

He looked startlingly calm as he rocked to the song of his old chair and it began to seem inevitable that he was the one to go, inured as he was to the bad news he was always expecting.

"I didn't know you had kids," I said.

"Two girls."

I nodded like I knew something about kids.

"Do you like them?" I asked.

"Like them?" He tossed a highlighter into the trash. "I love them."

I rode the elevator back up to nineteen in a trancelike state and bought a one-way ticket to Berlin. It was embarrassing to realize that the cost of my freedom was less than half of my monthly rent, but that didn't make it any less exciting. I'd spent $390 on a chair that would fly over the ocean and make everything different. I would learn to like espresso. I would say *gesundheit* in the country where it actually made sense. I would wander through a city full of signs I couldn't read but that would be part of the fun. It would be like being a kid again, fascinated and illiterate.

We'll be expats together in May, I wrote to **Madeline.** You need more $ for rent?

She responded with a picture of her unmade bed, coffee-stained and covered in charging cords. I wrote back:

For us?

Duh.

Can I use one of your pillows?

Don't push it

I packed up my things to leave early for the night and called my dad. I was excited to hear his voice and tell him my news.

My stepmother answered.

"Hello?" she croaked into the phone. "I don't know where your dad went. We weren't expecting you to call."

A minute later my father picked up. "Did you read the article I sent?" he said, sounding as chipper as ever.

"Election or earthquake?"

"Earthquake."

Cloaked commuters drifted past me and I wondered if I could lie. I'd meant to read the article, but it was long and the first paragraph contained the word *logarithmic.*

"Half the country's going down," he said. "East and West Coasts. It'll happen in your lifetime. Guaranteed next fifty years."

"Don't say that."

"But it's true. People you know and love are going to die."

Hot pretzel smoke blew in my face and I imagined the island of Manhattan sinking into the Atlantic. Buildings collapsing, people drowning. Everyone everywhere pushing each other into the waves.

"I just called to say I'm quitting my job," I said.

He was unfazed. "Makes sense. I never could see you working in an office."

"I might also move to Europe."

"You can afford that?"

"I can make it work."

There were more things to talk about, like where I might go, what I might do there, and how I might avoid becoming a destitute bag lady, but my father wasn't interested in unknowns. He didn't seem too worried about anything at all.

"Well," he yawned into the phone, "I better get back to my book."

Laurel talked me into going to Market Hotel, a decrepit second-floor venue at the edge of Bushwick that was hosting the one-year anniversary party for a magazine about hot people. It was also about art and fashion and maybe photography, but that's all the magazine was, just a really glossy catalog full of pictures of hot people.

"A bunch of bands are playing," Laurel said, talking herself into a sweat as she power walked to the venue. "Addy's headlining, and I think Yaritza is gonna be there too."

"Okay, so that's why we're going."

"I haven't liked someone this much in a long time," she said, ignoring me. "All I want to do is text her, like all the time, but it's hard."

"Why's it hard?"

"She told me not to text her."

We got tickets and went up the stairs, and Laurel instantly abandoned me to look for Yaritza while I went over to Addy setting up her merch. She was bent over a folding table in the back of the room, arranging her pins and patches across a wrinkled tablecloth.

"I'd buy a fridge magnet," I said, "but I'm about to not have a fridge."

She looked up at me with narrowed eyes.

"Going somewhere?" Her voice was low and she kept setting up her things, but I could tell she wasn't really doing anything. She was just moving stuff around.

"I'm quitting my job and going to Berlin," I said. "So, yeah. Big change."

Addy didn't look surprised. She just picked up a T-shirt with her name across the front and started folding it against her chest.

"I love Germany," she said. "I've been there a bunch of times."

For a second, I was annoyed. I had one exciting thing to share and she'd already been there, done that.

"You have to try currywurst. It's this kind of gross sausage they sell on the street and it comes cut up with toothpicks, and of course you have to see the Brandenburg Gate and all that, just be careful with the bars. There's still smoking inside. And don't jaywalk. Nobody jaywalks because Germans are very ethical and they love rules."

Addy was still talking about my trip, which now felt like her trip, when she interrupted herself to say that she was leaving too.

"It's just a support tour," she said, "so nothing crazy, but it's across the US and parts of Canada so I'll have to be careful with my voice, resting it and all that. Speaking of which." She dragged a box of her T-shirts under the table. "I should go to the greenroom and make tea."

I looked down at her box of shirts, half sticking out from under the table.

"You're just going to leave those there?" I said.

"Nobody's going to steal them."

"You're very trusting."

"I guess I have faith in people."

She turned toward the greenroom and then paused, adjusting her glasses.

"I don't get it," she said. "I felt like we had something, but you wouldn't let me in. You pushed me away. And it pissed me off, actually, because I'm about to turn twenty-seven and I'm feeling really over chasing after people who don't respect me or my time."

I wasn't sure whether we were fighting or flirting but I liked it. She was being brutally honest, and it gave me permission to be just as honest in return.

"I like you," I said. "I really do. But I'm a terrible person to date." Addy tilted her head and I felt like I had a small window in which I might be able to redeem myself. "I don't cook, I can't cook, and every time I try to cook something, like hard-boiled eggs, I forget the stove's on and the fire alarm goes off and both the eggs and the pot are burned to a crisp. I don't own any spare towels. I hate roller coasters. I'm afraid of ghosts. I don't understand health insurance. I can't speak any foreign languages. I hate sharing. And I'm not that nice."

"You think I'm nice all the time?"

I nodded.

"Fuck nice. I'm no 'nicer' than anyone else."

"You literally just said you thought people were good."

She smiled at me, still a little mad, but also not.

"I should," she said.

"Go," I said. "Go have your tea."

She went into the greenroom while I looked for Laurel and eventually found her curled up in a windowsill with her head in her hands.

"I didn't know I could feel this sad about one stupid person," she said.

"At least you know she's stupid."

Addy's first song came on while I was still comforting Laurel and I wanted to go up to the stage just to stare at her like an idiot, openmouthed in the front row, but I couldn't move or go anywhere because Laurel had abruptly started to cry.

"Why is she in Mexico?" She held out a photo of Yaritza on the beach. "I don't get it." She kept repeating herself and I tried to sympathize, but Yaritza was a notorious player and I'd secretly always known this was coming.

"Yaritza's selfish," I said. "Stop thinking about her. You don't need to keep chasing someone who's unavailable and objectively not good for you."

"I just don't get it," Laurel said. "We spent an hour dry-humping in her bed. Does that mean nothing?"

Laurel was still talking and it was my duty to listen, but that didn't mean I wasn't also watching Addy. Her voice was low and crooning and she sounded less like a singer than a poet who'd just happened to learn how to sing. Stress, circular thoughts, loneliness, missing—she sang about simple things, but seeing her live, I understood something new about her, and the power of her music's rawness and truth.

The set turned out to be short, only three or four songs, and after waiting in Addy's merch line and watching her sign records and take pictures with the sort of frazzled-looking twenty-two-year-olds I was glad to no longer be, I told Addy that I'd enjoyed her set and I thought her music was great.

"You don't mean that," she said. "I could see you from the stage. You were talking through the whole thing."

She dumped her unsold merch into a large rolling suitcase and zipped it shut.

"Let me carry that down the stairs for you," I said.

"I got it." She yanked it away.

"Fine," I said. "Then I'm carrying the box."

She carried her suitcase down the stairs while I carried her shirts and I ran back up to get her guitar with a giddy feeling of purpose.

Even the bouncer gave me a nod, as if I might've been a real roadie, following some rock star around on her scrappy tour. When I got back down to the street, I was prepared to mend things with Addy once and for all until I saw Cassandra's floppy hair and teacup face bounding toward me in the venue's buzzing neon light.

"Jane?" She wrapped her arms around me and squeezed. "I'm with a bunch of people from Brown and we're about to go to Trans-Pecos. Do you want to come?"

"I'm right in the middle of something." I looked at Addy, loading gear into the back of a car. "It was good to see you though."

"I'm actually hungry," Addy said, turning toward us. "Does Trans-Pecos serve food?"

Cassandra laughed. "It's a club," she said. "Dancing. Sweat."

Addy shuddered and got in the backseat of the car. Then she looked at me with permission in her eyes and I got in next to her, hastily ignoring Cassandra and closing the door.

"I never dance," Addy explained. "Unless I'm being forced."

She buckled her seat belt and looked down at mine, making sure it was buckled too.

"You should get over that," I said. "The whole not-dancing thing."

"Why? Are you some amazing dancer?"

"No, I just think people should dance because it's fun. It's fun to look like an idiot sometimes."

"I disagree."

I looked at her eye makeup, smeared around the edges. "It seems like you're pretty hard on yourself," I said.

"Maybe I have to be."

The car bumped over Atlantic. Addy put her hand on my knee. "I'm glad you're coming over," she said.

I felt the warmth of her palm seeping through my jeans. "You just want me to carry your stuff," I said.

"Hey, I can carry my own stuff, thank you very much."

I carried Addy's merch suitcase up the stairs of her building, through her kitchen, and into her room in the back, where she turned on a lamp and rushed over to the window, anxious to show me something out there in the dark.

"This morning I woke up and gasped. It's hard to see right now, but if you look really hard, you can see the tiniest little bud."

My instinct was to leave. My breath was foul, my clothes felt soggy, and my bladder hurt because I was afraid of going to the bathroom and letting Addy hear me pee through the wall. But I was trying to do things that I might not have done before, and when Addy came over to me, she for once didn't speak. She just stood motionless and stared at my ears.

"Should we," I said.

I looked at the freckles around her mouth.

"Should we what?"

I was hyperaware of the grime between my toes, the sweat in my armpits, the blood moving around my head.

"I don't know," I said.

I touched her arm and we kissed. Tentatively like colonial women and then rabidly like teenagers in a basement and then finally like ourselves, slowly and deliberately and with more tenderness than my body seemed capable of producing. We took off each other's clothes and climbed onto her bed. She'd put it on wooden risers so it was unusually high off the floor.

"It creates room for extra storage," she explained, lying on her side and looking completely at ease with her naked chest out.

I crossed my arms, feeling more self-conscious, and she reached for my wrists, wanting me to lower them.

"I'm just nervous," I said. "I'm really sober."

"Do you not have sober sex?"

"No, it's just . . ." I was lying. I had no idea how to have sober sex with Addy. She seemed so much more mature than me, with her music career and her past relationships and her apartment that had a blender.

"I think I just want to make sure this is okay with you," I said. "With me going to Berlin and all."

"It's not like you're moving there."

She pulled me onto her and we started to kiss. Her body was small but firm and I felt around her back, wanting to know all of her bumps and bones and dents.

"I really like you," Addy said.

"I like you too," I said.

She pushed me over and crawled on top of me. I leaned back, needing a pause. I wasn't used to lying on my back.

"You should let me," I said, sitting up on my elbows to take back some control.

"Stop." Addy was insistent. "We can take turns."

She pinned me to the bed with all the strength she could muster and went in for a hard kiss. Tiny but mighty, she was making it clear that she wasn't a pillow princess or a timid femme, and I let it happen. Not because I wanted to be submissive but because it felt good, and maybe even necessary, to be the one who was wanted, at least for a while.

Laurel's light was on when I got home. I crept past her door, wanting to avoid her, and she shouted, "WHERE HAVE YOU BEEN?"

With some hesitation about sharing good news and thus inviting a curse, I told her I'd been at Addy's. "But nothing happened," I said. "We just talked."

"Liar."

"I'm serious," I said. "She's cute but she's not my type."

"I know what you mean," was all Laurel said before retreating into her room. "She's so *good*."

If I were being honest, I would have told her I thought Addy was beautiful, but I couldn't imagine using that word. Beautiful? Never. It would have sounded like I was in love.

april

TYLER WAS IN THE BREAK ROOM WASHING A BIG CUP THAT SAID *I LIKE BIG CUPS AND I CANNOT LIE.* I pressed the button for medium blend and hummed the chorus of one of Addy's songs.

"You're in a good mood," he said, like an accusation.

"It's because I have good things going on outside of work," I said, feeling like a spiritual leader ever since I'd bought a one-way plane ticket and spent the last week in Addy's bed. "It's important not to let the office become your whole life."

He flicked his cup dry and leaned against the microwave stained with spaghetti sauce.

"I have good things going on outside of work too," he said. "I'm working on a novel. It's a Middle-earth fantasy set in outer space so it's sort of like *Star Wars* but with wizards and elves."

Normally I would have fled at the mention of warlocks, but for the next ten minutes I gladly listened to Tyler recite the plot of his epic unwritten tale of good versus evil and remembered a random weeknight months ago when I'd seen him sitting in the window of the Chipotle on Thirteenth, alone and eating a burrito. He looked so childlike, scooping up rice with a plastic fork, that I almost went in there just to sit next to him and ask about his day.

"The whole final act is the dream of a planet that doesn't exist," he said. "If you want, I could send you the outline."

"Please do," I said.

Addy had been writing to me in a stream of consciousness since eight in the morning, when I'd left her bed to go straight to work.

If I can't stop thinking about you
Do I keep that shit to myself?
I got you a toothbrush
Do you hate that?

I turned my chair away from Ellie to draft a response, a simple task that took three hours because it involved finding the perfect words and arranging them in the perfect order while taking frequent breaks to look out the window and wonder if Addy was the girl I'd been waiting for. The one who would turn me into a real adult who had an emergency contact and flossed twice a day and never left parties without saying good-bye.

Tom flew by the station and whistled for me. It felt shocking to see him. I had forgotten he existed.

"Won't take long," he said, "with all the numberless goings-on of life."

I followed the patch of sweat on his back down the hall and into his office, where he put his feet on his desk and listed his friends who worked in the music industry. Producers, bookers, promoters, DJs. He recited their full names like I should know them.

"You know the Black Eyed Peas? I worked with them in the nineties. They were good but they weren't *great* so I said to Will, 'You know what you need? You need a white girl.'"

He paused to let this sink in.

"You're the reason they had Fergie?"

He nodded. "I'm the reason they had Fergie."

I turned to leave, having known Tom long enough to know that the sharing of a semidelusional story was reason enough to be called into his office.

"Wait," he said. "Armani came back. They want the campaign in print. Can you send me the contract?"

He kneaded a knot in the back of his neck and picked up his phone. The cracked one that he'd dropped down the elevator shaft.

"Tom," I said, "that's amazing. That campaign is worth a half million dollars."

He was already calling someone, content to ignore my praise and pick up wherever he'd left off, chatting loudly about bottom lines and the Moody Blues. It occurred to me then that Tom was an old-fashioned salesman whose talent lay in talking to people. The other managers were all so eager to please and stay on top of the latest technological thing while Tom couldn't stop reminiscing about that old venue on Houston where the stage collapsed in '85, and maybe that was his strength. He might have turned his stories into a Bukowski-esque novel, but he got married, had kids, and threw his energy into work.

"Open or closed?" I said, standing in the doorway.

He swayed in his chair and waved me away. It made no difference to him.

I was pouring Pine-Sol all over my bedroom floor, getting ready for Addy's first potential visit, when a crash came from Laurel's room. It sounded deadly and I rushed in there to make sure a can of paint hadn't fallen on her head. She was grunting on the floor in purple lipstick, dismantling a papier-mâché sculpture too big to fit through the door.

"I'm having a crisis," she said. "I can't find anyone to punch me in the face."

I stood in the doorway, afraid to go any farther because her room was in shambles. Ever since she'd begun to pack, it had devolved into a hazard, bursting with enough wood scraps, matchbooks, power tools, and oily rags to turn the apartment into a serious bomb threat.

"Why do you want to get punched in the face?" I said.

"For an art show."

She tossed a chunk of newspaper over her back, conspicuously indifferent to where it might land, and gave up on dismembering her once-prized work of art to scratch her head with alarming vehemence. Flakes of stress-induced eczema flew off her scalp and I wondered if she was okay. Her skin was dry, her hair was thinning, and the stick-and-poke tattoos that went up and down her arms looked more than ever like a cry for help.

"Maxine's busy, Bhumi says it's a good idea but she can't do it, and Zinc says I shouldn't do it but you know Zinc, she's such a mom."

My feelings were hurt that she hadn't asked me to punch her in the face, but I tried not to dwell on it. I didn't go to art school and I probably would have punched her wrong and ruined her art.

"What are you going to do if you don't find anyone?" I said.

"I'll find someone," she said.

She got a hammer and started pounding on the sculpture that had been turned down by fifty or sixty art shows and I drifted back to my room, feeling rattled by the rejection she seemed doomed to face.

Addy was waiting for me outside the bar in her red plaid coat. It felt good to be waited for, different and somehow earned, as if all the other girls were just practice for this abrupt arrival, this perfect pair of eyes.

"I can't believe I'm in Bushwick," she said. "I hate Bushwick."

She leaned in to kiss me and I leaned back. Bushwick had its weedy lots, noisy trains, piss puddles, chicken bones, and rained-on trash bags that never got picked up, but it also had men who sold flowers out of grocery carts and an illegal art gallery called Cunt Hole in the back of my laundromat and bombastic thumping music that blew out of open car trunks.

"Don't insult my neighborhood," I said.

"Why not?" she said. "You insulted mine."

"Just because it's covered in trash . . ."

"It's not the trash," she said. "It's all the boys with bleached hair and girls in jumpsuits. It's like everybody's on display, performing all the time."

A girl walked by pushing a rack of wind chimes. She was followed by a man on Rollerblades, texting and playing ABBA out of a portable speaker.

"See? Everybody's posing," she said. "Everybody's following some *trend*."

"What's so bad about trends? Trends unite people. They're meant to be playful."

She opened the door of the bar. "Can we go inside? I'm starving and I think they serve food."

Addy cued up a bunch of songs on the jukebox and it suddenly didn't matter what we said to each other in the next few hours so much as when David Bowie sang "the church of man, love," and I heard "the church of mad love." That's where I was. Not real love but mad love, like grabbing someone by the neck and kissing them and tasting their sweat and not knowing the time.

"Language creates boundaries where there were none before," she said, because our third round of drinks had nudged us into the realm of the metaphysical. I nodded along, happy and boozy. Subatomic particles disappeared in one place and appeared in another. Time was made of light. It curved around us—elevators, cookies, clouds—it was all miraculous and it always had been.

"Food," Addy said, handing her card to the bartender. "We're getting food."

We walked to a nearby place on Evergreen that was open late and I warned her in advance this was a onetime thing. I didn't want to become one of those couples that picked at a bread basket and had nothing to say. And I didn't like sitting in the window of the restaurant either. It felt too much like we were on display, flaunting something in front of all the lonely people walking by.

"You sound crazy," she said. "This is what people do. They sit together and eat. It's not the end of the world."

She ordered a cheeseburger with onion rings. I ordered a sandwich with goat cheese. We didn't run out of things to talk about, and when the check came, we let it turn gray in the table grease just so we could keep talking.

"My grandma on my dad's side was left on a doorstep and my mom was adopted but she says she *feels* Irish, whatever that means. It makes sense though because I love potatoes. I could never have survived the potato famine." She touched her napkin, folding it into a box, and I wished I could take it and bring it with me to Berlin.

"Wait," she said. "The potato famine. I know it was a crop failure, but was it all potatoes or no potatoes?"

I had to think about it for a second, which is funny to think about. How little we know. How dumb we really are.

"No potatoes," I said.

The lamplight bounced off the walls and shone in her eyes.

"I'd be dead," she said, raising her fork for one last bite before letting out a surprisingly unselfconscious yawn. I reached across the table and felt her fingertips, plump and callused from playing guitar.

"Would you want to," I said. "You don't have to. But if you wanted to."

"I'm coming over," Addy said, grabbing the check.

We walked in silence down the long residential blocks that led to my building, and when Addy checked the time, I felt a pang. I could tell she was thinking about other things. Her music. Her tour. Her creative and fulfilling life.

"You can still change your mind," I said, unlocking the door.

"Stop doing that," she said. "Stop trying to take things back. I'm here. I want to be here. I don't do things I don't want to do."

I rushed us through the kitchen and into my room, where it was dim and clean but eerily empty, with nothing on the walls and even less on the floor.

"It's because I've been going through things," I said. "Getting ready to leave."

Addy looked around and I wanted to shrink. The windows were covered in their usual towels and all of my used books were in crooked, leaning stacks.

"I like it," she said. "It's very you."

She took off her jeans and placed them neatly next to the lamp. Then she got under the covers and I got in next to her and I thought we might start kissing but no, she wanted to talk.

"Have you thought about what you might want to do," she said, "when you get back from Berlin?"

We were lying on our backs, looking up at the water-stained ceiling, and I sat up on my elbow just to better see her face, all the freckles across her nose.

"I've thought about nothing," I said. "I have no idea what I'm doing."

"I feel that way about my music."

"I've been meaning to ask you," I said. "Where does it come from? Your inspiration or whatever."

She took off her earrings, the two squares of red glass from her neighbor in Maine.

"I always write the lyrics first. They come to me at random times, usually when I'm walking, so I write them down in my phone. Then I spend months building out the instrumentation one layer at a time. I add violin, a trumpet, maybe some harp." She took out her phone to play a song and froze, her thumb stuck on her artist page.

"I'm embarrassed," she said.

"Don't be."

I made her hit play, and when she did, I looked at a crack in the wall and listened to her song that was like a staircase leading into a room full of eyes.

"Now forget that ever happened," she said.

"I really liked it."

"You're just saying that to butter me up."

"I actually couldn't hear it," I said, reaching for her phone. "I actually think you need to play it again."

The train's emergency brakes were activated on my way to work and I fell onto a stranger's lap. We were stuck underground for the next twenty minutes—me and this woman and a hundred other people in a tunnel in the dirt—and I should've been annoyed or embarrassed or scared for our collective mental health but I wasn't. I was too filled with life. I loved the construction worker holding his metal lunchbox and the sleepy teenager rushing to finish his homework, and the professional lady wearing grubby tennis shoes she would probably take off as soon as she got to her desk.

I threw down my bag and was about to make coffee when Ellie got up with her notebook and pen.

"We have a meeting," she said, "with Arthur."

My stomach dropped. "Just me and you?"

"No," she said. "The whole department."

I followed Ellie into the big conference room where all the managers were already sitting, and Arthur and Helen Zeller walked in behind us mid-laugh. Helen sat at the head of the table in a fur-lined vest with a four-inch-tall bottle of Pellegrino. Arthur stood beside her with his hands clasped behind his back like some kind of reptilian manservant.

"Arthur has resigned this morning," Helen said. "He will be missed."

Arthur looked around the room with plump, watery eyes.

"He will be taking over as the chief revenue officer of *Luxury Voyager*, a new travel magazine featuring branded VR content."

Arthur lowered his head in reverence to something—himself, I guess.

"I'm on vacation next week," he said. "Then I'm back for one final week." He droned on about how much he had learned from everyone and Helen used his farewell speech to segue into one of her sound bites about how our work in sales formed the lifeblood of the Paper.

"You're the best Luxury team this company has ever seen," she said. "You are single-handedly bringing in the revenue this company needs to stay alive in the twenty-first century." I leaned against the wall and tasted phlegm in the back of my throat, thinking only of how good it would feel to spit.

In a matter of hours Arthur's office was filled with so many bouquets you'd think Coco Chanel had risen from her grave and died again in his rolling chair. They bloomed in radiant profusion all morning and began to die in the afternoon and Ellie made a point of blowing her nose.

"Allergic?" Karen asked.

"Getting there," she said. "I'm just surprised he gave the company only two weeks. Standard policy is four or five."

Suppressing the panic I felt over my own looming departure, I disagreed, having forgotten that an integral part of leaving was telling people you were.

"I'm sure two weeks is fine," I said. "People come and go all the time. He's the one who will miss us. It's hard to leave places. They're everything you know. It's kind of like growing up. But you can't stay young forever."

Ellie wasn't listening and I wondered if this was what Karen felt like, day after day, talking into a void.

Laurel's room had nothing left but her bed, her desk, and her paint-splattered folding chair.

"My gift to you," she said, kicking it toward me.

She went into the kitchen to light a joint on the stove and showed me some pictures of Yaritza, including a naked one. The full-length mirror she was standing in front of cut off her head but I could still recognize her pierced nipple and chiseled abs, imbued as they were with her chronic playboy swagger.

"I won't tell her I saw that," I said.

"Don't because she'll love it," Laurel said. "She's such an exhibitionist."

Feeling sentimental, we went to our favorite deli for sandwiches, and a cross-eyed man who seemed drunk and didn't smell good followed us inside. He stared at us while we ordered. Laurel was nice to him.

"That's Ghost," she said. "He's always here."

We sat across from the handball courts at Maria Hernandez Park and unwrapped our foil sandwiches while sitting on our napkins to keep them from blowing away.

"Tasha said she'd punch me in the face," Laurel said.

"Tasha wears a lot of rings," I said.

"She said she'd take them off."

I still felt hurt and a little confused as to why Laurel hadn't asked me to punch her in the face, but I was afraid of what she'd say if I were to ask her. *You're not creative. You're too conventional. You're too basic. You're too dull.*

"I'm still seeing Addy," I said. "It's getting serious."

"Of course it is. That girl's a serial monogamist."

Laurel was looking at her sandwich, studying the different parts of it, and she seemed so much more invested in her roast beef and watery lettuce that I felt pathetic for wanting to share anything at all.

"It doesn't matter," I said. "I'm leaving anyway."

"Oh yeah," Laurel said, scrunching up her nose as she chewed a big bite. "Where are you going again?"

Addy wrote to me in another stream of consciousness and it felt not only good but revelatory. I'd never met anyone so willing to make her desire known.

I feel it's important to voice my goblinesque interest in seeing you

Come over tonight?

We don't have to stay up

I sneaked out of the apartment while Laurel was in the bathroom and took a car to Addy's place, where we rolled around in her bed, kissing each other's eyes and ears, and taking long breaks just to stare at each other in the dark.

"Someday when I'm seventy-two," I said, "I'll remember this room and you next to me in it."

"What about when you're seventy-three?"

"Then I'll forget."

I got up to close the room-darkening curtains, and as soon as I leapt back into bed, Addy yelped. "You smashed my leg!" I apologized and leaned in to kiss her but it was hard to find her face.

"This is like that Halloween game where you're blindfolded and you have to eat a donut off a string."

"That's funny," she said. "I thought you were going to say it was the one where you're blindfolded and you stick your hand in a bowl of skinned grapes."

I lay on my back and looked up at the ceiling. "How do you skin grapes again?" I wondered out loud.

"I don't know," Addy said. "A machine?"

I was an hour late to work the next morning and nobody cared. It was the First Warm Day and everyone was happy. The pizzeria on

Forty-First propped open its door. Commuters unzipped their coats. Whole rivers of snow melted off the tops of buildings and streamed down in glistening streaks that made hard slapping sounds against the pavement. I tried to act normal but I kept laughing at stupid little things, like when Diana's purple ball rolled into the break room, and Tyler farted in his cube and tried to pass it off as his chair, and Karen talked endlessly to no one in particular.

"The old boys in Classifieds sure knew how to party."

"My kid's a ham. He refuses to wear underpants."

"A homeless man attacked a woman with a machete in Bryant Park. The *Post* said he was obsessed with women. He asked them out and they always said no. You'd think he wouldn't attack someone he liked. And where did he even get that machete?"

It was almost time to leave for the night when Robin hoisted herself onto the filing cabinets, back for another visit and bold enough to sit on the furniture. She looked at me with big eyes and I knew she was going to ask me to do something for her, like fill out a form or talk about shoes.

"Jane, would you mind covering for me tomorrow? Dylan asked me to take the day off."

"*Oooh.*" Karen batted her eyelashes. "*Romantic.*"

"Better get your nails done," Ellie said. "He's obviously going to propose."

"Shut up, you guys." Robin hopped back down to the floor. "It's not a thing. He just has a ton of days off and he doesn't want to spend them alone."

Ellie and Karen started humming "Here Comes the Bride" while Robin stormed off in her heels.

"Nothing is going to happen," she said. "Stop singing."

Addy was waiting for me under the arch at Grand Army Plaza in faded denim overalls and red Converse high-tops. When she saw me coming she ran toward me and threw her arms around my neck and I had to straighten my back so we wouldn't fall over.

"This is why people hate couples," I said.

"I know," she said. "I hate us."

We walked into Prospect Park and down a gravel path busy with bushes and leaves. The stones crunched beneath our feet, and as we passed the boathouse and the pond covered in scary-looking algae, I held on to her hand and squeezed it, just to feel the bones.

"Your phone's buzzing," Addy said. "Do you need to get it?"

We were in the Long Meadow, the light was fading, dog walkers all around us were calling out the most ridiculous names ("Cashew!" "Matilda!" "Bikini!"), and Addy—sweet Addy—was worried about my phone.

"You're adorable," I said. "You think I care about my phone?"

"It might be important."

"It's not."

"What if it is?"

I took out my phone and saw Madeline's name.

"Who's Madeline?" Addy said.

"No one."

"Then why's she texting you?"

I stopped and hid my phone in the deepest part of my bag, as if Addy might be able to read Madeline's message through the fabric.

"She's a friend," I said. "A friend I don't want to talk to right now."

"Well, she wants to talk to you."

Addy sounded irritated and I remembered how quickly tenderness, at least in Addy, could turn into something else.

"What was your first job," I said, reaching for her hand. "Was it in Maine?"

"Just text her," Addy said. "I know you want to. I know you're thinking about it."

"I'll do it later."

"Do it now."

I took out my phone and read Madeline's text.

Is this a good outfit for a date I don't want to go on?

She'd sent a picture of herself standing in front of a full-length mirror in a white crop top and high-waisted jeans.

You look incredible, I wrote. Your date is going to piss himself he's so nervous.

She wrote back right away.

Why are you assuming it's with a guy?

"There," Addy said, watching me put my phone away. "That wasn't so hard."

"Why are you acting weird?"

"You're the one who's weird! You're treating a text like some sacred thing you have to look at in private."

"That's not what I was doing."

"That's what it seemed like."

Her nose was scrunched and she was clearly angry, but still, it was cute. I wasn't used to girls being angry or jealous and it felt, in a demented way, like a form of love.

"Come on." I took her by the hand. "Let's ride the swings."

I dragged her over to the empty playground and we got on the swings. Whatever tension we'd been feeling vanished as we pumped our legs and rose up to the sky.

"I feel old!" Addy shouted at the peak of her swing. "How did I do this as a kid and not want to barf?"

Robin came back from her no-big-deal day off with a diamond ring.

"Dylan surprised me at our favorite diner," she said, holding out her hand in waist-high salute. "My whole family was hiding in the kitchen. The ring was in my omelet."

Karen tilted her head. "What if you got pancakes? Would someone have put the ring in the pancakes?"

"Probably," Robin said. She looked at Ellie, who was eating oatmeal. "I wonder what they would have done for you."

"I'm not worried about it," Ellie said. "My boyfriend would never propose to me in food."

My phone buzzed with another text from Madeline. She'd sent me her address in Berlin along with a picture of herself wearing a bra and drinking a Club-Mate in bed.

I was saving this bottle for you but you're taking too long

                                 I'm touched by your one second of generosity

Don't be. They're like two dollars at spätis

                                         What are spätis?

Spätis are like delis

I wasn't overthinking who or what Madeline was to me anymore. I was just accepting that life felt exciting again. I could be with Addy, I could fly to Europe, I could do, basically, anything.

We gathered in the big conference room at the end of the day to surprise Robin in honor of her engagement. The Stepford Planners poured gummy candy and chocolate Kisses across the table. Ellie taped a banner to the TV. We yelled, "Surprise!" when Robin walked in and she covered her mouth and jumped up and down, getting proposed to all over again. The next twenty minutes were spent eating candy and asking Robin questions: "Where is the wedding going to be?" "How many people are coming?" "Where is he from?" "Who are your bridesmaids?" "Where will you honeymoon?" "What kind of dress?" I was thinking of an excuse to leave when the tone of the conversation shifted.

"I changed my mind," Samantha said. "I used to want a big wedding but now I don't care."

Ellie nodded. "Why is everything for women about weddings anyway? Why not promotions?"

The Stepford Planners cupped their hands over their wrappers to hide how many candies they'd eaten, and it made me like them. How badly they wanted to fit into their summer bikinis but couldn't resist a chocolate Kiss.

"When I was in high school," Robin said, "I told my dad, 'My wedding is going to be the most expensive day of your life.' I feel totally different now that I understand the value of money. I don't get why we act like it's the biggest day of a woman's life. I mean, bridal showers are antifeminist. It's thirty women watching another woman open pots and pans. Why don't they have *groom* showers? And with all the energy you're supposed to put into it, what are you supposed to do *after* the wedding?"

"Get divorced and start over," Karen said.

Robin nodded. "We should live with our friends."

I rode the train to Addy's place with huge feelings stuck in my throat. There had been a profound shift in the coordinates of my being. Every moment that didn't include her was marked by an awareness of her absence, and if that was what love was, it wasn't a gift. It was the constant fear of future pain.

I let myself into her building with the spare key she'd given me—a key that I felt certain had once belonged to her ex—and was overpowered by the smell of home, or some idea of home I sometimes smelled in the hallway of my apartment building. It was like a warm cooking smell, which made sense the moment I opened Addy's door and saw her pulling a pan of biscuits out of the oven.

"The recipe said ten minutes but I only cooked them for eight because I wanted to check on them and make sure they weren't getting burnt."

I pulled her toward me and kissed her on the cheek.

"I like how you don't say hi to me anymore," I said. "I like how you just start talking about bread."

"I'm stress-cooking," she said. "I needed something to do instead of practicing."

"I'm doing the same," I said. "Seeing you instead of packing."

"But your trip's not that long. You'll come back in, what? Three weeks?"

"I don't have a return ticket."

Addy laughed. I thought she'd be mad.

"That's great," she said. "You deserve a break."

"I still have to tell the Paper I'm leaving."

"Just tell them tomorrow. It's not a big deal."

She closed the oven door with her lobster-claw oven mitt and I reread the fortune cookie message taped to her fridge. *To love what you do and feel that it matters—could anything be more fun?* I liked the message all right but hated that it had come from a cookie, like proof that life's greatest lessons were all factory-made.

"You must be getting excited for your Berlin adventure," she said.

Anxiety flared up in me and I held back from venting my contempt for that phrase. Adventures were for people who scuba dived and smiled with their teeth, who cut off all their hair and didn't question it later, who lived in the moment because they'd read some books and watched some movies and that's what life was all about. Living in the moment. Carpe diem. Good vibes only. All that shit.

"It doesn't matter how I feel," I said. "It's happening and I can't take it back. What about you? Are you ready for your tour?"

Our conversation was stilted, bordering on small talk, and it was Addy's fault. She'd brought up the future, which we weren't supposed to talk about. It opened some kind of temporal abyss full of questions we couldn't answer, thoughts I didn't want to face.

"It's all big theater shows so the setup's gonna be nicer than what I'm used to," she said. "My agent just sent me a picture of the tour bus. It's one of the nice ones with TV's and tons of snacks."

I couldn't tell if she was trying to show off or if her life really was perfect.

"Your life is like a movie," I said. "It's kind of annoying."

She opened the oven door and released a wave of heat. "It's not my fault that your life choices were different from mine."

She put her biscuits on the stove and I reached for one of them.

"Not yet!" she said. "They have to cool."

"Do they?"

"Yes. For twenty minutes. That's what the recipe says."

She went into her room and I followed her in there.

"Go away," she said. "I have to make my bed and I don't want you to watch."

"Too bad," I said. "I want to see you do everything. Cook, clean, pee."

"You're never going to see me pee."

I stood off to the side and watched as she tucked her sheets into her mattress, fluffed her big white comforter, and stuffed her pillows into their clean cotton shells. Then she arranged her pillows along the headboard and stood back to survey her work, a chapel of clean white lines, and I don't know why but I loved Addy in that moment. She had put so much effort into making her bed that I knew she was good.

"Don't look so sad," Addy said, cozying up to me and misinterpreting the look on my face. Or maybe she wasn't. Maybe loving her was making me sad. "We can go on tour together someday."

"Across the US and Canada?"

"And Europe."

I put my arms around her. I didn't want to let go.

Alvin was in the mail room, bent over the counter and eating a slice of pizza with his rosary dangling over the cheese.

"Miss Jane," he said, wiping his hands clean. "How are you today?"

I happened to be infatuated with a girl who had come out of

nowhere and unmoored me from the rigid outline of my being, so I offered up the god-given truth.

"I feel so so so so so so so so so blessed."

Alvin nodded, unsurprised by a blessing too big for words.

"God dwells in unapproachable light," he said, lifting the lid of his pizza box to offer me a slice.

It was after five when Tom called me into his office and I went in there determined to tell him I was leaving. Then I saw his rosy cheeks and rumpled shirt and he looked so inept, typing with his puffy index fingers, that I didn't want to tell him anything. I just wanted to disappear.

"Here." He handed me a pair of headphones with earmuffs as big as bagels. "Put these on."

I sat and put on his headphones and a song by the Beach Boys started to play.

"Close your eyes!" Tom shouted so I could hear him through the muffs, and it made me feel self-conscious but I did what he said. I closed my eyes and listened to the tambourine and the maracas and the many whirling layers of sound.

"And *that's* your music lesson for the day," Tom said, taking back the headphones that I suddenly wanted to keep. "Now send me the plan for Prada." He looked at his screen.

"I actually have some news," I said, but Tom wasn't listening. He was wearing his headphones, already gone.

Laurel's room was empty when I got home and her keys were on the counter. Jangling things I used to hear in the hallway, the keys were her way of saying *I will never come back here again.* I couldn't stand to look at them so I shut them in a drawer and went into my room, where I sat on the bed and tried to prevent my insides from turning to mush as I realized that everything I was seeing was just another place I would leave.

Addy wrote to me, telling me to come over.

It doesn't matter if it's late.

I just want to see you.

Don't make me sleep alone.

Her messages were buried under a text from Madeline, who'd sent me a photo of herself lying in bed in lacy black underwear. I stared at her photo for a long time, wondering, among other things, how many pictures she'd taken before arriving at that perfect one, with the sleepy look in her eyes and her butt rising ever so slightly over the sheets.

HOT, I responded carefully to her picture before switching back to Addy's more wholesome thread.

I don't want to sleep alone either

I'll be over at ten

The day before I had to put in my two-week notice, I sneaked out of the office at noon to meet Addy in Times Square. We walked in the blazing sunlight until we found a corny Italian place with a thirteen-dollar "business lunch," where we sat in the window under a speaker blasting opera.

"How's business?" Addy asked, straightening her back.

"At the end of the day," I said, "we have to circle back, think outside of the box, and nail down the low-hanging fruit."

She ordered spaghetti bolognese. I ordered angel hair with shrimp. The waiter made a ceremonious show of pouring the olive oil for our bread, and when our food arrived, it was terrible, overcooked and bland, but we ate it all anyway, grateful for the light, the warm plates, the red-checkered tablecloth, and everything else about that abominable restaurant that was making us happy to be alive.

"It feels strange not to be at work," I said.

"Do you feel guilty?"

"Not at all."

I took out my phone to check the time and then decided against it, putting it down on some spilled parmesan.

Addy frowned. Her face was red. "Are you cheating on me?"

"No."

"I'm serious," she said. "Are you?"

She picked up my phone and showed me six messages from Madeline. I grabbed my phone back and shoved it away.

"Why are you hiding it?" she said. "That makes you look more guilty."

I knew that if I could just explain my irrational crush and laugh about it, like a normal person, it would be fine. But I couldn't. There were no words to describe how it was possible, and maybe even a good thing, to be able to love two people at once.

"Go ahead," she said, smiling in a creepy way, like she might be mad enough to flip the table. "Read what your little friend sent. It's not like I care."

I took out my phone and read the messages from Madeline, careful not to react or seem remotely excited by the sight of her words.

Guten morgen

I'm in the city for a minute

I want to see you

Meet me for a drink?

Helloooo

Are you mad at me?

Addy was staring at me. Her mouth was clamped shut and she was breathing audibly through her nose.

"She wants to get a drink," I said. "Catch up. It means nothing."

"I thought she was gone."

"She came back."

"You're a messed-up person, you know that?"

"That's true," I said, "but I'm also good-looking and fun to be around."

She got up so quickly that her chair banged against the wall. The businesspeople turned. We were breaking the rules of the business lunch.

"Don't be so dramatic," I said. "It was just a fling. It's over and done."

I looked around for the waiter.

"If it's really over and done"—Addy buttoned her coat so slowly that it felt like a threat—"then let me meet her."

I scratched my chin, pretending to consider this ludicrous proposal in which my entire future might crumble.

"I don't think that's a good idea," I said.

She turned to leave.

"Fine!" I called after her. "Tonight! You can meet her tonight!"

Addy shot me a nasty look. "Fantastic," she said. "I can't fucking wait."

Madeline told me to meet her at the Strand after work, and when I got there she was nowhere to be found. I knew she was probably just late, but a part of me hoped she'd never show up. I didn't want to have to tell her about Addy. Not that she'd care. If anything, she'd be bored. I'd been dulled and beaten by the tenderness of a well-behaved musician who sang about her family, drank in moderation, separated her lights from her darks, and watered her plants with a Brita.

Madeline walked in with an armful of college textbooks. She looked anemic and lost in her too-tight black jeans and I made no effort to get her attention. But people always want you most when you don't want them so she immediately found me, handed me all the books she'd been holding, and guided me to the resale counter in the back.

"I want ten percent," I said.

"You get nothing," she said.

A man in a lanyard went through the books and gave Madeline a coupon good for four dollars cash. She was thrilled.

"I've been traveling, so I'm broke. Never go to Switzerland," she said. "A latte costs fourteen dollars. Amsterdam was amazing though. I would totally live there if everyone wasn't so high all the time."

"That can't possibly be true," I said. "Lots of normal people live there."

"Not really. People are high all the time. They're high everywhere. Parks, sidewalks, restaurants. When my friends went to the Anne Frank Museum, they were still high from the night before."

"That's awful."

Madeline shrugged. "Everyone goes to the Anne Frank Museum high."

A librarian's ingratiating voice came over the loudspeaker. "The Strand is now closed. No more browsing."

We imitated the woman's voice as we passed Biography, Poetry, and Theater.

"Please stop browsing."

"Stop fucking browsing."

"Put the goddamn book down."

We went outside and stood for a second on Broadway just to look at each other. Madeline had the same thin eyebrows, delicate nose, and cherry-shaped mouth that always looked a little pouty and ready to judge.

"You have to change," she said.

I thought she meant change into a different person. More generous, more kind.

"Your coat," she said. "We can't both be wearing jean jackets."

I looked down and saw that she was right; however, my jacket was old and hers was new but made to look old.

"Don't you want to match?" I said.

"No."

"But it's cute."

"It's not cute."

We were already falling into our old roles where I said dumb things and she contradicted them in a deadpan voice. I walked toward Union Square and she followed. It felt natural to walk and talk, like no time had passed.

"How've you been," I said, not really a question, more like a mood.

"Bored," she said. "Cassandra's moving to Montreal, the Paper still owes me money, and I came back here to get some stuff but then I realized I hate all my stuff and now I'm jet-lagged for no reason."

We were walking east on Fourteenth Street and in the blue half-light of dusk she looked so beautiful that it suddenly felt cruel to have to tell her about Addy. Life would be so much simpler if I could keep Addy separate and still fly to Berlin, staying with Madeline and sleeping with her while continuing to check on Addy and make her feel loved.

She held up a chunk of her smooth black hair.

"I forgot to tell you," she said. "I got a German haircut and it was the most German thing ever. The hairdresser finished and he was like, 'Do you want to blow-dry your hair?' He pointed at a station in the corner with all these blow-dryers. I was like, 'Um, can you do it for me?' He did, but still, is that not the most German thing you have ever heard?"

"Are you seeing anyone?" I interrupted her.

Madeline looked confused and then leaned into me slightly, as if she needed my waist for support.

"No," she said. "Nobody likes me."

When I didn't rush to reassure her of the opposite, she straightened her back and focused on the crosswalk. I think she knew something was wrong.

"I am," I said. "Seeing someone."

Madeline didn't react. She just kept walking.

"She's a musician," I said. "She wants to meet you."

"Did you tell her I was your mistress?"

"Don't joke like that. This girl has a temper, and for your own well-being, I need you to act like we're over."

We turned right onto Third and Madeline slowed down, letting herself get lost in the crowd. She put on her sunglasses and I got the feeling she didn't want me to see her face. Then she looked at me and seemed fine and I wondered if it was all in my head, all this longing and waiting and wondering what to do.

"When I texted you earlier and you didn't respond, I was like, it's fine, she's busy, her phone's dead." Madeline stopped. She took off her sunglasses so I could see her eyes. "But still."

"Still what?"

"I don't know." She looked at the traffic. The people passing. Nothing was happening. There was nothing to see. And yet my body was beginning to melt because I knew what she was going to say.

"I think I'm in love with you."

Addy grabbed me by the arm. "There you are," she said. She was supposed to have been waiting for us at the bar on St. Mark's but she must have gotten impatient. She must have thought I'd run away.

"You're here," I said in a weird, high-pitched voice.

She looked warm and wholesome in her L.L.Bean boots and beige flannel shirt, and a part of me was mad at her for not wearing something cooler, like her ripped-up Stevie Nicks shirt or her faded denim overalls that hung low and showed off her tits.

"Of course I'm here," she said. "I wanted to meet your friend."

My friend? Who was my friend? She turned to Madeline, who raised her arms and went in for a hug, and it felt insane. I couldn't tell whether I was witnessing a collision or something amiable and necessary.

"So nice to meet you," Madeline said, rushing to fill the air as she clutched and let go of Addy, whose arms never left her sides.

"Nice to meet you too," Addy said. Standing stiffly, she examined Madeline in such a steely way that it felt like a violation, making all the nights I'd spent with Madeline collapse into a worthless pit.

"Welp," I said, "Time for that drink."

We walked single-file to the only bar in the East Village that I actually liked. It was a rowdy Polish place run by women with huge craggy faces who looked pained if you ordered anything other than beer. The door was closed when we got there but we could hear loud music and shouting through the glass. It was some kind of wordless electronic polka and Madeline, who gravitated toward dark and boozy places, went right in while Addy stayed where she was and covered her face with her hands.

"Don't make me go in there," she said.

If I were a better person, I might have put my arms around her and led us away from Madeline and alcohol and all the other pathways in life that seemed objectively not good. But that wasn't me. I wanted to be with Addy in New York and Madeline in Berlin and I didn't see why I had to choose.

"One drink," I said. "Then we can go."

We went inside and the place was packed. And everyone looked so different from one another, it was like a train car that had turned into a drinking game with hairy old men and art school brats and old women wearing shawls.

"Find a table!" I shouted at Addy. "I'll get the drinks!"

She covered her ears and made a face.

"I can hear you," she said. "You don't have to yell."

Madeline was already at the bar, squeezed between beer bellies, looking lost and sad.

"You can sit," I said. "I got this."

One of the ladies behind the bar spoke to me in Polish and I had to disappoint her by ordering a vodka for Madeline and a bourbon for Addy and nothing for myself because I forgot. Then I bumped into Madeline as soon as I turned around because she was standing only a foot away. She'd taken off her coat and I saw that she was wearing a black dress over a long-sleeved velvet shirt with a black choker around her neck, and she looked so good that I couldn't speak.

"I'm scared of your girlfriend," she said.

"Me too," I said.

We nudged our way to the back and found Addy sitting in a booth under a faded photo of a meadow that had probably been there for at least twenty years. Madeline sat across from her and started asking her questions in the manner of a seasoned dinner guest, eager to make a good first impression, and I willed myself into being a dispassionate spectator, watching and listening and preparing, between handfuls of peanuts, to break up a fight.

"So you're a musician?"

"I sing and play guitar."

"Do you go on tour?"

"When I can."

"Do you have any tours coming up?"

Addy leaned back and crossed her arms. "I'd say it's good to finally meet you but Jane never talks about you. I didn't actually know anything about you until today."

I looked around for my drink that wasn't there. "I said a few things," I said.

"No, you didn't." Addy looked at me. "You said nothing. If anything, I feel sorry for Madeline."

Madeline pushed up her sleeves, exposing her arms. They were so different from Addy's, so thin and willowy. They could never hold the weight of an electric guitar.

"You look young," Addy said. "Are you still in school?"

"I graduated last year and moved here for—"

"I didn't go to college." Addy cut her off. "I had to work."

Madeline finished her drink and went to the bathroom. As soon as she was gone, Addy exhaled.

"I don't get how you could like her," she said. "She's a *baby*."

"She's younger than us. That's true."

"I'm just curious. Did you hang out with her to feel good about yourself? Was it, like, an ego thing?"

"I was lonely, okay? I hung out with her because I was lonely and she gave me a reason to not hate going into work, but if you were to tell me right now to never talk to her again, that would be fine. Because I don't actually care about her. You're right. She's a baby. I don't need her in my life."

Addy looked over my shoulder and there was Madeline, standing behind me.

"I better go," she said, reaching for her coat.

As cruel as it might sound, seeing her about to leave made me want to clap and cheer and do a somersault, because even though her feelings were hurt, I knew I could make it up to her. Buy her a drink. Kiss her on the cheek. Beg for forgiveness. The important thing was that she was leaving and my relationship with Addy could be preserved.

"So how long are you here?" Addy asked her.

"I fly home tomorrow," Madeline said.

"Where to?"

Madeline's lips formed the sound of a *B* and I wanted to grab her by the choker and shout, *Belarus!*

"Berlin," she said.

Addy looked at me with black holes for eyes.

"Are you fucking kidding me," she said in a voice so low and calm that it felt like being gracefully stabbed. Slowly she got up and put on her coat. She folded her lips into her mouth and held them there as she shook her head. "I knew something like this was going to happen. I should've known you were going to Berlin just to fuck around."

I stayed where I was and said nothing. All I could do was watch her face.

"You are the most selfish and immature person I have ever met."

"I would have to agree," Madeline said.

Addy ignored her and everything else going on around us. In fact, her voice was getting louder, and I wondered if this was how people got killed. If that phrase—*a crime of passion*—really did start with love.

"You are such a fucking asshole, do you know that?" She stuck her nose in my face. Her nostrils were flaring.

She was having a meltdown in the middle of a crowded bar, yet nobody was watching, so maybe this was normal. Maybe all I had to do was reach for her hand.

"Don't you dare touch me." She whipped her hand away. "I don't ever want to see you again."

She stormed out the door and I felt like I had three seconds to decide what to do. I could either chase her down, tackle her in front of Walgreens, and beg for forgiveness, or I could sit and do nothing and finish her drink.

Madeline was standing next to me, holding her coat. I gulped down the rest of Addy's drink and got up.

"I like her," Madeline said.

"She's likable," I said.

Madeline rummaged around in her tote bag.

"I'm paying you back," she said, taking out her wallet.

"Just go," I said. "I'll see you in Berlin."

"That's not a good idea."

"I don't understand."

"I mean I think you should find somewhere else to stay."

"Is this about Addy?" I said, raising my voice, because the bar had suddenly become very loud. "Don't worry about her. She has tantrums all the time. It's not a big deal."

"Good luck, Jane."

She backed into the crowd, and just like that, I was alone.

I walked south on Third with no thoughts in my head. Everything about my life was a symptom. My fear of commitment, my cagey personality, my raging indecisiveness, my unchecked selfishness. The city appeared to be equally ruined with its run-over pigeons and broken windows and endless agglomeration of depressing chain stores. I made it to the J train and was holding on to the pole with a strong desire to not exist when I heard my name. It felt like a joke. I didn't want that name anymore.

"Jane?! This is crazy." The voice was coming toward me. "I live in Williamsburg now, isn't that funny?" I looked up and there was Bekah Rake, towering over me in her leather jacket with the zippers and belts. Her hair was shorter, more like a bob, but still blond and shimmering.

"I got a job at *WaPo*. Can you believe it? I'm a planner so it's basically the same but the pay is better and they give us commission. Are you still at the Paper? God, I was so glad to get out of there. Tom was a lunatic. He basically threw me under the bus, and everybody I talked to said what happened was totally unfair." She looked me up and down and it was nauseating. Just being seen. Why did we have to look at each other all the time? Looking was mean. "I knew it was you from far away," she said. "You're always wearing those baggy pants."

The doors opened at Marcy and she leaned over to hug me goodbye. I had every intention of recoiling from her touch, yet for some reason I savored the way she squeezed me. It felt like I hadn't been touched in days.

"Tell everyone I said hi," she said. "Tell them I miss them."

The train bumped back to life and my phone buzzed with a

notification from Madeline. Hundreds of dollars had been returned to my account. It came with a message. I opened it right away.

Madeline Navarro has removed you as a friend.

I hit refresh and her message disappeared. She must have blocked me. Her face was gone.

The next morning I went straight into Tom's office to tell him I was leaving, but the walk I had to make past the filing cabinets, the copy room, and the break room that smelled like tuna made me feel like my throat was being pinched. Tom's door was open. All I had to do was go in there and make a perfectly sane announcement about "moving on to my next journey," but my feet were stuck to the floor and the happy, secure life I'd made for myself in the office came back to me with astonishing force.

"Oh no," Tom said as I slid the door closed. "Bad news."

I moved a stack of newspapers onto the floor and sat with my elbows on the desk. I'd never leaned on his desk before but my insides were ravaged and I needed the support.

"I'm putting in my two weeks," I said.

His face sank. "No," he said. "No, no."

I tried to smile to let him know I was happy and it made me want to cry.

"Where are you going?" he said. "Don't tell me Condé."

"I'm going to Berlin. I'm going to travel."

Tom sighed. "You're doing the right thing. You have to do that sort of thing before it's too late." I held my breath to keep from crying while he launched into a story about his friend Barry who lived in Berlin and was related to someone in a band called the Pogues and how once, when they were leaving a club in Dublin, they found Kate Moss's wallet.

"Be safe," he said. "Amsterdam is great during the day but get out of there at night. It's the creepiest red-light district you've ever seen. And you have to buy a first-class Eurail ticket because it's worth it. It seems like a lot but you can sleep and nobody will steal your passport."

He got up from his chair and we hugged. I could feel people's eyes looking at us through the glass. "And journal," he said. "Or else you'll forget."

All I wanted to do after work was be alone and feel sorry for myself but I couldn't. Not when I had to go to Cubbyhole, the scummy lesbian bar in the West Village, where Maxine had summoned our friend group to surprise Zinc with a birthday cake that said *Happy 30* even though she was turning twenty-eight.

I got there as Maxine was presenting the box with the cake, and Zinc burst into tears.

"I hate you all," she screamed before collapsing into Maxine's arms for a hug.

"I heard about Addy." Tasha kicked me in the shin. "You sure fucked that up."

She played with the end of a silk scarf she'd tied around her neck, some designer thing she probably wore to impress the trust fund kids she worked with at the gallery.

"I think I know what your issue is," she said, patting me on the head. "You have impostor syndrome. But for relationships."

"I don't have impostor syndrome," I said. "I feel completely confident in how inadequate I am."

Bhumi appeared in an argyle sweater and handed me a piece of cake.

"Sorry, no forks," she said. "You gotta eat with your hands."

Tasha leaned over and took a bite. Frosting and yellow cake got all over her lips and mouth and she licked herself clean with her tongue.

"Or do that," Bhumi said, "and literally repulse everyone here."

Tasha and Bhumi laughed and I laughed too but without really laughing. I was too busy looking at all the coats, looking for the one that might be red.

"I heard you're going to Berlin," Bhumi said, opening her backpack. "I printed you a list of all my favorite places. Number one is obviously the Audre Lorde archive."

Tasha grabbed the paper and started crumpling it. "KitKat, Sage, About Blank, Loophole."

"I have no idea what you're saying," I said.

"They're clubs! We went to Berlin last year. It was amazing. I didn't sleep for forty-eight hours."

"Has everyone already gone?"

Tasha and Bhumi looked around.

"Everyone but you," Tasha said. "And Donna."

Sitting alone at the end of the bar was Donna, the big, sad Canadian girl whose pale moon face and tiny puckered mouth seemed to be calling out for human contact.

I walked over to her with my shoulders back and said, "Hi, Donna," and she smiled at me, her big, dopey grin.

"Jane! I'm so glad you're here. You have to meet Linda." She squeezed the arm of the woman in stuffy business clothes standing next to her. "Linda, baby. This is Jane. Jane, this is Linda. I feel like you two will get along."

Linda rubbed small, protective circles into the back of Donna's neck. "Why's that, sweetie?"

Donna blinked. Her clumpy mascara left dots above her eyelids.

"Jane works in advertising and so do you, so I don't know, I thought you'd have a lot to talk about."

"I don't work in advertising per se," Linda corrected her. "I work in data analytics and market research."

Donna shifted her legs and her coat fell on the floor. I knelt to pick it up and had the urge to stay down there. It would be so easy to curl up and rest my head on a stranger's foot.

"What about you?" Donna said. "Are you still seeing Addy?"

Linda smacked herself on the mouth. "You're the one dating Addy? Is she here? I've seen her live like ten times. She signed my tote."

"She's not here," I said.

"You should call her. You should tell her to come."

I wanted to call Addy. It was all that I wanted. I wanted to call her and go on a long walk and talk until she liked me again.

"I will," I said. "I'll call her right now."

I went outside and took out my phone and there was Yaritza.

"How funny," I said. "I'm actually calling your friend right now."

Yaritza took a deep breath. I thought she might be acting.

"You shouldn't do that," she said. "You should probably give her some space."

Handsome, smoky-eyed Yaritza flicking away a hand-rolled cigarette in her cool white T-shirt—what right did she have to tell me what to do?

"I don't think it's up to you," I said. "I think you, all of people, should understand how easy it is to hurt people you don't mean to hurt."

"I still don't think you should call Addy. Or text her. You should give her some time. She'll come around."

"Will she?"

"I think so."

The door of the bar swung open and Yaritza looked over my shoulder, trying to see inside.

"Laurel's not in there," I said. "She's not coming."

"She's not?"

"No," I said, and when a look of genuine sadness passed across Yaritza's face, I knew that I should listen to her, and we both went back inside.

News had clearly spread because as soon as I got to the office, Ellie looked up at me with quivering lips. She got up and raised her arms for a hug. "I'm gonna *cryyyyy*." I felt her bony shoulders.

"You smell good," I said.

She let go of me and beamed. "It's my homemade organic shampoo," she said. "I'll send you the recipe."

Diana came over in a frilly pink tutu clutching a laptop and a bunch of folders.

"You're leaving?" she said. "Where are you going?"

"Berlin," I said.

"Guten tag!" she said, perhaps thinking it meant good-bye.

Tyler came over next and thumped me on the back. "Ah, adventure and self-discovery. I wish I had done that in my youth."

Tyler couldn't have been older than thirty-one or thirty-two, but there was no point in correcting him. He'd reached a level of entrenchment in the professional world that was hard, if not impossible, to break.

"China is where you should be going," he said. "They're the ones with twenty billion in buying power. I'm actually learning Mandarin. . . ." He was beginning to mansplain but there was something vulnerable about it. The way he clung to his one-sided conversations, his eternal need to be liked.

Karen was so hyped up on her creamy iced coffee, standing up, sitting down, and jabbering about the glare on her screen, that she hugged me so hard we almost fell over. "It's great that you're getting out of here," she said. "This place is shit when it comes to vacation time."

After I texted my mother that I'd quit and there was no way of taking it back, she responded with a barrage of baby photos. She sent them as pictures of pictures and they piled up in my phone, an uninterrupted chain of the past with each physical image outlined by the pattern of the living room rug as well as a thumb, soft and painted, that could only belong to my mother. After hours of receiving these photos, unprompted and unexplained, I got a call from my mother saying that she and Doug were on a break, and in her newly discovered free time she'd been organizing our old photo albums. It had been a longtime goal of hers—this massive overhaul of two decades of life—and just talking about it took an audible effort on her part not to cry.

"I'm fine," she said, her voice shaky. "Everything's fine. I'm just so happy I got to be your mom." She made a snort and wiped her nose. "I just wish I could hold you again. I wish I could go into your room and scoop you up and carry you around, just for a day. When it's happening, it's like, you think it'll last forever—all the feeding and diaper changing—but then it doesn't. And now I keep wondering, did I hold you enough?"

The kitchen cupboards banged. The faucet hissed. Whether my mother knew it or not, the backdrop of her life was speaking to me, it was saying *home, home, home,* and I was on the verge of confessing all manner of sappy things when she interrupted herself to ask about my savings account.

"It's all right to have dreams but you've still got to be able to support yourself. What if you got into an accident? What if you needed surgery? What if you broke a tooth? I can't believe you're going to Berlin, of all places. In a way, you've been there before."

"How is that possible?"

"I was pregnant with you when I went there for work. They were taking down the wall. I still have a piece of it in my dresser."

"You just picked it up and took it?"

She laughed. "I bought it. They were selling scraps of it at all the shops."

I hadn't heard from Laurel in weeks, but that was normal. She was busy getting ready for her performance, hyperfocused on the world of her art, and when I got to her friend's storefront gallery in Greenpoint, I felt like I was the one who should apologize. I'd come from work in a button-down shirt and everyone around me was wearing latex and chains.

The performances started at eight and they were boring. An Australian girl dressed as a mime read a long poem about love and mirrors. A person named Dragon Slayer sang a song that went "I am the moon and you are me and I am you and I am everyone." Then it was Laurel's turn and she didn't get punched in the face. She put a plastic tarp on the floor and poured black paint over her naked body and sang along to a Beyoncé song in slow motion. It was long and repetitive but vulnerable and true, and when it was over, she wrapped herself in a towel and I helped her fold the tarp.

"You did great," I said. "You made the whole room go quiet."

"I'm mad at Tasha," she said. "She flaked at the last minute so I had to scramble to get this performance together. I spent a hundred dollars at Home Depot. And I sent a mass text but nobody showed up."

We left the gallery and wandered into a nearby park, where we sat on a bench facing grass and trees. It was after eleven so the park was dark but it wasn't empty. There was a guy walking his dog, a girl talking on the phone, and an old man walking in circles with his wrinkled arms pumping.

"I feel like I want to kill myself," Laurel said. "Curators hate me. My friends hate me. Nobody likes me. Nobody calls me back."

"Nobody hates you," I said. "People will call. Your art keeps getting better all the time."

"It's getting bigger, not better, and I don't have the space for it. And nobody buys anything. Not that I care about that stuff, but still."

The old man walked past us, huffing and puffing.

"What about your art school friends? They're stylish and cool and I know they love what you do."

"No, they don't," she said. "They just like it when I take pictures of them." She rubbed at the black paint still smudged across her forehead.

"What about Marcel," I said.

Laurel sighed. "He wants to kill himself too."

The woman on the phone looked like she might be crying but it was hard to say. She was just a shadow, full of feeling, on a bench across the way.

"And whenever I try to tell people how I feel," she said, "they just get scared and push me away."

I wanted to say something perfect and wise, but the more she insisted that she had no reason to keep living, the more I felt like she might be right and we were no different from the dog in front of us, running in circles and barking at a tree.

A garbage truck stopped on the other side of the fence and its rotten-egg smell was strong. It almost felt as though we were in the truck with banana peels and cigarette butts. Two men in thick gloves started tossing heavy garbage bags into the back of the truck. Their mouths were open and they seemed happy to be throwing their smelly bags around in the middle of the night.

"I wish I could be a garbageman," Laurel said.

"If you become a garbageman, I'll become one too and we can garbage together."

I scooted closer to Laurel, ignoring the dried bird shit stuck to the bench, and put my arm around her. We sat like that for a while, not saying anything, and I can't say we were happy but I knew we'd be okay.

acknowledgments

Thank you, Alison Lewis.
Thank you, Frances Yackel.
Thank you, Taylor Rondestvedt.
Thank you, Gallery Books.